DEAD MONEY

FORTHCOMING BY RUDY STEGEMOELLER

Deep Water

A NO-LIMIT POKER MYSTERY

DEAD MONEY

RUDY STEGEMOELLER

MIDNIGHT INK
WOODBURY, MINNESOTA

FIRST EDITION
First Printing, 2007

Book design by Donna Burch
Cover design by Gavin Dayton Duffy
Cover gun image © 2006 by Stockbyte

Midnight Ink, an imprint of Llewellyn Publications

Library of Congress Cataloging-in-Publication Data
Stegemoeller, Rudy.
 Dead money : a no-limit poker mystery / Rudy Stegemoeller.
  p. cm.
 ISBN-13: 978-0-7387-1091-4
 ISBN-10: 0-7387-1091-1
  1. Poker—Fiction. 2. Casinos—Fiction. I. Title.

 PS3619.T448D43 2007
 813'.6—dc22   2006046941

This is a work of fiction. Names, characters, places, and incidents are either the product of the author's imagination or are used fictitiously, and any resemblance to actual persons, living or dead, business establishments, events, or locales is entirely coincidental.

Midnight Ink
Llewellyn Publications
2143 Wooddale Drive, Dept. 0-7387-1091-1
Woodbury, MN 55125-2989, U.S.A.
www.midnightinkbooks.com

Printed in the United States of America

For Mary.
After twenty years, still too good to be true.

dead money: in a poker tournament, an inexperienced player who is almost certain to be eliminated

PROLOGUE

June 14, Brooklyn, New York

GENERAL TSO'S CHICKEN AND cold lumpy white rice might not be the breakfast of champions, but it was the best I could scrounge from the refrigerator on a Monday morning. Already late for work, I wolfed down the food and fumbled with the buttons on my shirt while flipping through the copy of *Card Times* that was on top of the mail pile.

Eileen had thrown her work clothes into a gym bag and filled her travel mug with coffee. She gave me an exasperated look. "Newcomb, if we're gonna take the subway together, you have to get your butt moving. I'm not waiting if you're just wasting your time with one of those idiotic gambling magazines."

I had tuned out everything after "Newcomb." I couldn't believe what I was reading. "Hey, Eileen, look at this." I folded the magazine and thrust it at her.

She looked as though I were offering her a shovelful of dog droppings. "Mark, c'mon, we have to get to work. What's in there that could possibly interest me?"

"Just read it!"

She managed to scowl, roll her eyes, and sigh all at the same time as she took the magazine and scanned the article.

TABLE TALK
By Zip Addison

So who is the best poker player in the world today? For my money the top cardmeister is still **Shooter Deukart.** On a Friday night in early May I had the pleasure of watching Shooter play $100-$200 no-limit Hold'em at the **Trinidad** in Atlantic City. Chewing on his trademark toothpick, the wily Texan had both barrels blazing, and anybody foolish enough to stick their chips into the pot walked away with "nuthin' but a bellyful of lead." **Tim O'Byrne,** who won last year's NPF event in Biloxi, caught a few slugs. **Barracuda Gant** sat in for some hands, but even he could see that "the Duke" owned the table that night.

Shooter saved his best ammunition for **Mark Newcomb,** a talented amateur from New York City who must have dropped fifty large to the crafty old bandit. I'll give credit to the hapless Newcomb, he kept coming back for more, sort of like **Rocky** in his first fight with Creed. And like Rocky, he left everything he had, and I mean everything, on the mat.

She looked up from the magazine. "Hapless! You got your fifteen minutes of fame, and they called you hapless."

"What? Let me see that." I snatched the magazine back from her and reread the article. *Hapless?* Yep, there it was. *Bastard.*

"Don't feel bad, Rocky. You'll get more chances." Eileen came around the table and put her hand on my shoulder. "And hey," she whispered into my ear, "*I* don't think you're hapless." Her hand slid down to my belt. Abruptly, she yanked on it and pulled me toward the front door of the apartment. "Let's go, talented amateur. Try to remember you've got a day job too."

I dropped the half-eaten breakfast into the sink, grabbed my briefcase, and followed her out the door.

1
—

Monday, September 27, Ludbury, Massachusetts

THE LOBBY OF THE Humpback Hotel and Casino always made me smile. Twelve miles from the old whaling town of Yarmouth, Massachusetts, it looked more like a nautical museum than a gambling palace. Antique maritime artifacts decorated the walls. Coiled ropes, harpoons, belaying pins, life preservers. The lobby was dominated by a twenty-foot boat that looked as though it had just come off the water from a whale hunt.

Who puts a harpoon and a life preserver in the lobby of a casino? These were not the subliminal signals normally used to bring in the suckers. A proper casino was decorated with lots of glitz and mirrors, big-money images, no windows or clocks to remind the players that time was passing, and *certainly* nothing to remind them that they were about to be harpooned.

But the rustic décor of the Humpback proved that a casino could ignore all those rules and still make a fortune. Turns out gamblers didn't need to be snared with tricky subliminal enticements. The clicking of the chips, the warm felt expanse of the tables, and the babbling of the slot machines were enticement enough. Just make the action available, and people would come.

They'd come, the casino pros would tell you, for one simple reason: gamblers are just big mindless invertebrates with wallets. Prod them with the right stimuli and money will gush from every opening.

Taken as a general rule, this is probably true. As a poker player, though, I flattered myself to think that I had advanced beyond the rank of mindless invertebrate. My gambling instincts had evolved to a higher level, like that of, say, a laboratory rat. Smarter than the rest, maybe, but still chasing the cheese.

The cheese this particular week would be the three-million-plus in the prize pool of the Northeast Open, sponsored by the National Poker Federation. I hoped to win a good-sized piece of it. My bankroll had been flattened four months ago during an unfortunate encounter in Atlantic City with one of the top players in the world, a sly old rounder named Shooter Deukart. Deukart had taken me down, to the tune of forty-seven dimes, with a breathtaking series of plays that ranged somewhere between brilliant and clairvoyant.

Forty-seven thousand dollars. That was a tough one to explain to my wife, Eileen. Since every penny of it was profit that I had won in earlier poker games, she couldn't complain too much. Even so, there are people who just don't get the concept of "easy come, easy go," and I happened to be married to one of them.

Starting over with a small stake, I spent four months grinding my way through a number of medium-sized games in the New York City area. These were games that I could quietly dominate most of the time, and I patiently played my bankroll back up to a respectable twenty-eight thousand.

Now, in my ordinary, non-gambling life, twenty-eight thousand dollars was a hell of a lot of money. Far more than I would ever dream of spending on a car or a vacation, or anything else for that matter. I was, in fact, something of a cheapskate when it came to spending money on everyday things like clothing and restaurants.

But gambling wasn't the same as spending. Gambling was more like breathing. And the high-stakes poker scene was pure oxygen. The Northeast Open would be my first trip back into that rarefied atmosphere since the disaster in Atlantic City.

I walked across the lobby and joined a line of fellow invertebrates waiting to check into their rooms. From a large opening at the far end of the lobby came the blinking and jangling of the slot machines in the casino. Deeper inside were the crap tables and the poker room, and I was feeling the gentle gravitational tug that they always exerted on me. After four months away, it was a welcome sensation.

A voice came from behind. "Excuse me, sir, is this the check-in line for the big-shot professional poker gods?"

I turned and regarded the elegant figure of Wilson J. Hopkins III, who was looking up at me from his wheelchair. As usual, he was immaculately dressed and flawlessly groomed. His haircut and his pencil-thin mustache were perfect. In his mid-sixties, shading toward the portly side, he sat in an old-fashioned wooden wheelchair, and despite the warmth of the September day, he had a woolen shawl pulled over his legs. Whether he intended it or not, I always thought that Willy Hopkins looked like he had rolled right off the set of a 1940s movie.

"Well, yes, it is. But I think you want that line over there, the one for the sheep heading to the slaughter." I grinned. "How are you, Willy?"

"Peak form, dear boy. Thank you for asking. The brain still hums like a finely tooled machine, the legs are not functioning, and all things in between are in various stages of graceful degradation."

Willy Hopkins was what the casinos referred to as a "whale," a very big player. Retired after turning his father's fortune into several more fortunes, he now spent the better part of his time following the poker circuit and playing as many high-stakes games as he could. When he wasn't playing poker, he favored baccarat at a thousand dollars per hand, played in exclusive rooms set aside for the super-rich.

"And you, Kenneth. You're looking well, as usual," I offered. Kenneth was Willy's attendant, a bull of a man nearly as wide as he was tall. His smashed-in nose and visible scars indicated a colorful past. As far as anybody could tell, though, his only job for the last five years had been to push Willy's wheelchair and fetch him sandwiches and drinks. Although Willy could afford the most high-tech motorized wheelchair on the market, he preferred to display his wealth by using an old-fashioned chair that required the services of an attendant. Kenneth glared at me and said nothing.

"Kenneth is overwhelmed with pleasure to see you." Willy smiled. I tried to imagine Kenneth feeling the slightest pleasure at seeing me, but I couldn't. "He has missed you lately, ever since Master Deukart cleaned your clock a few months back. And how are all your hoodlum friends doing?"

I looked away with faint annoyance. "Most of my hoodlum friends seem to be here in this hotel at the moment. Why don't you ask them yourself?"

"Very droll." Willy waved a hand dismissively. "Of course, I was referring to your clients, the criminal scum on whose behalf you work so diligently."

"I just get them a fair trial, Willy. The jury decides if they're guilty or if they go free." I had had this conversation hundreds of times with my law-and-order friends and relatives. Especially the relatives.

I was, by profession, a criminal defense lawyer. For eight years, I had worked for a legal service organization in Brooklyn, providing free legal defense to criminal suspects who could not afford to hire their own lawyers. The pay was crap, the hours were long, and the emotional demands were excruciating. The budget was always overstretched. More often than not, my clients were uncooperative and ungrateful. Also more often than not, they were guilty as sin. Saving the occasional innocent person from prison used to be enough to keep me going, but it was harder every year to stay motivated.

"As it happens, my hoodlum friends didn't have a very good time of it last week. Everything I touched turned to 'inmate.'"

"Glad to hear it, glad to hear it," Willy said. "And your lovely wife? I still haven't had the pleasure of meeting her. Will she ever stoop to appear at anything so tawdry as a poker game?"

"Eileen is great, thanks. She has nothing against gambling," I lied. "She's just busy with her family all the time. Today it's a birthday party for a nephew."

"She needs to get her priorities straightened out, I think. Do you have any dinner plans? Why don't you join my table in the Nantucket Room around seven. I'm sure it will be a beneficial change from your usual diet of takeout Chinese."

"Glad to." As it happened, I loved takeout Chinese, which was fortunate because it did constitute somewhere between 50 and 80 percent of my diet. But a dinner at Willy Hopkins's table was always a welcome treat. Most evenings during a major tournament, Willy hosted ten or twelve players at the most expensive restaurant in the hotel. He made it a point to order every appetizer on the menu and several that were not, along with the finest wines to be had. Sitting with friends around a table loaded with food, listening to poker pros talk shop, was his idea of pure pleasure.

"And tell that miscreant friend of yours, that Shea fellow, that he's welcome to join us as well, if he can mind his manners." Willy motioned to Kenneth to wheel him away. He never had to wait in line to check into a hotel room; his complimentary luxury suite would be arranged for him by the casino host.

"I haven't seen Jack, but I'll mention it to him if I do. See you at dinner." I smiled at Willy's retreating back as Kenneth wheeled him toward the elevators. Then I turned toward the reception desk and waited, bouncing softly on my toes. I felt good. Miles Davis was playing over the hotel's sound system—"So What." As usual at the beginning of a gambling trip, I was brimming with energetic cheerfulness and optimism. No matter how many times I did this, and no matter how seasoned a veteran I thought myself to be, my brain still fooled me, each time, into believing that *this* trip would be the biggest win ever.

2

AT NOON, THE CARDS were shuffled and dealt to begin the pre-tournament "satellite" games. Satellites are a way for people to play into the big Hold'em event without having to put up the $10,000 entry fee. Put down a thousand dollars, play against ten people, and the winner gets into the main event on the cheap.

Though seldom played around kitchen tables, Texas Hold'em had long been the reigning game in the world of high-stakes poker. It is a variation on seven-card stud in which each player is dealt two cards—face-down—and five more cards are dealt face-up in the center of the table. The five face-up cards are common to all the players, so the winner is the player who can make the best poker hand by combining his two face-down with the common cards. There are four rounds of betting in a hand—first after the two face-down cards are dealt, second after three common cards have been "flopped" face-up, next after the fourth common card, called the "turn," and finally after the fifth common card, the "river."

I usually played in one or two satellites before a big tournament. The quality of play tended to be lower in the satellites, which increased the chances of winning for a would-be semi-professional like me. Or so I thought, until I went to my assigned table and found myself sitting across from none other than Shooter Deukart.

Deukart's eyes lit up with cunning delight when he saw me. "Newk!" he exclaimed. "Welcome back to high society!"

"Shooter."

"Ain't seen you around too much lately. You been on safari?"

"Busy with my day job, Shooter."

Deukart proceeded to entertain everyone at the table with the story of how he had taken me apart at our last meeting, culminating with a brilliantly timed maneuver of slow-playing his pair of kings and trapping my queens. He didn't hesitate to rub my nose in it. "Y'all shoulda seen the look on this ol' boy's face," he cackled. "He looked like the man who jumped halfway over the barbedwire fence." I smiled gamely through the humiliating story and changed the subject at the first opportunity.

"What are you doing playing in a satellite, Shooter? I thought a $10,000 buy-in was pocket change for you."

"Jus' limberin' up," said Deukart, chewing on his toothpick, as usual. "Spent the last three weeks at my house in Hawaii, so I'm feelin' a bit rusty. Hawaii's the only place in America I kin go to git away from poker. Ain't a game worth playin' on any one a them damn islands." He was tall and angular, with a weathered Western look straight out of a Marlboro ad, but I was fairly sure that the drawl was an act. One time I had overheard him talking on the telephone in a flat voice that sounded vaguely Minnesotan.

The first hand was dealt and Shooter gave his cards a long look.

"Say, Newk, hep me out here. Like I said, I'm a little rusty." He paused dramatically to make sure everybody was listening. His toothpick shifted from one side of his mouth to the other. "These cards with the K on 'em, they're kings, right? So if I have two of 'em, that's pretty good, ain't it?"

Several players around the table chuckled. I pretended not to notice.

When his turn came, Deukart tossed his cards into the muck pile. "Guess I better fold these kings, there might be a tough ol' pair a queens lurkin' out there." The rest of the table grinned broadly at this, and several players watched for my response.

Under certain times and circumstances, I adhere to the doctrine of turning the other cheek. But a poker game is not one of them, so I came back with the first thing that entered my mind. "Shooter, one day somebody's gonna take that toothpick and stick it right up your ass." It wasn't profound, but it met the needs of the moment.

Shooter Deukart smiled. "They try every day, pardner. They try every day."

I began to suspect that the real reason Deukart played in the satellite was to have a fresh audience for his old stories. Before ten hands had been dealt, everybody at the table had heard about Deukart's days as a Navy flier in Vietnam and how he was shot down and spent three years in a North Vietnamese POW camp.

"Look at these gold teeth here," he said, baring the right side of his mouth. "Guard knocked out the real ones with a rifle butt. Know why? 'Cause I didn't bow down low enough when he walked past me. Take a look at my arms." His arms were bare beyond the rolled-up sleeves of his gingham shirt. He held them both out, in parallel, and it was plain that his left forearm was set at a weirdly crooked angle. "They broke it when they tied me to a truck and dragged me around the yard. Just for fun. That was at Cam Phu."

Although I had heard this story many times, it remained compelling. Shooter always finished the routine with the same punch line. "So when I put all my chips in the pot and I'm holdin' nuthin' but a deuce-seven, you think I'm scared you're gonna call me? Ain't nuthin' ever gonna scare me at a card table."

Scared or not, it wasn't Shooter's day. Midway through the third level of the satellite, with the blind bets up to $50 and $100 and the pressure to gamble beginning to mount, he found himself low on chips and staring down a heavyset man wearing a "Life is a Beach" T-shirt. Deukart had made a big raise before the flop, the Beach Man had called, and the flop had come out K♣ 8♣ 3♦. Shooter moved all of his remaining chips into the pot. Beach Man rubbed his jaw for a minute, and then called. "Turn 'em up," said the dealer. With Shooter's chips all in, no more betting was possible, so the cards were turned face up. Shooter showed A♥ K♠.

Beach Man flipped over his cards—K♦ 8♥. His two pairs gave him a big lead; Shooter would need an ace to win. The turn was a five and the river was a ten, and Shooter Deukart was eliminated. "Yeah!" howled Beach Man, pumping both fists into the air, when he saw the river card. "*That's* what I'm talkin' about! Tex-ass *Hold*'em, baby!" Maybe Shooter *was* a little rusty. Or distracted. He sure didn't read that guy for two pairs.

As abrasive as he was when he won, which was most of the time, Deukart was always honey-smooth when he lost. It was good business for him. He smiled, rose from his chair, and walked around the table to shake Beach Man's hand. "That was a hell of a play, ol' buddy." I knew that behind the smile Deukart was thinking, *The man called my raise with a king-eight! Is there a special God that watches out for idiots like this?* But I also knew that whenever a lucky chump like Beach Man walked around with a story about how he took down Shooter Deukart, dozens more dead money players were motivated to get in line and have their chance. Every time Deukart lost a hand like this, it paid for itself many times over.

I wasn't doing too much better than Shooter. I couldn't catch any playable cards, and my bluffs were running into power hands, with unfortunate results. Late in the fourth round, my stack of chips becoming dangerously short, I managed to get all my chips into the pot holding a pair of tens against another player who had the ace and three of clubs. When the board came with a two, four, five to give my opponent a straight, I was finished.

"That's poker," I said, smiling. "Nice hand."

By this time, Beach Man had long since lost all of his chips. He was already mingling in the crowded poker room, bragging to anybody who would listen about his brilliant play against Shooter. At that time neither he, nor I, nor anybody else at the table could have known that Beach Man was describing Shooter Deukart's last hand of poker.

3

DINNER AT WILLY HOPKINS's table was sumptuous and entertaining, as usual. Willy held court in regal style, leading the conversation and laughing at everybody's jokes. Kenneth was not there to tend to him, but the casino had eagerly provided a nubile hostess to serve in Kenneth's absence.

Above everything else, Willy Hopkins wanted to win a major poker tournament, with the fierce desire of a rich man who had nothing left to prove. Willy was the most sought-after card player on the high-stakes circuit, and not just because he was liberal in picking up dinner tabs. The pro players loved him because he played fearlessly for very large stakes and because he had a fatal weakness. Willy found it difficult to fold a strong hand, even when he knew in his head and in his gut that he was beaten. When the decisive moment came, his money usually seemed to find its way into the pot. He frequently lost big hands holding the second-best cards. The pros knew this, which is why there was always an open seat for Willy at every high-stakes game. They loved him the way a gang of crocodiles loves a leaky rowboat.

Conversation around the table was lively. The highlights of the day's poker action were chewed over, and I took pleasure in describing Shooter Deukart's downfall at the hands of the Beach Man. There was general agreement with my idea of a destination for Shooter's toothpick, and a hilarious debate as to the best method of putting it there.

As dinner broke up and I thanked Willy for the meal, he pulled on my arm and spoke to me in a confidential tone. "If you're interested, Mark, there is a private game being held tonight in the penthouse suite of the hotel. The stakes, I'm told, will be astronomical. And the skills of several of the players highly questionable."

I sat down. "In *your* suite, Willy? An illegal game?" The casino operators did not want their high rollers playing up in the suites; they wanted them down on the casino floor where the house would get its percentage.

"No, of course not. This suite is taken by a gentleman—and I use the term loosely—whose tastes are … a bit more exotic than my own."

"Ah, I see." The casino's poker room had more than enough high-stakes action to satisfy a pure card player. What a private game had to offer were the peripheral diversions—hookers and drugs— without which, for certain types, an evening is just not complete. These events could be riotous, orgiastic affairs. Imagine the Roman Empire at its worst and you start to get the picture. Cold-blooded pros like Shooter Deukart, though, *lived* for games like this. Keep a clear eye and a sober head while your opponents are doing lines with the cut card and getting hummers under the table, and you can earn a year's living in one night.

"Willy, I'm a little bit shocked. You're the last guy I would imagine being mixed up with that kind of low-class stuff."

He wrinkled his face. "Not my idea, I assure you. The host and his entourage are visitors from Spain. Barcelona, I think, or thereabouts. He is an … associate … of somebody with whom I'm trying to do a small bit of business."

"Wiseguys? Willy!"

He sighed heavily and didn't deny it. "Strictly innocent on my part, I assure you. I volunteered Kenneth to work the door for them, that's all. He has your name, if you care to partake."

"Pass. Thanks for asking, though." I smiled. "I guess I'm just an old married man."

"To your everlasting credit. Does your wife know what a good boy you are? I'm not sure she deserves you."

"Funny, my father-in-law tells me the opposite every time I see him."

I said good night to Willy. Ten paces from the door of the five-star restaurant, I was in the middle of a blinking, jangling sea of slot machines, heading toward the center of the casino. It looked as though there was some pretty good action going in the craps pit, and my pace quickened. I had my hand on my wallet when I remembered that Eileen would be expecting me to check in. There was a row of pay phones around the corner from the cashier's cage—I was, possibly, the last lawyer in America who didn't carry a cell phone—and I called home.

"Hello?" came a soft answering voice.

"Hi, sweetheart. It's me."

"Oh, I'm glad you called, Mark. I was just starting to miss you."

"Miss me already?"

"Well, I miss my nightly foot massage, anyway."

"I'm sorry, honey. I'll give you a super-special when I get back."

"Oh, don't worry, there's a cute carpenter guy working across the hall at the Johnsons' apartment. I'm thinking about recruiting him to give me my massages while you're gone."

"Why don't you try that guy who fixed our refrigerator last month? He had a pretty appealing pants droop going, if I remember."

"So how did it go today? How are all the little Lost Boys up there in Never-Never Land?"

"I got knocked out of the satellite. Broke about even in the side games. But I had an excellent meal, courtesy of Willy Hopkins."

"The Chairman of the Board."

"Yes, he is. He asked about you. Always complains that he's never met you."

"Tell him to show up at Liam's graduation party on Saturday and he can meet me in all my glory."

A familiar edge had crept into Eileen's voice. It was the I'm-mad-as-hell-that-you're-missing-more-family-functions-but-I've-decided-not-to-say-anything-about-it edge.

I clamped my left hand over my ear to block out the noise from the casino. "So how was the birthday party?"

"Mark, it was so much fun. Paul was adorable, he blew out both of his candles and got cake all over everything. Little Mikey sang 'Yankee Doodle Dandy,' and Ann Marie danced a reel."

"Ann Marie?"

"Yeah, you know, Kathleen Anne's little cousin from New Jersey. The one who wins all the trophies?"

I tried to place this one within the jumble of Anns, Marys, Ann Maries, and Mary Annes that populated my wife's huge, extended Irish-American family. I gave up and decided to fake it.

"Oh, of course. I'm sorry I wasn't there to see it."

"So am I." The edge grew a little sharper and a little closer to the surface. I scrambled to change the subject.

"So do you have a good bedtime book to read?"

"I do, but no substitute for my hubby," she pouted. "You get some sleep for yourself, okay? Don't stay up all night playing craps with Jack."

"I haven't seen Jack. I didn't think he was coming."

"He's not. Or he better not, anyway. Brigid put him on a three-month ban and told him they were finished if he did any more gambling this year."

"Ouch. I'm lucky *you're* so tolerant of my gambling."

"You *are* lucky. But then aside from the one vice, you're a fairly acceptable companion. Aside from Jack's gambling, he's still an irresponsible jerk."

"But fun to be around."

"Okay, fun to be around."

"I love you, Eileen."

"I love you too. Have you called Roger?"

I rolled my eyes and groaned inwardly. "Not yet."

"He's your brother! He practically lives right there, you have to call him!"

"Eileen, please. It's not the right time for this. He'll come out, and he'll have some big project going on, and he'll needle me into doing him a favor or something. I just don't want to deal with him when I'm trying to get back into the game."

"Promise me." There was a distinctly uncompromising tone in Eileen's demand.

"Okay, I'll call him," I sighed. "Have a good sleep. I'll talk to you tomorrow."

"Night, darlin'."

I was very much in love with Eileen Donnelly. She had a warm heart and a lively mind, and by some miracle she had agreed to be my wife. The fact that she was nice-looking and physically fit was icing on the cake. We had been married for just over two years, after a respectable engagement of eighteen months. ("Mustn't be hasty about these things," the prospective father-in-law had cautioned, probably hoping that his daughter would come to her senses.) I also enjoyed her family, a spirited bunch of first-generation Irish-Americans headquartered in the Greenwood neighborhood of the Bronx.

The family social calendar, on the other hand, was a problem for me. It rotated around a seemingly endless series of commemorative events, attendance at which was pretty much compulsory. Take seven brothers and sisters, twelve aunts and uncles, forty-six cousins, dozens of nieces and nephews, assorted in-laws and other outliers, multiply by birthdays, christenings, first communions, eighth-grade graduations, wedding showers, bachelor parties, and weddings, and you had a calendar that was pretty well packed. Not much room for weekend jaunts to Atlantic City without pissing somebody off.

The way I solved this problem was to go ahead and piss *everybody* off by missing large numbers of family events. This way, no one person could take offense. Strangely, my beloved spouse did not see the excellent logic of this solution. She would argue that I didn't appreciate the value of family. Then I would point out that the Declaration of Independence promised me the pursuit of happiness. That one always got her mad. It was clear to both of us that this would be a source of tension for years to come.

During the early days, when our relationship was just starting to become serious, the stakes that I gambled had been something of an issue. It wasn't that Eileen and her family were opposed to gambling. But gambling was something you did around a kitchen table, for dimes and quarters, with a case of beer. Or buying a chance on the fifty-fifty drawing for the Holy Name Society dance at the Saint Rose of Lima parish. That was gambling.

My hard-edged world of casino gambling had an air of moral delinquency about it. Blackjack and crap tables where the minimum bet was ten dollars, poker games where thousands of dollars changed hands in an evening—those were horrific risks, a reckless waste of money.

Of course, what is waste to one person is necessity to another. For Eileen, spending three hundred dollars on a bridesmaid's dress for a cousin's wedding was a solid investment with years of return—not because the dress would ever be worn again, but because the event was part of the glue that held the family together. But taking three hundred dollars to a casino and coming home with nothing was no different than flushing the money down a toilet. Not surprisingly, I tended to see it the other way around. Family was great, but the countless thousands of dollars squandered on ceremonial events could have been much more wisely invested in, say, a hard eight at the crap table.

As time went on, an uneasy détente was established around the subject. I kept a separate bankroll for gambling, only playing with the winnings that I was able to accumulate. If I went bust and had to dip into the family finances to start a new roll, I would pay it back with interest. In theory. Eileen, for her part, tried to keep the annual cost of birthday presents, wedding gifts, and Christmas shopping to a total that was no higher than the payroll of the New York Yankees. After two years of marriage, our "saving for a house" fund contained about enough money to buy a bathroom fixture.

I hung up the phone. Eileen's night might be ending with a good book and an early bedtime, but I valued my free casino time far too much to waste it on sleep. Within thirty seconds after hanging up, I was standing at a crap table laying out bets.

The table was nearly full. I played small bets for a couple of hours, waiting for the dice to get hot. As usual when the dice were running choppy, I had to fight the urge to double up my losing bets, which was a sure way to lose big money.

I was just on the verge of giving up for the night when I felt a hand on my shoulder. "Hey, girlfriend, whaddup?"

"Jack! Hey!" I nudged over to make room so my friend could squeeze into a spot at the table. "What've you been up to?"

"A little of this, a little of that." Jack Shea enjoyed being mysterious even when he had nothing to hide. He was a compact, well-groomed man in his late twenties, slightly below average in height at five-foot-eight. Jack's erect posture and vigorous manner gave him a dynamic presence. His attire was usually just a bit snappier than it needed to be.

I suddenly recalled the conversation with my wife. "Hey, are you supposed to be here? I thought you were under a ban."

Jack shrugged in a nonchalant way and threw a handful of chips onto the table. "Thirty each six and eight, buy the four and ten, ten each on the hard ways," he said to the dealer. "And put ten on the hard eight for the dealers." Jack played the game with an aggressive gusto no matter what the dice were doing, and he generally lost more than he won. He turned back to me. "I told Brigid I was going to a nanotechnology conference in Albany. Do you let Eileen tell *you* what to do?"

"Yes," I responded without hesitation.

"Well, I don't. Brigid, I mean."

"Yeah, right. No fear whatsoever."

Jack shouted as an eight was rolled. "Nicely, nicely, shooter!" Then, to the dealer, "Press up my six and eight and put me back up on the hard way." Without looking at me, he casually said, "You won't mention this to anybody, of course?"

I grimaced. Brigid Corrigan had been Eileen's closest friend for years, all the way back to high school. Both women were New York City police officers, and it was through them that Jack and I had come to know each other.

"Aw, hell, Jack, you're putting me in a bad spot. I don't think I can lie to Eileen for you."

"I'm not asking you to *lie* for me," Jack explained patiently. "I'm just asking you *not* to tell the *truth*. Surely an esteemed defense counsel such as yourself can appreciate the subtlety of this distinction."

"Okay. If your name comes up, I'll change the subject. But remember, if you get busted, I get busted."

"Yeah, but if *you* get busted, you won't end up broken into little pieces drifting around on the bottom of the ocean with the whale shit, like I will."

As far as I was aware, his girlfriend's anger was the only thing in the world that Jack Shea had ever been afraid of. Brigid was a diminutive woman—just a bit over five feet tall and no more than one hundred pounds—but extraordinarily powerful in both mind and body. She was a martial arts instructor at the police academy, and many a cocksure cadet with years of street-brawling experience had been humbled in her class. She had a ferocious temper to match her prodigious fighting skills. Most of the time, she managed to keep the temper in check, but on occasion Jack was exposed to a full blast of it. He tried hard to keep those occasions to a minimum, though not going so far as to actually change his errant behavior.

"But of course it's not like Brigid can tell you what to do," I said.

"Up yours. Hey, listen, I have a new theory on poker that is going to win me this tournament."

I rolled my eyes. "You *always* have a new theory on poker. Here's a theory for you: bet your good cards and fold your bad cards. How about trying that one out?"

"Doesn't work for me. But listen. I read an article by this psychologist, and he says poker is all about sex."

"Huh. Well, everything else seems to be about sex. Why should poker be any different?"

"Exactly. So you have a bunch of guys sitting around a poker table, right? Basically trying to hump each other's brains out, only using cards and chips instead of their natural equipment."

"A bunch of guys?"

"Yeah, that's the whole point. This article says inside everybody who thinks he's as manly as they come, there's a little bit of queer trying to get out. And poker is one way to let it out. 'Giving free play to our suppressed homoerotic tendencies,' the guy says."

"Or in your case, autoerotic tendencies."

"Funny." Jack grimaced as the dice came up seven and wiped out his array of bets. He threw more chips onto the table. "But really, think about it. According to this article, nobody is completely heterosexual or completely homosexual. Most people are about 95 percent one way or another. So the 5 percent of you that wants to go the other way is the part that you're really afraid of, right? *You* try to pretend that it doesn't exist, but *it* is smoldering away in there. And that's one reason why guys love poker so much. It gives that 5 percent a chance to step out and slam it around a little bit."

"Sounds so crazy it might even be true."

"It *is* true! Listen. In poker, when you make a big aggressive move on someone, you're 'coming over the top of him,' right? Where do you suppose *that* came from? And did you know that the word *poker* comes from the French word *pouchettier*, which means, literally, to impale with a stick?"

"Really?"

"Well, no. Actually, I just made that up. But it sounds plausible, doesn't it?"

"If you say so." I made no attempt to hide my skepticism. "So how does this theory translate into winning?"

"Here's the beauty of it. You have all these guys, they're all trying to prove to themselves and to everybody else what tough men they are, right? But all the time, without knowing it, they're really letting their gay parts out for some fresh air. So what *you* have to do is put the gay stuff right in their face. Show 'em the part of themselves that they're terrified of. They can't handle it, they go on tilt. They're putty in your hands."

"You could have chosen a better metaphor than that last one. I still don't know what you're talking about."

"It's simple. You just throw a little bit of effeminate stuff at them. A wink, maybe a little hand slap. It's like holding up a mirror in front of their faces, and they freak out when they see it. I think I'll call it my 'Queer Eye for the Straight-Flush Guy' method."

"Uh-huh. And this is the plan that will let you beat the world's best poker players?"

"No, sir. This is the plan that lets the world's best poker players beat themselves."

"No pun intended, I'm sure. Of course, aside from being insane, your theory has a major flaw."

"What's that?"

"Well, a certain number of the people you run into will actually *be* gay. And then there are the female players too. Your plan won't work on them."

"Yeah, you're right. Not much I can do about that. I'll just have to beat those players the old-fashioned way. Fall back on superior intelligence and superior firepower. And that's all she wrote." When pressed, Jack was always good for a quote from *Caddyshack*.

"Uh-huh. Well, this ought to be fun to watch, anyway. I hope you'll have a team of medics standing by for when somebody hauls you out back and pounds the crap out of you. So what's your gimmick gonna be at the next tournament? Astrology? Taking your guidance from the movement of planets and celestial orbs?"

Jack grabbed me by the arm. "Hey, I'm looking at some celestial orbs right now. Let's switch tables, Anita Wilson just started her shift over there."

"You go. I'm gonna stick it out here for a little bit longer."

"Suit yourself," said Jack. He scooped up his chips and sauntered to the next table, where he took a spot immediately to the right of a dealer, who happened to be an astonishingly beautiful woman. Anita Wilson was famous among all the regulars at the Humpback for her sheer, unabashed gorgeousness. She had glowing cocoa skin, a brilliant smile, and huge deep brown eyes, with a voluptuous body that, in the words of Groucho Marx, would make a shambles out of a monastery in five minutes flat.

Wherever Anita Wilson went, most of the men within fifty feet were keenly aware of her presence. Her magnetism definitely made it hard to play craps in an intelligent way. Men tended to make a lot of macho plays: chasing big losses by doubling up, or putting big money on the hard-way bets with ridiculous percentages favoring the house. Men, it turns out, are prone to doing a lot of amazingly stupid things when they think that a beautiful woman might be watching them. The casino had to be paying Anita well in excess of the standard wage for a craps dealer.

Jack chatted her up. I had no firsthand knowledge of Jack ever screwing around on Brigid. But he was such an outrageous hound around women, it was hard to believe that he didn't.

"Never gives up, does he?" asked a voice at my shoulder. I turned and smiled at Evelyn Gibbs, who was holding a tray of drinks. "You want anything, Mark?"

"Beer would be great."

Evelyn Gibbs had been a waitress at the Humpback since the day it opened, yet she seemed to be incapable of remembering individual drink orders. As far as I could tell, her strategy was to load a tray with a variety of beverages and hope that she would be able to get rid of them to thirsty gamblers who weren't too particular.

Unlike most of the cocktail waitresses at the casino, Evelyn was a mature woman in her mid-fifties. She was in reasonably good shape for a woman of her age, but the skimpy outfit that the casino forced her to wear looked ridiculous, through no fault of her own. The almost-thong bottom and the push-up top were ludicrous on her. Nobody deserved that kind of humiliation, I thought. Evelyn was just a nice lady trying to make a living.

Evelyn looked around on her tray for a beer. I settled for a watered-down ginger ale and handed her a five-dollar chip as a tip.

"You working the poker tournament?" I asked.

"Yeah," she replied. "I'll look for you in there."

"Thanks, Evey," I said as she hurried to respond to the impatient glowering of another gambler.

Maybe the fact that Jack and I were on a first-name basis with so many of the staff at the Humpback should have been a disturbing sign that we were gambling a little too much. If so, the fact that there were four or five other casinos where we were on similar terms of familiarity should have been even more troubling.

But it wasn't, at least not to us.

4

I SHOULD HAVE GONE to bed. The dice at my table were cold, a couple of the other players were annoying, and I was tired. I picked up my chips and made the move toward the cashier when Jack noticed that I was leaving and beckoned me over. *Okay,* I told myself, *maybe just a few more rolls to see if we can get something going.*

There was a much warmer atmosphere at this new table, a lot of friendly chatter between the crew and the players. My mood picked up immediately. Thirty minutes later, as I took the dice to begin a new shoot, I remembered Eileen's admonition: "Don't stay up all night playing craps with Jack." *I guess she knows me,* I thought.

As often happens around a slow crap table at three in the morning, the talk developed into a cheerful dispute over a totally meaningless question. How we got onto the subject of oceans, I don't remember, but a spirited disagreement erupted over how many there were.

"There are four oceans," I maintained. "Atlantic, Pacific, Indian, and Arctic. Everybody knows that."

Jack, naturally, agreed with whatever position was being taken by the nearest beautiful woman. In this case, that was Anita Wilson. "Listen to me," she said in crisp English that carried just a trace of her Caribbean origin. "There are five oceans. Atlantic, Pacific, Indian, Arctic, and Antarctic. This is elementary."

The consensus at the table was against me. Everybody was in on it—the stick man who was in charge of the dice, the box man who monitored all the action, and the lone gambler at the far end of the table. They all agreed with Anita. Her opinion on the matter carried great weight, of course, because she had perfect breasts and a slender waist that sloped out marvelously into hips that were just ever-so-slightly too full. This fantastic toboggan ride for the eyes gave Anita more authority—among that particular group of gentlemen—than if she'd had multiple PhDs. If she had said there was a sixth ocean called the Sahara Desert, they would have reached for their scuba gear and dived in.

"I know how we can settle this once and for all," Jack said. "I have a world atlas in the back seat of my car."

"You have a *world* atlas in your car?" I asked. "What, in case you suddenly need to drive to Kazakhstan?"

"Stranger things have happened. Like I said, it's in a pile of stuff somewhere in my back seat. Anita, I suggest that you and I go out to look for it."

She laughed. "You are a funny man, Jack Shea." Jack had propositioned Anita so many times that she'd long since stopped taking him seriously.

"Actually, if there really is an atlas, I'll go and get it myself," I said. "I'd love a little fresh air after all the bullshit you guys have been talking."

Jack handed me the keys to his Audi and said, "G11."

"Watch my chips, all right?" I turned to go.

"Thank God. I thought we'd never get rid of that guy," Jack said in an exaggerated voice as I walked away from the table.

I navigated the complex of parking lots, looking for Section G, Row 11. Walking outside in the crisp night air felt great. *Life* felt great, come to think of it. A full week of gambling stretched out in front of me like summer vacation to a ten-year-old. No ill-fated clients, no aggressive prosecutors to square off with, nobody to keep out of jail or bail out of trouble. This week was going to be about me.

I was somewhere between E4 and E5 when all that came to a crashing halt. A woman was screaming in terror in a far corner of the parking lot. *What the hell!* I craned to see what was happening, but it was too dark and there were too many cars. The hotel was at least a hundred yards away. It was either go back and grab a security guard or run forward to the rescue. I hesitated for just a moment; then my inner Boy Scout took over and I dashed off toward the screams.

It was a long way to run, which gave me plenty of time to consider the likelihood that I was heading toward a confrontation with an armed, violent criminal. Because I was neither armed nor violent, it occurred to me that fetching security might have been the better move. Too late for that now.

The woman had stopped screaming after just a few seconds, well before I reached the edge of the lot. The fact that the screams had ended, however, did not mean that the trouble was over or that the bad guy was gone. The first thing a rapist would do would be to shut up the victim. I knew that all too well.

I was crossing cautiously between rows of cars, trying to move as quickly and quietly as possible while a small but vocal part of my brain was urging me to get the hell out of there. The closer I got to the edge of the parking lot, the harder I could feel my heart banging away in my chest. *What am I doing? Go get a cop!* I strained to hear some sign of a struggle, but there was nothing except the soft sound of my sneakers on the pavement and the pounding of the blood in my ears.

Closer to the hotel, the lot had seemed well lit. Out here on the fringes, it felt awfully dark. Beyond the parking lot there was a black wall of forest, and behind every car was a pool of shadow that promised to shelter a murderous thug.

A gunshot exploded inches from my ear and I cried out in mindless panic. Then nothing happened. Five seconds later I recovered myself and realized that the sound was not a gun at all. It had only been a car door slamming, a good fifty yards away. I stood still, waiting for my heart to slow down, while the car started up and its sound receded into the distance. Was it connected somehow to the screaming? There was no way to know. But if somebody had told me it was the bad guy escaping, I would have kissed the ground in gratitude.

Since I'd already given away my presence by yelling at the sound of the car door, I had nothing to lose by shouting, "Hey! Whoever's out there, I called the cops! If I were you, I'd get out of here!" Silence. I advanced, slowly, through the rows of cars.

Section R, Row 25, was the far end of the lot. There were no cars parked in the last two rows, just empty spaces. I didn't have anything to hide behind, but then neither did he, if he was still lurking around. The lamp at the end of Section R wasn't working and there was a wedge of darkness where the light from the neighboring lamps didn't reach. Directly beneath the non-functioning light pole was the figure of a human being, slouched in a half-seated, half-lying position.

I approached warily, looking over each shoulder, until I stood ten feet away from the slumping figure. Even in the darkness it was easy to see that he was dead. There was no question of shouting for somebody to call 911 or making a heroic attempt to administer CPR, which I didn't know how to do anyway. The four holes in the chest left no room for doubt.

A woman's scream, a man's dead body, and a scared-shitless would-be hero. But no bad guy. *Okay, it is definitely time to go get a cop.*

Human beings are drawn to human faces, and somewhere I've read that a person confronting a corpse has an almost irresistible urge to look at its face. It's true. I couldn't help drawing closer. About four feet from the body, I stopped and squatted down to eye level, getting my first look at the dead man's face. *Holy shit.*

Then a blinding spotlight shone in my eyes.

"Freeze! Right there!" came a man's voice. I was frozen, all right.

"Stand up slow and hold your arms straight out at your sides."

I did it.

"I'm not armed!" I shouted. Behind the man a pair of headlights was rapidly approaching, and the revolving red and blue lights of a police cruiser shot out suddenly from above them. Within a minute there were three cars there.

"Damn!" said the first man, the one with the flashlight, as he approached the dead body. He wore the uniform of a hotel security guard. "What did you do to this guy?"

"I found him, that's all I did. I was across the parking lot and I heard a woman screaming. I came running over to help, and this is what I found."

He looked at me suspiciously. He seemed excited about the prospect of catching a bad guy, and I was the only guy around. I would have to disappoint him.

"I didn't hear any scream," he said. "I heard a man yelping like a scared dog."

"Uh, that was me," I said sheepishly. "I got startled when the car started up."

"Car? What car? So where is this woman? The screamer?"

"I don't know. Maybe she took off in the car."

"Maybe she's the one that called in the alarm." This was a different voice, and an older uniformed man stepped forward. "I'll take care of this, Jimmy. Good job being first on the scene." He sized me up. "There's an easy way to test this. Any of these cars around here belong to you?"

Obviously, I had found the clever one in the bunch. I began to relax just a little. "No. I was heading for an Audi in G11." I held up the keys. "Belongs to a friend. He's inside the casino right now at a crap table. You can go and ask him."

"Won't be necessary. You don't mind if I check to be sure you aren't carrying?" He patted me down quickly and expertly. Obviously a retired cop, and a good one. "Gerry!" he called over his shoulder at one of the guards. "Take a look in all the cars around here to see if any have the keys in them. And don't touch anything. Jimmy, come over here a minute. Look at those wounds. No, don't touch him, for Chrissakes! This guy has obviously been dead for hours. And where is the blood? Somebody must have dumped him here."

He turned back to me. "Anything else you have to say?"

"I heard a car start up and leave the lot a couple of minutes ago. Might have been the woman I heard screaming."

"Where was it?"

I pointed in the general direction. "Hard to say. Maybe fifteen or twenty rows over there."

"We'll let the state cops sort this out when they get here. Meantime, why don't you go over and wait by my vehicle while I secure the scene."

"Sure thing. Thanks for being so professional. Your guy there with the flashlight had me a little nervous."

"Jimmy? He's a good kid. I'm George Crow. Tribal police."

"Mark Newcomb. Listen, you should know something. I recognize the victim. He has a pretty big name around here."

He looked at me without any expression, waiting.

"You ever heard of Shooter Deukart?"

His eyes widened. "Him?" He gestured with his head.

I nodded.

"Holy shit."

"Yeah, that's what I said."

I spent the next five minutes leaning against a security car, staring at Shooter Deukart's murdered body and trying to absorb the fact that this was really happening. When the state police arrived, I turned my whole attention to the pressing matter of not getting arrested. I gave them a detailed statement, and George Crow backed me up. This seemed to satisfy the police, but it didn't satisfy me. I insisted that one of them go into the casino to take statements from Jack Shea and Anita Wilson in order to corroborate my story. I had represented enough people who were wrongfully accused due to sloppy police work, and I sure as hell wasn't going to let that happen to me.

5

Tuesday, September 28

BY THE TIME I squared everything with the state police and got back to my room, it was after five a.m. I did my best to sleep in late, but by nine I was wide awake. I tried a quick call to the narcotics unit office where Eileen was stationed. She was out, and I was not allowed to call her cell phone when she might be working undercover. After leaving a message for her, I shambled down to the coffee shop for my usual casino breakfast of eggs and hash browns. I sat there pretending to read the morning paper, but really I was still trying to come to grips with my experience last night.

"Mark, did you hear?"

I looked up. "Oh hi, Maddie. You mean about Shooter?"

Madelin Santos dropped into a chair. She was a tall, auburn-haired woman in her mid-twenties. She had begun attracting attention as one of the growing number of women who played cards professionally. Strikingly good-looking, with brilliant green eyes set off against a cinnamon complexion, she was exactly the sort of person that the new publicity-minded promoters of professional poker wanted to have in the spotlight.

"Yeah. I heard they found him out in the woods behind the hotel with four bullets in him. Wallet, watch, rings gone. They say he was taking a walk and got robbed."

"Actually, it was the parking lot. R25. I was the one who found him." My chest puffed up, just a little bit, with self-importance. For reasons that would be understandable to any male above the age of seven, it gave me no small thrill to impress this beautiful woman with the fact that I had stumbled across a bloody corpse.

"Oh my God, I had no idea. That's unbelievable." She put her hand on my arm. "So, tell me the whole story." The touch of her fingers on my arm was not unpleasant, but precisely for that reason I politely pulled it away.

I told her everything, only exaggerating a little bit when I got to the part about rushing heroically to the rescue of the mysterious screamer. Maddie had a dozen questions that I couldn't answer, about how and why it all happened. "Hey, how should I know? All I did was find him. I didn't shoot him. So, have you heard anything about what's going to happen with the tournament?"

"Bob Herr's telling everybody not to worry, the games will go on."

"Good. Have you seen Jack this morning?"

"He's over playing craps. I asked him if he'd heard the news and he barely looked up, like it was an old story already."

"Yeah, Jack learned about it last night from the cops. He's my alibi."

"*You* need an *alibi*? Please don't tell me they think you had something to do with it."

"Nah. Of course not. But when the cops find a person standing over a dead body, they generally would like to know what he's been up to for the past few hours."

Attendance at the day's poker events was very low. To play cards as though nothing had happened just didn't seem the right thing to do. Like me, most people that morning found that their main reaction was shock, but not sadness. Deukart had not been well-liked by those who knew him best. He was a poker legend, a war hero—and a disagreeable guy. People were milling around, wondering what they ought to be doing, not wanting to appear inappropriate or disrespectful but, for the most part, not experiencing anything resembling genuine grief.

Bob Herr, the director of the tournament, was almost beside himself. Like everybody else, I'm sure, he felt the need to appear sincerely devastated despite the lack of much real feeling. I have no doubt that one corner of his mind was already calculating the increased publicity and TV share that were likely to result from this sensational new development. He was everywhere that day, juggling hurried conversations with police, reporters, players, and the financial backers of the tournament.

State police investigators were prominent throughout the morning as they sought out anybody at the hotel who might have useful information.

The better part of my day was spent in the Nor'easter, which was the Humpback's coffee shop. The nautical décor of the Nor'easter was highlighted by photos of fishermen standing next to huge, trophy-sized swordfish juxtaposed with pictures of big slot winners posing next to their jackpot machines.

I was quite the celebrity that morning. Naturally, everybody wanted to talk about how I'd found the body, but after the third or fourth telling it became a bore. The only person I really wanted to talk with was Eileen, but after leaving three messages I gave up on reaching her.

Around eleven o'clock Steve Brown, otherwise known as Buddha, sat down and ordered a late breakfast. Tran Le Binh, one of the many pros who had immigrated from Vietnam, joined us for a while. Binh chain-smoked a brand of filterless cigarettes that I didn't recognize. Anywhere else, I would have found the presence of a smoker to be highly annoying. Inside a casino, though, it seemed perfectly normal.

I was glad for Buddha Brown's company, because he had no morbid curiosity about Shooter's body and he was always good for an interesting conversation about cards. "Don't think of a poker tournament as a bunch of individuals fighting it out for the big prizes," he said. "That leaves a handful of winners and a whole bunch of losers. Think of the tournament as a communal event. Everybody throws their money, their skills, and their luck into a big pot, and Fate sorts it out from there. If the game is played beautifully, everybody wins."

I was way too polite to say, "Bullshit," which was my initial reaction to Buddha's notion. "Tell me something, Steve," I asked. "Is that really how you feel the moment you get knocked out of a tournament?"

He smiled. "Let's just say I'm still working on it."

Binh was more to the point. "You talk like somebody who has never been hungry," he said. Buddha nodded thoughtfully.

Binh was a quiet man who kept to himself. It was unusual for him to be sitting around socializing like this. When I asked him a few questions about Vietnam, Binh was obviously uncomfortable talking about it.

Buddha Brown graciously changed the subject. "The closest I've ever come to Asia is Hawaii. Great place. I spend as much time there as I can manage."

"I've heard there isn't much poker action out there," I said.

"What do you mean?" asked Brown. "Hawaii is a poker paradise. All those rich tourists—there are games all over the place."

"Really." I frowned. That was odd. Before I could ask another question, though, Jack Shea plopped down next to me and heaved a sigh.

"Cold table?" I asked.

"Brutal. Numbing. Hyperborean." Like an Eskimo with fifty-six different words for snow, Jack had an impressive vocabulary when it came to describing an inhospitable dice table. "Went bad on me and just never turned around."

"When are you going to learn to walk away from the table when you're losing?"

"When are you going to learn that stubborn idiots like me are the happiest people on earth?"

He had me there. Buddha Brown laughed.

"Hey, look who's coming," Jack said. "It's Assahola Gant himself."

I looked up toward the entrance to the Nor'easter and watched Jim "Barracuda" Gant walk energetically into the coffee shop. He ignored the hostess, who was trying to tell him that there was a wait for seats. Gant was a twenty-three-year-old professional player who had nominated himself as the leading young gun on the circuit, and he was happy to tell anybody, at any time, how great he was. He was dressed raffishly in baggy jeans, an oversized athletic jersey, and a backward-facing baseball cap—the unofficial uniform of too-cool overprivileged suburban white kids. Self-consciously brash and bold, Gant had given himself the nickname "Barracuda" to enhance his star value. He was, in fact, a pretty good player, though not, in my opinion, anywhere near as good as he made himself out to be.

"Hey, Jim, we've got an empty chair over here," called Jack in a voice loud enough for everybody in the café to hear. Barracuda hated being called Jim. "Come on over and teach us how to play poker."

Gant swaggered over and pretended to smile. "Jack Squat, how you doing? Why aren't you giving away your money at the crap tables?" He had a low opinion of anybody foolish enough to gamble at a game in which the casino had a statistical advantage. Poker, Gant was fond of saying, isn't gambling. It's a contest of skill where the strong devour the weak. Barracuda Gant was never invited to Willy Hopkins's dinner table.

"Have a seat, Barracuda," I said in an attempt to be polite. I gestured toward the empty seat that Binh had quietly vacated.

Barracuda glanced at me blankly for a moment and did not acknowledge my invitation. "Buddha, whassup?" he asked as he turned away from me. In Barracuda's world, only full-time professional poker players were worthy of attention. The only reason he bothered talking to Jack was that he enjoyed calling him "Jack Squat." I really hated this guy.

Buddha Brown coughed softly, using his hand to cover a smile. "An unsettling day, wouldn't you say?" he asked.

"Hey, out with the old, in with the new. I mean, bad shit and all, but when your game starts going, then what's left to live for anyway?"

"Shooter Deukart had more game left than you'll ever have," I fired out. In my irritation, I had stooped to a playground cliché.

Gant ignored me completely. "So, Buddha, you playing in any satellites?"

"No, I think I'll pass today," said Brown, a patient smile still playing on his lips.

"You're missing a killing, man. There's almost no pros at the tables. I won one this morning already. Worth getting up for, even after an all-nighter with those Spanish dudes up in the penthouse. *That* was a wild scene. They had a couple of bitches up there, called themselves Prancer and Vixen. Un-fucking-real what they could do ..." He cocked his head, obviously waiting for one of us to ask.

"Somehow I managed to miss the festivities." Buddha took a sip of his coffee. "I wasn't invited, anyway."

"Neither was I! I crashed it! That big fucking retard who works for Meals-on-Wheels Hopkins won't let me in, right? So I come back later and he isn't there and Prancer opens the door for me. Two minutes later I'm bare-assed in the fucking hall closet with her and Vixen, and you won't believe what they're doing to me."

Gant paused again, but none of us prompted him to continue. I'm sure Jack was dying of curiosity, but even he wouldn't give Barracuda the pleasure of telling his story.

Buddha turned pointedly away from Gant. "So, Mark, how are things in the criminal defense world?"

"Too busy, always," I said. "Heroin is making another comeback."

Gant stood there awkwardly for a moment. "Anybody seen Maddie around?" he asked finally. Without waiting for a response, he walked away, head high, pretending to scan the room for somebody important. Of all the annoying traits that Barracuda Gant possessed, the most intolerable was his pretension that he and Maddie Santos were fated to be the glamour couple of the poker world. Despite what seemed to be an utter lack of encouragement from Maddie, he liked to pose in card player circles as her sometime lover.

"Man, that is one detestable shitwad," said Jack, shaking his head. "He's given me a wicked idea, though. Where exactly was it that you found Shooter's body, Mark?"

"In the parking lot, Section R25," came a voice from behind me. "Why do you ask?"

I turned around in my seat and faced Zip Addison, intrepid reporter for *Card Times* magazine. I had a bone to pick with him.

"Hapless?" I asked. "You had to write that I was *hapless*?"

Addison sniffed. "You *were* hapless that night. Shooter played you like your cards were made of rice paper. Ooh, I like that, I'm gonna write that down." He scribbled into his notebook. "Besides, I said some nice things about you too."

Zip Addison was a thin man with fine features who would have been considered very attractive to women if it weren't for a slightly pinched expression and a ghostly complexion that gave him a weasely look. He also had an annoying habit of shifting from foot to foot as though he had to go to the bathroom.

"So what do you know?" Buddha Brown asked him.

"Well, the cops are asking a lot of weird questions. This wasn't any robbery, that's for sure. Billy Birds is already laying three-to-one that the murderer is another card player. Not you, though, Mark."

"Well, be sure to tell Billy thanks for me."

Billy Birds was the unofficial oddsmaker for the professional poker circuit. He would place a bet on absolutely anything, and he had an uncanny sense for the probabilities of seemingly random events. Point to two birds sitting on a telephone wire, and he would bet you which one would fly off first and somehow be right about 80 percent of the time.

"Hey, Zip," Jack said. "You went to a really good college, didn't you?"

"Swarthmore '98," Addison said proudly.

"So how come you're the only one in your class who couldn't get a decent job?"

He stiffened. "I don't know if any of my classmates are covering a major murder case right now," he said.

"Yeah, well, when you crack the case, let me know," Jack said with obvious disdain.

I was much more interested than Jack was in the progress of the investigation. "So really, Zip, what else are you hearing about all this?"

Addison's eyes narrowed, and his already pinched face tightened into a stingy sneer. "You give me something and I'll give you something," he said.

I shrugged. "I don't have anything to tell you other than what you've already heard."

"Well, then I guess I'm wasting my time here, aren't I?" He walked away without saying goodbye.

A few minutes later Jack had just about persuaded me to give the crap tables a try when we were approached by a uniformed officer.

"Are you Mark Newcomb?"

"Yes, I am."

"Sir, I'm Trooper Schmidt of the State Police. Would you mind coming with me to one of our conference rooms so we can ask you a few questions?"

"I already told everything I know, last night."

"Captain DiCarlo is the chief investigator on the case. He'd like to talk to you in person if you don't mind."

"Sure." I shot a glance at Jack, who raised his eyebrows.

6

I was led down a wide gallery that skirted the casino floor. In keeping with the overall theme of the establishment, the walls were trimmed with thick nautical rope. We passed a glassed-in collection of model whaling ships. I wondered how many gamblers had taken time away from the slot machines to appreciate the display. I guessed very few.

Beyond the casino host's station, there was a door that opened onto a narrower corridor. With the door closed behind us, the noise and atmosphere of the casino were shut out. Over the loudspeakers in the ceiling, Diana Krall was crooning "Cry Me a River." Here was another thing that I loved about the Humpback. Apparently, the president of the Missequa Tribal Council was a stone cold jazz fan. So, instead of the canned soft rock that filled most casinos (complete, the rumor went, with subliminal messages whispering, "Lose"), the patrons of the Humpback were treated to Miles, Diz, and Ella. Most of them, of course, couldn't have cared less.

Trooper Schmidt ushered me into a comfortable room that was normally used as a temporary office by business clients of the Humpback. There was no music, just an ominous quiet. I sat in a padded chair. Schmidt stood in a corner, and we were joined by a plainclothes officer who wore the ill-fitting, nondescript suit of an honest cop. I stood up and he shook my hand.

"Captain Frank DiCarlo, Massachusetts State Police."

"Pleasure."

His eyes were level with mine, which put him at about six feet tall, like me. But that was where the physical resemblance ended. Everything about DiCarlo was a hard angle, including his military haircut. I thought I was in reasonably good shape, for a man who wore a tie to work and spent most of his leisure time sitting at a card table. But the captain was a chiseled fitness nut, probably a triathlete or decathlete or something overbearing like that. He had to be twice my age, but he definitely could have kicked my butt in any sporting event I might name. I made a mental note to start doing sit-ups.

DiCarlo took a seat behind the desk, glanced at a notepad that lay open in front of him, and looked up at me. He didn't waste any time with small talk.

"You knew Warren Deukart pretty well?"

"His name was *Warren?* I had no idea." I sat down again and described for the captain the extent of my relationship with Shooter. I had played cards across from him and lost money to him. We had occasionally shared a meal at one of Willy Hopkins's feasts, but that was about it. I was not particularly fond of the man. DiCarlo wanted to know quite a bit about my background. When I mentioned that I was a public defender, the captain interrupted me.

"So you think cops are the bad guys, right?"

"Not all cops. I'm married to one."

His eyebrows arched in surprise.

"Okay, tell me where you were last evening, from six o'clock on."

"I gave a complete statement to your men last night."

"I'd like to hear it for myself, if you don't mind." He was looking at a file that contained, I assumed, my statement from earlier. He was going to be listening closely for any inconsistencies.

"All right. From six to seven I was in my room watching TV Land. *The Addams Family*. Uncle Fester got his high school diploma. Gomez ran for mayor, and Pugsley was his—"

DiCarlo looked up sharply and interrupted. "Okay, okay, I get your point." He closed the file and put it down on the desk.

Score one for me. I continued. "At seven I joined a big table for dinner: Willy Hopkins, Pete Kuhler, seven or eight other people."

"Names, please." I provided the names and continued.

"Dinner ended sometime between nine and ten. I made a call to my wife from a pay phone, then played—"

He interrupted again. "Why didn't you use your cell phone?"

"Because I don't have one."

He frowned, not sure what to make of that. It was as if I'd told him I didn't own a toothbrush. "Okay. Did you use a calling card?"

I gave my card information, and Trooper Schmidt wrote it down.

"Go on. What happened then."

"I played craps until around three o'clock, when there was a friendly argument about a question of geography and I decided to walk out to my friend's car to get his atlas. The time I spent at the crap table was all recorded on the casino's security cameras, of course. Oh. You need to know, the casino doesn't hold that tape for more than a day or two, so you should probably talk to them about securing all the tapes from yesterday, to make sure nothing gets erased."

"When I need you to tell me my job, I'll let you know. My men are already on that."

From the way that Trooper Schmidt was frantically scribbling a note to himself, I could see that they were *not* already on that. I allowed myself a tiny smile.

"All right," he said. "Tell me what happened in the parking lot."

I carefully described the entire sequence of events leading up to the time when the security guards arrived on the scene.

"I don't suppose you've made any progress in finding the mysterious screamer, have you?" I asked.

"I was about to ask you the same question."

"Oh. I didn't realize I'd been assigned to the case."

"Just thought you might have done some poking around on your own."

"No thanks. I plan on being very busy this week. Can't you trace her cell phone number from the 911 call?"

"Ordinarily we could, but this call seems to have been made on one of those throwaway phones. No way to identify the caller."

"Figures. Probably another loser who puts her paycheck into the slot machines instead of paying her bills. But you know," I said slowly, "there might be another way to do it. Let's assume that she was a gambler who was leaving for the night, was walking to her car, and discovered the body. She freaks out, decides she doesn't want to get involved, so she takes off. But then she makes a 911 call from her car. Right?"

He leaned forward, his elbows on the desk. "Reasonable assumption. But from what you tell me, the car was pretty far away from the body. Which was in shadow. So how does she accidentally come across the corpse when it's that far out of her way?"

"Maybe she couldn't remember where she was parked. Maybe she lost a lot of money so she was blowing off steam with a walk around the lot. Maybe she's an exercise freak. Hell, I was wandering around the parking lot looking for a world atlas. There's all kinds of nuts out there. Anyway, my point is, you can check the security tapes. They'll show any woman who walked out of the casino during the ten or fifteen minutes before I did. There probably weren't too many people at that hour. Then you can check the tapes for the whole casino floor from the half hour before that, and try to spot her at a slot machine or a table game. If she used a player's card, the casino will have her play on file and you can identify her."

DiCarlo looked interested. "Not bad. Could be worth looking into. Maybe I'll have to deputize you." He sat back in his chair and showed a trace of a smile.

That was a little too nice. Something was coming.

"Do you know anything about a private game that happened last night in one of the hotel rooms?" he asked. "Possibly one of the luxury suites?"

I wasn't going to get Willy Hopkins into any kind of trouble if I could help it, short of flat-out lying. "There was some buzz about a game. I wouldn't have paid much attention, I don't get involved in that kind of action. Why do you ask?"

DiCarlo didn't respond. He stood up and walked over to the window. He turned and faced me. With the light from the window behind him, his face was shrouded, intimidating.

Here it comes, I thought. *Whatever it is that he's got.* Having sat through hundreds of police interrogations, I easily recognized the old window ploy. Do your attacking with the sun in the other guy's eyes.

"Did you have any particular reason to dislike Deukart?"

"Other than that he took my money and wasn't very polite about it, no. But if that's a reason, then you're going to have a real long list of people to talk to."

"It appears he took a whole *lot* of your money. And embarrassed you pretty badly in the process." DiCarlo reached over to the desk, picked something up, and handed it to me. It was a photocopy of a page from *Card Times* magazine. I was amazed. This guy worked pretty fast. He took it back and read aloud: "I'll give credit to the hapless Newcomb, he kept coming back for more." He looked at me. The implication was obvious.

"Look, Captain, between then and now Shooter probably beat a dozen guys worse than he beat me. It's the nature of the game. You're saying I'm going to be a suspect because some reporter called me hapless?"

"It's a remarkable coincidence, don't you think? Deukart takes a lot of money from you, then you happen to discover his murdered body."

I had seen this game played so many times. After making nice for a little bit, now he was trying to rattle me, probing for a weakness. I wasn't going to show him any.

"First of all, I didn't discover the body. The screamer did, and the fact that security got an anonymous call supports that. Second, Anita Wilson and Jack Shea have already given a statement on why I left the casino to go to the parking lot. And third, it's hardly a coincidence that Shooter and I were both here for a tournament. With all the poker players around the Humpback this week, the odds were pretty fair that Shooter's body might be found by somebody who had lost money to him at some point." *Take that, copper.*

He fired back. "I have several people who say that you threatened Deukart yesterday."

"Excuse me?"

"To be more precise, you threatened to shove a toothpick up his ass."

Now I didn't know whether to laugh out loud or to be furious. Who would have said this? Who would report that to the police as a suspicious statement? Was this why the guy was playing games with me? After a moment of incredulity, my lawyer's instinct kicked in. I sat up straight and gave him the simple facts.

"Yesterday I was at a satellite table with Shooter. He was giving me a hard time, and the table expected me to come back with something, so I made an observation that someday his famous toothpick was going to find its way to a place where it didn't belong. That's all."

"Well, you turned out to be right on the money."

"What do you mean?"

DiCarlo was watching my face intently. "The coroner found a toothpick in the rectum of the corpse."

When the three cards of the flop are placed face-up, a good poker player does not look at the cards right away. Instead he studies the face of his opponent as the cards are revealed, watching for any sign of a reaction. A gleam of excitement, a slight grimace of disappointment, or a glance down at the chips could give away the opponent's cards. Just then Frank DiCarlo was studying my face with all the skill gained from years of experience as an investigator. He was going to decide on the spot how much interest he had in me as a potential suspect.

I don't think I gave his face-reading skills much of a challenge.

"You're shitting me," I said, my mouth hanging open. I was no longer a model of professional composure.

"I shit you not, as the poet said." He returned to the desk and sat down.

"Well, I don't know what to tell you. At dinner there was kind of a raucous conversation about the various things people would like to do with Shooter's toothpick. The idea was a pretty popular one."

DiCarlo didn't say anything.

"No way I could've had time to do that between the time I left the hotel and the time the security guards got there."

Still he didn't speak. He continued to watch my face with an unnerving stare. Somewhere in my mind I knew that I should be coolly assessing the situation and measuring every word I said. Just as I always advised my clients to do. "What the fuck? *I* sure didn't have anything to do with this!" is what I finally blurted.

DiCarlo leaned back and showed me his half-smile. "Don't worry. I don't think you're much of a suspect. It's a damn shame, though. Every cop on the East Coast would buy me dinners and drinks for the rest of my life if I could tag a public defender with a murder rap."

I was still flustered. I didn't say anymore. And I wasn't sure if I believed him.

DiCarlo spoke again. "Like I said, I have no serious suspicion that you are involved in this. For now. I would appreciate it if you'd keep the information about the toothpick to yourself, though. If you go shooting your mouth off, I might have to resume my interest in you."

This shook me out of my daze. "Look, Captain. Can I call you Frank?"

"No."

"Captain. First off, I know better than to disrupt a police investigation in progress. Second, if there's somebody out there killing poker players, I want him caught as much as you do. So of course I'm not going to tell anybody. But next time, remember who you're talking to before you pull that kind of police intimidation bullshit."

DiCarlo stared at me for a minute. "We're finished here."

I stood up to leave.

"Oh, there's something else that you might be interested in," I said. "A weird thing, maybe nothing at all."

DiCarlo waited. He had not risen from his chair.

"Yesterday Shooter told me that he had just come back from his house in Hawaii. Said he goes there to get away from poker, that there's no decent card games at all in Hawaii."

"So?"

"Just today I was talking with a guy who goes there all the time. He said the islands are full of terrific poker games. I don't know why Shooter would have lied about something like that, but maybe you should check out his house in Hawaii."

"I don't need you telling me what to check out. Poker in Hawaii. Right, that's going straight to the top of my list," DiCarlo said with mild sarcasm. He turned his attention to the notepad on his desk in an obvious gesture of dismissal.

"Just trying to help."

"You can help by keeping out of my hair." He didn't look up. "Thanks for stopping by."

I walked out of the office. DiCarlo had assured me that I was not on his list of potential suspects. This meant, of course, that I probably *was* on his list. You didn't have to be a poker player to understand that much.

7

THAT NIGHT MARKED THE conclusion of all the preliminary games, and the eve of the main tournament event. Dinner at Willy Hopkins's table was unusually quiet. Even Willy was subdued. I sat between Maddie Santos and Joel Simon, an amateur player who was one of Willy's old business pals. Jack Shea, who usually flirted with Maddie at every opportunity, was nowhere to be found.

There were a couple of mildly disgusting stories about the wild game with the Spaniards, but poker talk was mostly concerned with the new tournament schedule. In response to police concerns about players being unavailable for interviews, Bob Herr had agreed to provide much longer and more frequent breaks and would make up the time by starting earlier each morning.

I couldn't get my mind off of the meeting with DiCarlo. What kind of psychopath was on the loose in this place? Had somebody tried to set me up? What did DiCarlo mean when he said I wasn't a suspect "for now"? And the next morning was the start of the main event, the $10,000 buy-in Hold'em tournament. Should I cancel my plan to play?

This last question, at least, had a clear answer. The instant it flashed in my mind, I knew that I wasn't backing out of the tournament. The old whaling gear in the lobby of the Humpback really did stand for something. I had been mentally priming myself for this tournament for months, and it would take more than the death of a card player and an unsettling visit from a policeman to loosen the harpoon that was stuck way down deep in my gambler's soul. I was playing, all right.

I was so distracted at dinner that I somehow failed to notice Maddie Santos's several attempts to start a serious conversation with me. Finally, as dinner was breaking up and I was rising to go, she grabbed my arm. I sat back down and looked at her. Looking at Maddie was always enjoyable.

"Mark, you're a lawyer, right? I think I might be in trouble."

"What's the matter?"

She turned in her seat and faced me directly. "My gun is missing from my room."

Whoa. "You have a gun?"

"For protection. As much as I travel, the kind of cash that we carry around … the way I look." She blushed. "I mean, with the kind of creepy assholes you run into when you're gambling. You have no idea …"

"Don't be modest. It's okay. You have this gun registered?"

"Yeah, but I'm not licensed to carry it concealed or anything like that."

"Since when is it missing?"

"Since I changed my clothes before dinner. That's when I noticed it wasn't there. The last time I saw it was when I checked in yesterday afternoon and unpacked my bags."

"Has anybody else been in your room?"

Her green eyes didn't blink or waver. "No."

"Have you told the police?"

"Not yet. Mark, I'm afraid to."

"For God's sake, Maddie, you have to tell them right away! If there's even the slightest chance that your gun was involved in killing Deukart, you absolutely want *them* hearing from *you* instead of the other way around."

Maddie Santos didn't have to tell me why she, of all people, had a reason to be worried. Her history with Shooter Deukart was well known. Maddie's father had been a successful car dealer in Arizona who had developed a very destructive gambling habit. He was trying to kick the problem, and had succeeded in staying away from cards for a while, when Deukart enticed him into a big game. Four days later, Gabriel Santos was a ruined man. Deukart played him without mercy, ending up with all of his money, the deed to the car dealership, and a marker for $70,000. Maddie's dad disappeared the next week. Nobody had heard from him since.

That had happened eight years ago, when Madelin Santos was seventeen. She initially swore never to gamble. A couple of years later, she changed gears and devoted herself to learning the craft, eventually joining the ranks of respected pro players. But Shooter Deukart wouldn't sit at a table with her. He said that he would only allow himself to ruin one member of any given family. Typical Shooter.

"Have the cops talked to you yet?" I asked.

"No. After I saw you this morning, I went into town for the day."

I stirred sugar into my coffee. "Okay, Maddie. First off, tell me where you were last night."

"I had dinner with Jack. He walked me back to my room. Kidded around about wanting to come inside, you know, not serious. And then … then I just went into my room, and that was it."

"What time?"

"I'm not sure."

"Did you make any phone calls? Watch a pay-TV movie? Anything to show you were in the room?"

"No. Just read my book and went to sleep."

"What book were you reading?"

"What? Oh …"

Obviously, the question had caught her flat-footed.

"Madelin, you're hiding something. If you can't fool me, you won't fool the police."

She poked at her blueberry cobbler with a fork. I noticed that she had been nervously shredding her napkin into tiny pieces. These were not the nerves of steel that won her so many poker hands.

"I'm sure you weren't involved in that game upstairs …"

She looked horrified. "Jesus, no. How could you even *think* that of me?"

"So what is it, then?"

She looked vaguely across the room. "I can't talk about it."

"Okay, don't. But tell me this. Whatever it is, is there even a remote chance that it has anything to do with the murder?"

Maddie shook her head.

"Good. Then just be straight about it with the police. Seriously, you really need to. They're going to want an alibi from you. My read on DiCarlo is that he's a smart cop and a decent guy. I'm not saying you can trust him. But you really don't have any other choice. Don't try to bullshit him like you just tried to bullshit me. It'll come back to bite you."

"Oh, Mark, I think I need a lawyer. Will you be ... ?"

"I can't, Maddie. I'm not allowed to take outside clients. Besides, I'd have a conflict of interest. DiCarlo is looking at me too, you know. If you really want a lawyer, I'll find one for you. But I don't think you need one. I think you just need to put your cards on the table. So you hated Shooter Deukart, with good reason. Plenty of people did. That doesn't make you a murderer or even a murder suspect. So your gun is missing. Almost certainly it's a hotel employee who rips off guests on the side. On the other hand, lying to the police about what you were doing on the night of the murder, or holding out important information—*that* will get you in trouble real fast, and put you right at the top of their list."

Maddie appeared to be convinced, though not relieved. She leaned over and kissed me on the cheek. I watched her walk away.

It was then that I noticed another figure hovering nearby, at a respectful distance, obviously waiting to talk with me. I sighed. What I really wanted was to clear my head and get a good night's sleep before the tournament started, not soothe the fears of gamblers who were scared of Captain DiCarlo.

Tran Le Binh approached me hesitantly. "Mark, can I have a word with you?"

Binh must have wanted to talk with me earlier in the day but had never found a private moment. Now he had me cornered. I forced myself to smile patiently. "Sure, what's up, Binh?"

"I need your help. I could be in some trouble with this Shooter business."

Another one. "What kind of trouble, Binh?"

"The police detective want to talk with me tomorrow. He don't say what he want to talk about, but I think I know what." Binh's tentative grasp of English belied his spectacular card-playing skills, but it may have accounted for his tendency not to mix socially with the other players.

"Okay, tell me what's on your mind."

"I don't want to talk about it." Binh stabbed out a cigarette and immediately lit another.

"Ohh-kaay ... so what can I do for you?"

"I need you to come with me tomorrow to help me with the police."

"Binh, I can't—"

"Listen," Binh interrupted, "this thing about me, it looks pretty bad. It is not a bad thing I did and I got nothing to do with Shooter dying. But this thing, if police know about it, it can look real bad for me. I need you to help me talk to them." His nicotine-stained fingers were anxiously combing through his hair in an agitated repetition. I had never seen nerves like this on Binh before.

"Binh, I can't be your lawyer. First of all, I'm not allowed to take outside clients. More important, I'd have conflicts of interest all over the place."

"No, I don't ask you to be my lawyer. I just ask you to be my friend."

Ouch. Bull's-eye.

I sighed. "What time are you supposed to see them?"

"In the morning. During the first break I come to the captain's office."

Oh great. Another close encounter with Frank DiCarlo. "This had better be really important, Binh."

"For me, it could be matter of life or death, Mark. I never forget this thing you do for me."

"Okay. I'll see you tomorrow. And good luck with the cards."

Eileen was eager to hear from me when I finally reached her.

"Mark, I saw on the news that some big poker player got killed!"

"Yeah."

"I knew it wasn't you when the headline said it was a top money winner."

"Thanks."

I told her everything—how I found Shooter's body, my session with the state police, the panicky reactions of Maddie and Binh. The only thing I left out was Jack being there.

She seemed to take it all in stride, as though a corpse in a parking lot was something one came across on a normal day. Then again, for a narcotics cop like Eileen, I suppose it was. She had a lot of questions about my talk with DiCarlo. She wanted to be sure that I was taking care of my own interests. But her strongest reaction came to the news about the toothpick.

"Eeww, that is so disgusting! Why did you ever say something like that in the first place?"

"It was my insecure sophomoric side. The side you rarely see."

"Yeah, right. Really, though, do you think somebody is trying to get you involved? Was it a sick joke?"

"I really don't know. Nothing to worry about, though. I'm not under suspicion." *I hope.* I was sitting on the edge of the hotel bed. "God, I'm tired. I wish I were in your arms right now."

"Poor thing. Are you sure you want to play in this tournament? Why don't you just come home?"

"I couldn't now, even if I wanted to. I promised Binh I'd go with him tomorrow. But honestly, honey ... I want to play in this tournament. I want it a lot."

"A guy gets killed and all you gamblers can barely look up from your card game. It's a little pathetic, don't you think?"

I yawned. "No, I'd call it dedication to the craft."

"Did you call Roger yet?"

She was plainly not going to give this up. "Honey, I'm just really, really tired."

"If you have the energy to play poker and craps all week and keep your hoodlum friends out of jail on the side, I think you can make a five-minute phone call to your brother."

"What's all this with my hoodlum friends? Have you and Willy Hopkins been exchanging notes?"

"What?"

"Never mind."

"Just think of Roger as one of the good-for-nothings that you like to keep out of trouble."

"*Roger* doesn't get into trouble. Roger gets *me* into trouble."

"Just call him. Tonight."

Busybody. "Okay, I'll call him. What about you? Catch any bad guys today?"

"No, they all got away."

"Good. They won't be looking for me at the office. Night, darlin'."

"Good night. Hey, Mark?"

"Yeah?"

"Good luck tomorrow."

"Thanks."

When Roger's answering machine picked up, I had some hope that I could just leave a nice message and be done with it. But Roger himself came on when he heard my voice. Roger would not be able to come out to see me at the Humpback, which was a relief. I wound up talking with him for over an hour. I liked my brother, from a healthy distance. Although we had gone our separate ways as adults, we were never too far removed from the deep pool of childhood experiences that tied us together.

It had been Roger who introduced me to gambling. I remembered it well. I was five years old; Roger was twelve. Roger colluded with our nine-year-old sister, Casey, to lure me into my first game of poker, on the rug in the bedroom that Roger and I shared. Twenty minutes later, all of my cash—one dollar and twelve cents—had been lost. I was anguished, and furious. I attacked my older brother and sister with all my might. They just rolled up and laughed while I rained ineffective blows on them with my little fists. When our mother found out about it, she made them give my money back to me. I always wondered whether that had been a mistake on her part. Probably she should have let me learn a lesson the hard way. Somewhere in the back of my mind there was an irrational belief that if I lost everything, my mom would come in and make them give it all back.

I made one more phone call that night, to a former client who had a wealth of knowledge on all matters related to real estate fraud. I asked him how I could check out real estate records in Hawaii, and he volunteered to do it for me, no charge. Keep a red-handed criminal out of prison and you have a friend for life—yessiree, that's job satisfaction.

I really hadn't planned on solving a murder this week. Mostly what I wanted was for everybody to leave me alone so I could play poker. But it looked as though I was going to be in this case, whether I liked it or not.

8

Wednesday, September 29

THE MAIN EVENT OF the Northeast Open—the $10,000 buy-in no-limit Hold'em tournament—was not held in the poker room. It was played in the Showroom, an auditorium large enough to seat three thousand people. The satellites were finished, and a total of 387 players were entered. The tournament was scheduled to go on for four days. By the end of the first day, half of the 387 would be eliminated. The prize pool contained over $3.5 million, $1 million of which would go to the winner, with the rest distributed among the top thirty-seven finishers.

Ten years ago a tournament of this size would have been the biggest thing ever, but now it was just one of many. Even at this astonishing level of prize money, the Open did not attract all of the world's top players. Many of them were occupied with games of similar size occurring elsewhere. And some of them didn't even bother with the tournament, opting instead for the lucrative side games that were going on in the poker room.

I was always struck by the amazing amount of anxiety in the air as the players assembled for a tournament. There was almost none of the chatter that one would expect in a room holding four hundred people waiting for an event to begin. The hush was so pervasive that it was weird. Normal people didn't behave this way. I remembered nine years ago, waiting for the bar exam to start—a bunch of stressed-out ultra-competitive lawyers about to take the biggest test of their lives—but that had been like a cocktail party compared with the grim silence that hung over the room before a poker tournament started.

I usually made it a point to introduce myself to the players on either side of me and to make whatever small talk was possible within that smothering atmosphere. This was not to gain some sort of tactical advantage, but simply because it seemed like the decent way to behave. Apparently, Eileen's civility was beginning to rub off.

This particular morning I was feeling groggy from lack of sleep. Not only had I gone to bed late after my long talk with Roger, but once in bed I'd tossed and turned for hours. It wasn't because of the murder and my involvement in the investigation. I was a criminal lawyer and was fairly well inured against things like that. It was, quite simply, the fact that I had foolishly drunk at least seven or eight cups of coffee while hanging around the Nor'easter all day. *Stupid!* I'd sworn at myself Eventually, I'd given up and turned on the television. Thank God for TV Land. A *Dick Van Dyke Show* marathon had finally soothed me to sleep.

Despite my wooziness, I was feeling optimistic about the tournament. Certainly the large size of the field was encouraging. The advent of the "super-satellites" had done a great deal to enrich the winnings of the best poker players by loading the big tournaments with dead money. A super-satellite was a $50 buy-in tournament that could, with a lot of luck and a little skill, earn a player a ticket to the main event. Poker was the only professional sport (if you want to call a game played by a lot of really fat guys drinking beer and eating Fritos a "sport") in which a rank amateur could find himself going head-to-head with a top-name pro. The super-satellites had been held for several months leading up to the Open, producing dozens of lucky players who were in way over their heads.

I felt confident that between 100 and 200 of the 387 players were dead money—people whose lack of experience and knowledge left them with no realistic chance of winning. Then again, I had to remind myself, players written off as "dead money" had won major tournaments in the past. This was still gambling, after all. And some of the unknown dead money players had more skill than anybody gave them credit for. For that matter, I knew that I was by no means one of the best players in the room, and I would need more than my share of luck to get ahead in this field.

Every player started with $10,000 in tournament chips. The chips were not redeemable for cash; the only way to earn money with them was to survive into the final thirty-seven. During the first round, the blinds would be $25 and $50. Blinds are mandatory bets placed by the two players to the left of the dealer, before they receive their cards. Every couple of hours, the blinds would be increased. As the blinds became ever larger, players with short stacks lost the luxury of sitting back and waiting for premium cards.

My theory on how to play the first two rounds of a Hold'em tournament was not to play at all, unless I was dealt a prime hand like a pair of aces or kings. In a poker hand, the potential downside is usually bigger than the potential upside. The winner is most often a person who makes a large bet and causes all opponents to fold. That means that he has to risk a lot of chips to win just a few. In the later rounds of the tournament, a hundred or two hundred chips would count for almost nothing. So why get involved now, to win a couple of hundred chips, with a hand that could set me back thousands and put me into a deep hole? I was resolved to be patient and to resist temptation.

It didn't take long before temptation called. On the fifth hand, I found myself on the button holding an alluring A♥ J♥. This was a hand that I would have thrown away if I were in early position, but on the button it was playable. The button is the "dealer" position, last to act in the betting after the flop. The button passes one seat to the left with each new hand, so every player gets a turn at it. Because the player on the button has the privilege of waiting to see what everybody else does before having to make a decision, the button is the power position in Hold'em.

I was not excited about playing the ace-jack. It's a trouble hand that loses all the time to ace-queen and ace-king. But when the cards come, you have to play them, because who knows when they'll come again? If anybody had raised ahead of me, I would have tossed the hand. The first rule of tournament poker, or any poker for that matter: You usually need better cards to call a bet than you need to raise one. So when everybody had folded around to me, I raised the pot to two hundred.

There were only two players left who hadn't acted—the small blind and the big blind, who sat to the left of the button and already had their blind bets in the pot. The player in the small blind folded. The player in the big blind, with $50 already in, called the remaining $150.

The flop could hardly have been better for me. J♣ 9♥ 3♥. I had the top pair, my ace was the top kicker, and with four hearts I had a 35 percent chance of drawing a flush on the turn or the river. My face showed none of the satisfaction that I felt when I looked at the cards on the board.

The player in the big blind, now acting first, checked. I made my first mistake of the tournament by betting $400. The big blind was a middle-aged man I had never seen before, wearing sunglasses and a baseball cap. I had $600 in the pot, my opponent just $200. I would have been content if the guy had folded. Which he did not.

"Raise," he said from behind his sunglasses, and moved $1,200 into the pot.

Oh crap, here we go, I thought. *What have we got here?* The best-case scenario would have the guy on a semi-bluff with two hearts, hoping to knock me out of the pot but relying on his flush draw if I called. If that were the case, I would have him beaten both ways—with a pair of jacks and with a higher flush draw. The worst-case scenario was that he was holding nines or threes, or maybe even jacks, giving him three of a kind. I had a 35 percent chance of hitting my flush, which would beat three of a kind. It would cost me $800 to call, for a chance to win the $2,025 that was in the pot. A good bargain. But how much more would I have to pay after the next card? And even if I made my flush, I could still lose because there was a 20 percent chance that the guy would make a full house or better if he was already holding trips. Another possibility was that the guy had slow-played a pair of queens or kings. In that case, my chances of beating him were just above 50 percent, because hitting a third jack or a second ace would give me the winning hand, unless another queen or king appeared. The real danger was the set of threes or nines. Did he really have them? Would the guy have called my pre-flop raise with just a low pair? Maybe. Would he have check-raised me with anything less than trips? At this stage of a tournament, with unknown players of unknown skill, it was hard to read too much into a player's behavior.

It took me just a few seconds to process these thoughts. With enough practice, this sort of figuring becomes almost automatic. Having analyzed the possibilities, I took a little time to determine how I felt about them. My first thought was to kick myself in the ass for breaking another of my tournament rules: Never raise a pot if an opponent's re-raise might force you to throw away a promising hand. One thing was for sure; I had to decide right now whether this hand was worth risking all of my chips. Just calling would mean I'd have to face an even bigger bet after the next card. I had to raise or fold, and if I made a large raise it would become very difficult to get away from the hand if the guy raised back.

Did I bust my ass for the last four months to come here and get knocked out in the fifth hand by some guy with a pair of threes?

"Take it," I said, and tossed my cards, face-down, into the pile. My opponent showed nothing as he quietly added the chips in the pot to his stack. *Well, I butchered that hand. Damn.*

Things did not improve much after that, but then they didn't get worse, either. The rest of the morning went by without any major confrontations. After a few hands, I observed that the guy three seats to my right was a very loose bettor who was playing weak cards too aggressively. I settled in and waited for big cards that I could bust him with. Unfortunately, they never came. Someone else picked up the dead money, and the chump was gone before the break. I managed only to steal a couple of small pots by raising against the blinds. When the break came, I had $9,600 in chips.

––––––––––––

To accommodate the police, Bob Herr had extended the usual fifteen-minute break to an hour and a half. I was aching to go up to my room for a nap, but Tran Le Binh was waiting for me. Instead of a nap, I drank another cup of coffee.

In the cab on the way to the police station, I felt annoyed at losing my break time. Binh was plainly a nervous wreck, though, and I soon forgot my irritation in the effort to keep Binh on an even keel. The best thing that I could do was keep him talking.

"Beautiful out there, isn't it?" I asked. The New England foliage had started to show. The sumacs were red already; most of the oaks and maples were still green, with a smattering of early yellows and oranges showing in the bright sunlight.

Binh tipped his cigarette ashes out the open window of the cab. Smoking in a cab was illegal, naturally, but the driver didn't seem to mind. "We don't have this fall colors in Vietnam," said Binh. "Snow and ice are not for me, but I like the fall very much."

Inside the Humpback, of course, the seasons never changed. And most of the gamblers in there couldn't have cared less. They could have been at McMurdo Station in Antarctica, with high temperatures in the negative forties and wind chills down to a hundred below. It didn't make any difference to a guy hunched over a blackjack table praying for the dealer to bust.

I wasn't that far gone yet. When I got home to Brooklyn, Eileen and I would go for walks in Prospect Park and otherwise enjoy the normal life that existed outside the world of gambling. For a week, maybe two, it would be out of my system. Then the itch would return and I would be looking for a game.

"Why they make us come all the way to the police station?" worried Binh. "Why don't they see us at the casino like they been seeing everybody else?"

"It's about intimidation and control. Show you who's in charge, make you take the first step, then watch you and react to it. It's a little bit like playing from the button."

"Ah," nodded Binh. After a pause he said, "I would do the same thing if I was him."

9

THE MASSACHUSETTS STATE POLICE unit was quartered in a dusty-looking building on the western edge of Yarmouth. This part of town faced away from the sea; it was not the idyllic touristy section. Frank DiCarlo's office was as sparse in appearance as the captain himself was. The only decoration, on a shelf beneath the window, was a replica of a Navy destroyer. Next to it was a blue cap with an officer's insignia.

DiCarlo stared at me in surprise as Binh and I walked in.

"What the hell are *you* doing here?" he barked.

"Binh asked me to come along. I'm just doing him a favor."

"Are you his lawyer?"

"Er…"

"If you're his lawyer, then sit down. If you aren't, then get the hell out. This isn't a cocktail party."

Binh gave me a desperate, pleading look. I sighed and cursed myself. "Yes, I'm his lawyer." I sat down on a metal chair in a corner of the office, not happy. I was risking a serious disciplinary proceeding. For a lawyer to represent a client in an investigation that might involve the lawyer personally is *way* out of bounds.

DiCarlo turned his glare on Binh and pointed to an empty chair. As he had when he'd interviewed me, he jumped right into the interrogation without any small talk.

"Several people saw you talking with Shooter Deukart in the hotel bar before he was killed. Where did you go after you talked with him?"

"I go to my room, read a book, go to sleep."

"Anybody with you? Anybody see you?"

"I don't think so."

"Make any phone calls? Watch a movie?"

"No."

"What were you reading?"

"A book about the United State presidents. It helps me with my English and also I study for citizenship."

"Huh." DiCarlo looked skeptical. "What were you and Deukart talking about in the hotel bar?"

"Nothing, just gambling talk. I am sitting at the bar and he come by. Just small talk for a minute or two, then he leave."

"Small talk? About what exactly?"

"He tell me about the dead money player who took him down at the table that day. Ask me how my play is going. Who is hot on the tour right now. Just gambling talk."

"Anybody with him? Did he say where he was going?"

"No."

"Nothing at all? Just walked away without a word?"

"He look at his wristwatch. Said he had to be going."

"Do you know anything about a private high-stakes game that went on in the hotel that night?"

"No. I never hear nothing about that."

"So. Since when does Shooter Deukart make small talk with Tran Le Binh?"

Binh's eyes widened a tiny bit. "I'm sorry? I don't understand," he said. It seemed like a harmless enough question, but for some reason it had struck dangerously close to home. Binh was near to breaking out in a sweat. Like Maddie Santos the evening before, Tran Le Binh was showing very little of the cool reserve that made him such an effective poker player.

"Let me put it another way," said DiCarlo. He rose from his chair and stood over Binh. "Since when does a former POW make small talk with a former North Vietnamese soldier who worked as a guard in a POW camp? The same camp, it turns out, where that POW had his teeth knocked out and his bones broken?"

Binh said nothing. I looked at him in amazement. So this was the thing that Binh couldn't talk about.

"I checked you out with the federal Immigration and Naturalization Service. It took some doing; they have you in a classified file. But for a murder investigation, they were willing to give it to me." He returned to his desk and picked up a manila folder. "Second lieutenant in the regular North Vietnamese Army. Stationed 1968 through 1973 in the prisoner-of-war camp at Cam Phu. Arrived in San Francisco four years ago and granted political asylum on a provisional basis. Why the hell they're allowing you to stay in this country is a mystery to me. How many American soldiers did you torture in that camp?"

"I never torture nobody. Shooter Deukart could tell you I never torture nobody."

"Shooter Deukart can't tell me anything. You never knocked out anybody's teeth with a rifle butt? Never drove over anybody's arm with a truck?"

Binh looked DiCarlo in the eye and said nothing.

I broke in. "Frank, what does this have to do with Deukart's death?"

"Don't insult my intelligence, Newcomb. It's obvious this creates a motive. Deukart could have been blackmailing Binh with this information."

"Shooter Deukart blackmailing Tran Le Binh!? Shooter had a house in Hawaii. A ranch in New Mexico. Every time he walked into a casino there were twenty-five millionaires lined up to lose their money to him. He had no conceivable reason to be involved with blackmail."

"I'm not going to argue theories with you right now, Newcomb. Tran Le Binh had a potential motive. He was seen with the victim on the night of the killing. He has no alibi. That makes him a person of interest in this investigation."

DiCarlo turned his attention back to Binh. "So no torture, huh. Never hit a prisoner with your fist? Never slapped one around for not having his shirt tucked in or leaving his sandals on the wrong side of his cot?"

Binh spoke vehemently. "You tell me, what is torture? My sister and her family was blown to bits by American bombers. The only thing we find of them is little pieces. Then I get these bombers in my prison."

Binh fixed DiCarlo with a stare that the officer, against his will, could not break away from. "You tell me something, Captain. Some street gang kills half your family. Then you get some of that gang in your patrol car. You gonna knock them around a little bit? You gonna bring charges on one of your troopers if he knock them around a little bit?

"I never do no interrogations. I never break no bones or put out teeth like other guards. Why you think Shooter Deukart keep my secret these years? Because he knows this. We were not friends. But he knows I was a good soldier."

DiCarlo said nothing at all for a full minute. Finally, he asked, "How did you get to America?"

"That is a very long story. I will tell you the whole thing if you want to hear. I deserted my unit near the Chinese border, and got my way to Hong Kong. If they catch me, I go back and be killed for sure. In Hong Kong I work for many years until I have a chance to get to America. The American government give me political asylum.

"I am here for four years playing cards and now the poker is all over TV and people start to know my name. If newspapers find out about me, people think the worst and there will be clamor to send me back to Vietnam. They put me in prison there for sure, probably kill me."

Then why the hell do you risk the exposure of playing in the big tournaments? I thought. But I already knew the answer: *Because they're there. Why do people risk climbing Mount Everest?* To me, at least, that made perfect sense.

Binh looked earnestly at DiCarlo. "The American government keep my secret. Shooter Deukart keep it too." He glanced at me.

"Mark is my lawyer so he have to keep my secret. Captain DiCarlo. What do you do now?"

DiCarlo didn't speak for a while. His face was a mask as he thought through his options. In my experience, many cops would relish having this kind of leverage over a potential suspect and would play it without mercy. I was pleasantly surprised, and impressed, when DiCarlo finally spoke.

"I'll tell you what. You don't leave town until this case has been resolved or until I tell you that you can go. I don't know who killed Deukart yet, and I don't know that it wasn't you. I don't know if I might not think that punk guards who beat up American heroes shouldn't have their names splashed all over the newspapers. But if I decide that you had nothing to do with Deukart's death, then your personal story is none of my business."

I decided not to press our luck and gestured to Binh that it was time to leave.

"And listen," DiCarlo said as we reached the door.

We stopped and turned to face him.

"The U.S. Navy Air Wings are not a street gang."

I glanced at the model destroyer and the officer's cap that rested on the shelf beneath the window. I looked DiCarlo in the eye, nodded, turned, and left.

10

BINH WAS DRIPPING SWEAT as we walked out of the state police building and approached the cab that was waiting to take us back to the Humpback. I stopped Binh when we were out of earshot and took hold of his arm. He had already lit a cigarette.

"Listen, Binh. You need to get yourself a lawyer. It can't be me, I've already broken about five ethical rules by representing you in that room. You've got a serious situation. But I think you're going to be okay. DiCarlo is a smart guy, and he seems to be fair enough, as cops go. He isn't going to screw with you just for the hell of it. But you have enough vulnerability here that you could get pulled into this if they don't find anybody else to pin the murder on."

"You believe my story, Mark?"

"Binh, I've learned the hard way not to believe anything without proof. But I don't think that you killed Shooter." What I didn't tell him was that his story had set off my bullshit detector in a big way. Binh casually sitting around in the hotel bar? Unlikely. And there was something else nagging at me, a detail out of place, but I wasn't able to pin it down.

"Let me make a couple of phone calls and I'll find you a good lawyer in Boston," I said. "Money's not a problem, is it?"

"Not for this, no. Money is not a problem."

"Binh, I have a question. Do you own a car?"

He looked up at me. "No. Why?"

"Have you rented a car anytime in the last week or so?"

"No. I take cabs everyplace."

"You're absolutely sure about that."

Binh looked me square in the eyes. A puff of smoke came out of his nostrils. "You think I would lie to you?"

"I'm just trying to help. Whoever dumped Shooter in the parking lot had to use a car. Is there anything else I might need to know?"

He looked down the road. "You're not my lawyer anymore."

"I guess not."

By the time Binh and I had settled ourselves into the cab, my attention was shifting back to the tournament. I would have felt guilty about this, except it was clear that Binh was also returning his focus to cards. He looked anxiously at his wristwatch. "You think we have time to get back?"

"No problem," I smiled. After the excruciating stress and drama of the previous half hour, Binh's greatest worry was that he might miss a hand or two of cards. For my part, I found that the closer the cab got to the Humpback, the more matters like Shooter Deukart's toothpick, Maddie Santos's gun, and Tran Le Binh's military record faded to the same level of significance—none at all—as all other matters outside the card tables. Psychotic? Maybe. Pathetic, as Eileen described it? Probably. But you had to have that kind of focus if you wanted to play well at the highest level.

The cab dropped us at the entrance to the hotel. As we walked through the lobby, Zip Addison appeared from behind the whaling boat with his ballpoint and notebook in hand.

"Mark Newcomb and Tran Le Binh. Now there's an unlikely pair of sightseers. You guys out taking in the foliage?"

Oh shit, I thought. *This is the last thing that Binh needs.* "What's up, Zip? What are you hearing?"

"I'm hearing that a prominent Vietnamese card player needs to bring a defense lawyer with him when he talks to the cops. What's going on here?"

This was trouble. Everybody knew about Shooter's Vietnam experience. Even a dipshit like Zip Addison would eventually put two and two together and start digging around into Binh's history, and I didn't have much confidence that Binh's "classified" file would stay secret for long. I had to think fast. Despite being basically a truthful person, to this day I take pride in the lie that I made up on the spot.

"Okay, Zip." I took him by the elbow and steered him into a quiet corner. I spoke in a low, conspiratorial tone. "I'm gonna tell you something, but it didn't come from me or I'm in huge trouble."

"My sources are absolutely confidential."

"Okay, I'm gonna trust you. Here it is. Shooter Deukart had a love child. A Vietnamese daughter, from the war. They found a bunch of letters in his hotel room. They needed them to be translated. That's why they called Binh."

His eyes widened, then narrowed as he looked at me. "Why did he have to bring you along?"

"Green card stuff. Immigration won't let the state cops talk to a foreign national without a lawyer present. Strictly a formality. But it did let me in on some pretty juicy stuff."

"What juicy stuff? I want the juice!"

"Hey, I've already told you enough to get my ass thrown in jail. Maybe later. So what do you have for *me*?"

He showed a coy smile. "You're on somebody's list."

"What are you talking about?"

"It's not a list you want to be on. Toothpick man."

"Oh, for Chrissakes. Where did you hear about that?"

He stiffened. "My sources are strictly confidential."

"Yeah, yeah, yeah. So I'm on DiCarlo's list. I already knew that."

"That's not what I said. You're on the Vegas list."

"Vegas list?"

"Yeah, you'll see what I mean soon enough." Addison scribbled something onto a slip of paper and put it into my hand. "This is my cell number. Give me a call anytime." He walked off toward the casino.

Vegas list? I didn't know what the hell he was talking about. Then again, if his other sources were as full of shit as I was, he also didn't know what the hell he was talking about. He did know about the toothpick, though. I shook my head and double-timed it into the poker room, anxious that I might be running late for the next session.

An hour into the third round of the tournament, I was wondering why I had been in such a hurry to get back. The cards were running lousy and my play wasn't much better. Because the blinds had increased to $100 and $200, it was becoming harder to sit back and wait. Increasingly, I looked for opportunities to steal a pot with a bluff or a semi-bluff. But I wasn't feeling the confident rhythm needed to make that kind of play work well. So I hunkered down and waited for good cards.

Shortly into the fourth round, with the blinds increased to $150 and $300, I was in the first betting position with a slowly dwindling stack amounting to $8,400 when I peeked at my cards and found two red kings. *Finally.* I called the $300 blind bet, hoping that another player would raise me so that I could raise back. Two seats to my left, a young man wearing an orange Miami Hurricanes cap, who looked like a high schooler but must have been at least college-aged, raised the bet to $1,200. *Yes.* This was a very welcome development. Unless Mr. Miami had aces, my kings would be a big favorite over whatever he was holding.

I was considering how large a raise I would make and watching the other players fold when the player in the small blind said, "Raise," and pushed $3,000 into the pot. Bobo Helwig had been a thorn in my side all day. I knew him vaguely from several other tournaments and had played against him at high-stakes tables in Atlantic City. Why he was called Bobo was a mystery.

Helwig had been stealing the blinds from me with annoying regularity, and I hadn't had the cards to call his bluffs or the chips to bluff him back. Now I had to consider whether Helwig's large raise meant that he was holding aces. I didn't consider for long. There are various schools of thought on the question of what to do with kings when you suspect you might be facing aces before the flop, but my opinion on the matter was clear. If I had a pair of kings, I was going to play them hard. If somebody else held aces, then so be it. It was just as likely that he could be holding queens, or a suited ace-king, and I wasn't going to let the fear of aces screw up a rare chance to vault forward in the chip count.

Don't outsmart yourself, said my inner voice. "All in," I announced, and looked Bobo Helwig straight in the eyes.

Mr. Miami tossed his cards into the muck with a petulant flip of his hand. He had thought he had big cards, only to find himself ambushed by not one but two superior hands.

I knew I had the better hand, or at least a tie, when Helwig did not instantly call my bet. With aces, he would have had nothing to think about. Now the pressure was all on him.

Helwig looked at me, seeking some information. I returned his stare and raised my eyebrows. *It's up to you, fella.* Unlike many players, I chose not to wear sunglasses or a cap to mask my facial features. I wanted to use my expression as a weapon, not run away from it. In my way of thinking, if an opponent could read my cards by looking into my face, then I shouldn't be playing in the first place.

The longer Helwig fretted, the more I found myself enjoying the situation. I had the guy pinned down, squirming. I felt something that almost resembled an erotic thrill. *Maybe Jack is right,* I found myself thinking. *I really do want to hump this guy.*

After two minutes of deliberation, Helwig said, "I call."

"Turn 'em up," said the dealer.

I showed my red kings. Helwig turned over the other two kings.

"Ooohhh," the table moaned collectively, as the moment of high drama instantly devolved into farce. A split pot.

I was still stewing in my disappointment when the dealer turned up the flop—Q♠ 9♠ 8♠. "Ooohhh," came again from the table as the wheel turned around and farce was resurrected as drama. Helwig now had four cards to a spade flush, and one more spade meant that I was finished. *Oh shit,* I thought to myself. "Oh shit," I said out loud. The humper was in danger of becoming the humpee. The turn came—four of diamonds. Finally, the river card—eight of hearts.

"Split pot," announced the dealer, as I collapsed backward into my seat. Relief at my escape had wiped out my initial disappointment at not winning with the kings.

"Nice call, Bobo," I said.

"I was smelling aces all over you, man. Came that close to folding."

The brush with death now left me feeling strangely enlivened, and my game picked up a couple of notches. The slight timidity that had corrupted my play earlier in the day was gone. When the tournament broke for dinner, without any improvement in my cards, I had played my stack up to nearly $15,000.

11

I FIGURED THAT I could find Jack Shea either at a crap table or in the coffee shop. I was right on the second try. Jack saw me coming, called over his shoulder to the waitress, and waved me over. I pulled out a chair and seated myself.

"I've already ordered you a cheeseburger," Jack said, his eyes wide with excitement. "Guess what."

"What." I couldn't help but smile.

"It's working! I'm sitting on more than twenty-six thousand in chips! I had this guy at my table, ugly guy, incredibly intense. Looked a little bit like Charles Bronson in a bad mood. I get involved in a pot with him, and I give him a little wink. He looks at me like he can't believe it. So I give him a coy little smile, you know, like this?" Jack tilted his head and offered a small suggestive smile. "Next thing you know the guy comes at me like a bull. Smoke coming out of his ears. Goes all in. And he's got nothing! Doubled up my chips right there."

I let Jack patter on, enjoying the sheer absurdity of it all. It struck me that nothing had made me laugh since the last time I'd talked to Jack. It felt good.

Although we had been close friends for several years, I was never 100 percent certain of what Jack Shea did for a living. He made good money, I assumed, based on the amounts that he regularly squandered at the crap tables. It was a Wall Street job, I knew that much. It had to do with computers and trading derivatives, or something like that. Whatever firm Jack happened to be working for always seemed to be in the process of being bought out by some other firm, to the point where I had stopped trying to keep track. I knew that Jack traveled quite a bit, another aspect of his business that was foreign to me. My work revolved around my office and the county court-house that was three blocks away in downtown Brooklyn. There was more than enough trouble right there on my side of the East River to keep me busy for a lifetime.

"Hey," Jack said with mischief in his eyes. "You didn't happen to catch Assahola Gant this afternoon, did you?"

"No, I don't remember seeing him."

"I guess he got worked over pretty good by the state police guys."

"Worked over? You mean they beat him up?" I couldn't believe it.

"Nah. Nice thing if they had, though." Jack looked almost wistful. "I guess they got an anonymous tip that Gant was seen leaving the hotel with Shooter Deukart Monday night."

"Really! I wonder what that—" I stopped. There was something in Jack's expression. "Jack. You didn't."

He tried to suppress a grin. He never did have much of a poker face. "Of course not," he said. "Giving a false tip to the police would be illegal. And morally wrong."

I shook my head. "I really don't want to know about this." I was silent for a moment. "It's pretty damn funny though."

I turned the conversation to Eileen and Brigid. "How are you going to keep Brigid from figuring out where you are?" I asked.

Jack frowned. "That's going to get harder every day. Usually I would have been out of the tournament by now." It was true. Jack's lack of discipline ordinarily led to an early flame-out in the big tournaments. He clearly hadn't planned on fooling Brigid for more than a couple of days. "But thank God for cell phones!" he said. "I didn't have to leave her a hotel number. That would have been a dead giveaway. She calls my cell phone, thinks I'm in Albany at the nanotechnology conference."

"How long exactly was that conference supposed to go on? We could be here for four more days if your luck holds out."

Jack frowned again. "Yeah, I know. I haven't quite got that figured out yet." He brightened again. "Well, we'll deal with that problem tomorrow, won't we? The best lies are the ones that are made up on the spot."

"So what is this power that Brigid has over you, anyway? I've never been able to figure out whether it's love or fear that keeps you in line."

"Who says I'm in line? I'm here, aren't I? She can't keep me in line," he said proudly. Then, sheepishly, "She just scares the piss out of me, that's all. I mean, most of the time we get along great, but it can get pretty intense sometimes. Have you ever seen her do her martial-arts thing? It's phenomenal. I've watched her take apart guys who are twice her size."

"You're not afraid she's actually going to beat you up?"

"Nah. Of course not. But when she gets really mad, it's ... indescribably bad. You *wish* she'd use her fists on you."

I pointed across the crowded shop. "Hey, there's Willy Hopkins. I've got an idea. Why don't you try out your gay shtick on Kenneth?"

"Pass on that. I may be crazy but I'm not suicidal."

I waved at Willy, who gestured to Kenneth and was brought to our table.

"Slumming in the coffee shop?" I asked. "Isn't this place a little bit trashy for your taste?"

Willy sighed heavily. "These confounded tournaments don't allow time for a civilized meal. But, when in Rome, I always say. So, forced to rub elbows with a couple of cretins like yourselves, I can make do with proletarian fare."

"In other words, you'll have a cheeseburger."

"That is correct."

At a gesture from Willy, Kenneth turned to hunt down a waitress. Jack jumped out of his chair and put his hand on Kenneth's forearm. "Kenneth, you poor brute, he runs you around all day and you never get off your feet. Why don't you sit down and join us?"

Kenneth froze. His eyes shot over to Willy. Willy waved his hand. "That won't be necessary, not at all."

Jack spoke again, his tone just slightly higher than normal. "But honestly, doesn't the poor man ever get a day off? I mean really, Willy, what would you do without him?"

I tried not to grin at Jack's performance. Despite myself, I was taking pleasure in Kenneth's obvious discomfiture. "Jack, are you telling me you haven't met Kenneth's substitute?" I asked.

"I guess I haven't. Poor Kenneth, working, working, working," said Jack. He had not removed his hand from Kenneth's forearm yet. Kenneth stood riveted, his eyes bulging in his battered face, a vein throbbing wildly in his neck. He looked the way a highly trained German shepherd or rottweiler might while the master's two-year-old child pulled on his ears or punched at his nose—straining every nerve to be obedient and override the instinctive urge to slaughter.

"I believe it may be time for you to remove your hand from Kenneth now," said Willy, a slight smile playing at his lips. "You realize, of course, he could take you apart with ease."

Jack took his hand off of Kenneth's arm. "Sorry, Kenneth, didn't mean it," he said in a deliberately masculine tone. Jack offered Kenneth a handshake. Kenneth didn't move. He stared straight ahead, the vein in his neck still pulsing. "Ohh-kaaay," said Jack, retreating to the safety of his seat.

He pointed over my shoulder. "Hey, Mark, check out the love-birds." I swiveled in my seat and saw Maddie Santos and Barracuda Gant in a booth on the far side of the coffee shop. Gant was talking, as usual. Maddie looked bored.

"She must have lost a bet to him," I grinned, turning back around. "I can't think of any other reason she'd be sitting with that tool."

Behind Willy's chair I noticed that Kenneth's hands were clenched into white-knuckled fists. "Hey, unwind, man. Jack was only kidding around with you," I said to him.

"I don't think he's mad at *me* anymore," Jack said. He was right. Kenneth was staring across the room, at Maddie and Gant.

"Kenneth, would you be kind enough to track down a waitress and order me something to eat?" asked Willy. Kenneth moved off without a word.

"Wow," said Jack. "If I didn't know better, I'd say he has eyes for the lovely Ms. Santos."

"Not likely," said Willy in a dry tone. "I've never seen him show interest in anybody, of *any* gender. His only real passion is for cars, which he is a genius at fixing. If you had eight cylinders, he might find you tantalizing."

"Why exactly do you keep him around, anyway?" I asked. "He scares people."

"Then he has fulfilled his most important duty. A few years ago I was being harried . . . stalked . . . by an unstable man who was under the delusion that I owed him a large amount of money. My attendant at that time was a rather shapely young woman . . . a Swedish girl named Britta. She did not provide the deterrent force that I needed. So I hired Kenneth on the advice of a friend. He had run into some minor legal problems and was keeping a low profile, doing oil changes and brake jobs in the godforsaken desert—'Saintly Motors' the place was called, or some such unlikely name. It was love at first sight—between Kenneth and my Rolls Royce. Now I could hardly bear to separate the two of them. And even though the problem with the stalker is long gone, I suppose I've become used to the feeling of security that he provides me." Willy turned to Jack. "You really ought to meet Britta, though. She's still on my payroll and stands in for Kenneth when he has time off. Britta is six feet tall, blond hair, blue eyes, a staggering figure. Massage therapist with a certificate from the Waldstein Academy in Stockholm. She has hands that could melt steel."

"Really!" Jack said. "Mark, have you met her?"

"Yeah, she's not your type. A little too much on the Teutonic side. You know, razor-sharp cheekbones. Leather. Scary."

Jack waved his hand at me and turned back to Willy. "Suppose I were to have a temporary nerve spasm that confined me to a chair for a week or two. You think you could loan her to me?"

I was stunned at the audacity and sheer bad taste of Jack's joke, considering that Willy would never walk again. But Willy seemed unperturbed. "Doubtful. Doubtful. Of course, I'd be happy to arrange a transfer of *Kenneth's* services on your behalf."

The cheeseburgers arrived, the banter continued, and for a few minutes the world seemed almost normal. I enjoyed it thoroughly.

12

With twenty minutes left before play resumed, I borrowed Jack's cell phone and put in a call to Captain DiCarlo. It turned out that he was right down the hall in the hotel. He suggested meeting over a cup of coffee. By this point, I was so wired from sleep deprivation and caffeine that another cup couldn't hurt.

"Interesting chat with your client today," opened DiCarlo.

"Binh isn't my client anymore. As I said, I was just doing him a favor by coming along," I explained, stirring sugar into my cup. "Now I realize why he was so anxious. He'll be represented by another lawyer tomorrow."

"You stuck your neck out for him. Must've violated two or three ethical rules while you were at it. A pretty serious conflict of interest, I would guess."

Here we go, I thought. *Time for the squeeze.*

"I respect that," DiCarlo said simply.

I waited for the other shoe to drop, but DiCarlo sipped his coffee and didn't add anything.

"I made a few phone calls to an old friend," I said, happy to change the subject. I didn't mention that the "old friend" had several felony convictions on his record. "There is no house in Hawaii owned by anybody named Warren Deukart."

"We're way ahead of you. He didn't own a ranch in New Mexico, either. Didn't own a thing, in fact. As far as we can tell, he had no tangible assets at all. Just a lease on an apartment in a shitty part of Las Vegas."

I took a moment to ponder this information. Shooter Deukart had consistently won huge amounts of money at poker, yet he had died flat broke. Some of the big-time card players were borderline compulsive gamblers who blew all of their poker winnings on sports betting and craps. But Shooter wasn't one of them. That left only one likely explanation.

"You think the mob was into him?" I asked.

"That's our guess."

"Why would they kill Shooter, though? He must have been a gold mine for them." At some point in his storied past, Shooter must have gone broke and borrowed money from the wrong people. They had never let go of him, kept squeezing him for everything he earned playing cards.

"Who said they killed him? I don't think they did. For exactly the reason you said. But we'll be chasing this one down, believe me. And God knows how many other card players might be mixed up in the same type of business."

"Unbelievable. Shooter Deukart owned by organized crime."

"Not really unbelievable at all. Of course, if he had no money, it does revive the theory that he may have been blackmailing Tran Le Binh."

I put my elbows on the table and leaned forward. "You know, Binh is awfully small to be dragging Shooter Deukart's body around. Also, he doesn't have a car. If you're looking at Binh, you'll have to look for an accomplice, and that doesn't fit very well with your blackmail theory." DiCarlo offered a noncommittal grunt.

At the same time I was defending Binh to DiCarlo, the detail that had nagged at me clicked. Binh had said that Shooter looked at his wristwatch. I was pretty sure Shooter Deukart never wore a watch. A minor discrepancy. Maybe just Binh's nerves talking, maybe part of a bigger lie. Why the hell had I put myself into an attorney-client bond with him? What a mess.

DiCarlo was looking at me. "Something on your mind?"

"Huh? No."

After a long moment he said, "I'd like to ask you a favor."

"For you, Frank? Anything at all." I said it cheerily, in a lame attempt to lighten up the conversation.

"I believe there's a large Haitian population down there in Brooklyn. Correct?"

"There's a large *everything* population in Brooklyn. Why do you ask?"

"I assume you're on good terms with a lot of people on the wrong side of the street."

"If you're referring to my clients and former clients, then yes, I do have a fairly deep roster to call on."

"I need to find out what this means." DiCarlo handed me a drawing—a drum with a knife sticking out of it. "The experts we've asked say it's some kind of voodoo symbol, but they don't know what it means or where it comes from. While I wait for them to dig through their reference books, it occurred to me that you might know some people who can get me a quick answer."

I smiled. This was right up my alley. "I know just the guy to ask, if I can get hold of him. You wouldn't want to tell me what this has to do with Shooter's murder, would you?"

"I didn't say it did. I'm just asking you for a favor."

"Understood. I'll see if I can find anything out."

13

THE LAST SESSION OF the first day of the tournament was a tense time. Half of the entrants would be gone by midnight, and nobody wanted to go home on the first day. So a lot of the players tightened up, avoiding danger. This meant it was time for me to change gears, loosen up, and start risking a few chips to steal pots. After a full day of observing the players at my table, I had a good idea of which ones could be pushed off their raises. So I was able to pick up a number of small pots, even though my cards were still lousy. I was cruising along in this mode, concentrating nicely on my game and steadily increasing my chip stack, when disaster struck.

I heard my brother before I saw him, pushing his way to the rail, calling and waving. In tow with Roger was his son, an impish boy with unruly strawberry-blond hair, whom I had not seen in a couple of years.

"Yo, Mark! Over here a minute!" hollered Roger.

Aargh. If I left the table now, my cards would be automatically folded until I returned. Since I was folding most of my hands anyway and the stakes were still relatively small, that probably wouldn't hurt me. But of course, who knew if those two or three hands I missed might not be aces or kings?

Fortunately, I was in early position at that moment, which was a good time to fold my cards anyway. I got up and quickly walked over to where Roger was waiting, behind a blue rope used to cordon off the spectators.

"Roger! Glad you could come. As you can see, we're in the middle of playing right now—"

"Had to let Patrick see the master at work!" interrupted Roger. "Looks like you're playing awesome!" Obviously, Roger had not seen me play a single hand, but I accepted the glib flattery without comment. All I wanted was to get back to my seat before the blinds reached me. But two years of marriage with Eileen had trained me to be at least minimally polite.

"Hi, Patrick. Great to see you. How old are you now, thirteen?"

"Twelve," said Patrick. "My pubes are starting to come in."

"Er, great, great," I mumbled, my eyes shifting back to Table Nineteen, where fresh cards were being dealt. "Look, Roger, can we—"

"Hey, Mark. I can't stay very long. I have this amazingly awesome business deal going down, so I have to go to the Left Coast for a few days. I'm already late for my plane."

"Oh, that's too bad, I mean it's great, but too bad you can't—"

"The thing is, the ex is out of town, and none of my regular babysitters are around either. Not that Patrick needs a babysitter anymore, but..."

"Hey, wait a minute, Roger. I'm in the middle of a very big poker tournament here."

"Exactly! So Patrick can hang out with you and learn all your tricks! Thanks, bro, I knew you'd come through for me. Patrick, be good, okay? I'll see you in a few days."

"Roger! No way!" I protested, but Roger had already turned and gone. For the first time, I noticed that Patrick was trailing a small duffel bag. *What the hell is happening here?* The boy looked up at me eagerly. "Roger!" I called again, but my brother was just a distant retreating figure. At Table Nineteen, another hand had been dealt and folded. I looked around desperately for help. Maybe Mary Poppins would come floating down on a magic umbrella to make this problem go away. She didn't, and after a few seconds it sank in that this was real: I was in charge of this twelve-year-old, and I was going to have to find a way to deal with it. I closed my eyes and pinched the bridge of my nose between my thumb and forefinger. I bit my lip, choking off a stream of profanities. Strangely, I was angry at my wife, not my brother. *Eileen! I told you something like this would happen!*

Finally, I got control of myself and turned to the business at hand. "Look, Patrick, I'm going to go back to my table and play cards. This will probably go on for another hour or two. Do you think that you can stay here and watch, all by yourself?"

"Sure, Uncle Mark! I like watching poker. If I get bored, I'll play my Gameboy."

"That's the ticket. Good lad. Okay, you stay right here, okay, so I'll know where you are."

I ignored the disapproving stares of the spectators who were standing nearby and dashed back to my table, just in time to see another of my hands being folded. Standing behind my chair, I surveyed the room. Patrick was still where I had left him, surrounded no doubt by dozens of child molesters and dope fiends.

Panic was tightening my chest. High-stakes poker showdowns? I thrived on them. Murder investigation with my name on the fatal toothpick? Piece of cake. But taking care of a twelve-year-old boy in the middle of all this? Somewhere near the bottom of my rib cage there were respiratory muscles going into paralysis.

Across the room I saw Bob Herr, busy in conversation with somebody I didn't know. I hustled over to where he stood, weaving in and out between the tables and pushed-back chairs, and caught Herr just as he was turning to leave.

"Bob!" I said. Herr frowned and tried to remember if he was supposed to recognize me.

"Mark Newcomb." I stuck out my hand, which Herr took with an artificial smile.

"Of course, of course. How's it going?"

"Look, believe it or not I suddenly have a twelve-year-old boy on my hands. My nephew. Do you know if there's any kind of baby-sitting service or anything like that around here?"

"The hotel has a child-care center," said Herr, plainly not interested in the personal troubles of a no-name card player.

"Great! Do you think we could get somebody to take him over there right now?"

"I'm pretty sure you'd have to sign him in yourself. That might take a while. But they'll definitely be open in the morning, if you want to try then."

"Okay, okay. Thanks, Bob."

I made the return trip across the room, bouncing and jostling the chairs of several players along the way. "Sorry ... 'scuse me ... sorry."

I peered over at the onlookers' section. Patrick was standing there, beaming, exactly where I had left him. I sat down as a new hand was being dealt. *Okay. Okay. This is going to work out okay. And Eileen is going to pay big time.*

14

AT THIS POINT IN the proceedings, the quality of my poker game took a major turn south. Distracted beyond all imagining by this new responsibility, constantly glancing over to make sure that Patrick was still there, I found myself bluffing at the wrong players, betting too cautiously with good cards, and generally playing like an amateurish clown.

Then things got worse. At one point I thought I saw Patrick put his hand on the backside of a nearby woman spectator. From the way she reacted, I guessed that I had seen correctly. While deliberating whether I had to go over and deal with the situation, I underbet a solid hand and allowed an opponent with weaker cards to stay in the pot and run me down on the river. From a high point of almost $20,000, my chip stack was reduced to under $12,000 before the session was mercifully closed for the night. *Damn! Damn! Damn damn damn!!!*

I took Patrick by the arm and steered him through the crowd to where I could see Jack Shea talking animatedly with several other players. Apparently, things were still going well for *him*, at least.

"…so I made this little kissy face at him, and the next thing you know—"

"Jack! I need you for a minute."

Jack turned, the huge grin on his face freezing in stupefaction as he saw Patrick standing with me. To Jack, children were practically an alien species. Even at a family party he had little use for them; in a casino, they were simply not to be tolerated.

"Jack, I have to take care of Patrick here for a few days, and you're going to help me."

If I had scraped a dead skunk off the side of a road and served it to Jack on a platter, I couldn't have evoked a look of deeper revulsion. For once in his life, Jack Shea was speechless.

"Don't worry," I said. "Starting tomorrow morning, he can go to the hotel's child-care center and—"

"No! Way! Uh-uh. Not going to happen," interrupted Patrick. I turned to face the rebellious twelve-year-old. "That place is for babies! They sit around and watch *Barney*! Look, my dad brings me here all the time. I know how to take care of myself!"

I turned back to Jack, but he had taken advantage of the distraction to make himself scarce.

"Great," I grunted.

I took Patrick up to my room—our room—and tossed his duffel bag onto the spare bed. I ushered him into the bathroom to get washed and brushed, and called Eileen, who answered in a cheery voice.

"Hey, poker-star-slash-murder-suspect, how did it go today?"

"Eileen, I need you to come up here. Roger dumped Patrick on me and left town."

"Ohhh. That's not good, is it." She was silent for a moment. We didn't need to discuss her partial responsibility in the matter. "There's no way I can get away from work for the next three days. We're getting very close to a major bust. Maybe I can find somebody else who could come up and help out?"

"Anything. Anybody."

"How old is Patrick?"

"I'm not sure. He says he's twelve but he acts more like seventeen."

I was in my early thirties, two years older than Eileen, and the subject of children came up pretty frequently. We both agreed that we wanted to be parents. Eileen told me that I would have to spend less time gambling. I told Eileen that I was willing to do this, but she would have to give up working narcotics, because I didn't want to raise a family of orphans. Neither of us knew for sure whether I was bluffing, but Eileen was very clear that she wasn't ready to lay down her police duties. So we remained in a fidgety state of indecision, which obviously could not go on forever. This experience with Patrick was likely to set us back at least another couple of years.

"Well, what else happened today? How's the tournament going? You haven't been incriminated in the use of any more kitchen utensils on the body of what's-his-name, have you?"

"Not me, no. But a friend of mine is potentially in trouble."

"Oh?"

"I can't talk about it." *Oops.*

"Why not?"

106

I didn't answer. When you've done something really stupid, your spouse is the last person you want to admit it to.

"Why *not?*" Eileen was not the type to just let something slide.

"Attorney-client privilege." I said it quietly and fast, as if maybe I could sneak it by her.

"Mark. You agreed to be somebody's lawyer, in a case where *you* found the *body?*"

"Just for today. I'm already done with it."

"My God, Mark, you could get disbarred for something like that!"

She was right, of course, but I wasn't in the mood for a lecture.

"Listen, Mark. You have this compulsion to stick up for losers and scumbags. Okay. But this is a situation where you have to look out for yourself. Just stay out of this and let the cops do their job. Promise?"

I didn't promise. The "good nights" between me and Eileen were a little on the frosty side.

Patrick came out of the bathroom. He was showered, pajama-clad, and wide awake—certainly more alert than I was, anyway. *Do kids his age have bedtimes anymore? Is that my responsibility?* I had no idea.

"Uncle Mark," he asked, "will you teach me how to play poker?"

"Patrick, I'm really tired right now ..." He was looking at me with big, innocent puppy eyes. Eileen's voice sounded in my conscience: *He's your nephew, for crying out loud. When is the last time you did anything for him?* She was right again. Harpy.

I sighed softly and reached for the deck of cards that was on the nightstand. "Okay. Poker is designed around a five-card hand.

There's an order to the hands. If you have a pair, it beats a hand with no pairs. Two pairs beats one pair—"

"I know," Patrick interrupted. "And three of a kind beats two pair. Then after three of a kind is a straight, then a flush, then a full house. My dad taught me that much. What I really want to know is, how can you tell what your chances are of hitting the cards that you need? Like, if you have two pair after the flop, how can you know what your chances are of making the full boat?"

I was impressed. Maybe there was good in this child after all.

"Well, that's pretty easy, actually. All you do is count the number of cards still in the deck that will help you. We call those your 'outs.' You multiply the outs by twice the number of cards still to come.

"So let's say you have an eight and a nine in your hand, and the flop is eight, nine, jack. So you have two pair, eights and nines, and you need another eight or nine to give you the full boat. You have four outs—four more cards still in the deck that could give you the full house—two more eights and two more nines. If the turn and the river are still to come, you have two more chances to hit your outs, so you multiply four outs times two cards to come, which gives you eight. Then you multiply that by two and you get sixteen, which is, approximately, your chances of making the boat. Sixteen percent."

"Cool! How did you figure that out?"

"I didn't. Some computer math whiz figured it out, I just read it in a book. It's actually a little more complicated than that if you want to get the exact number, but this way is close enough most of the time. Anyway, the key is to compare your chances of making your hand against the odds that you are getting on your bet. So, back to our example. Let's assume you need a full house to win. If there are a hundred dollars in the pot, and it will only cost you ten dollars to call, then you are betting 10 percent of the pot on a 16 percent chance to win it. So it could be a good deal."

"I get it." He asked me a few more questions, demonstrating that he had a keen mind for this sort of thing. After a few minutes, I told him it was bedtime and was amazed when he didn't object. My first attempt at asserting authority was a success.

We had a quick negotiation about the next day, and a deal was struck. Patrick would not have to go to the child-care center. He would stay in the room all day, watch TV, and order food from room service. I had to admit to myself that the boy seemed pretty mature for his age.

15

WITH PATRICK FINALLY TUCKED in, I was settling in for a badly needed night's sleep when a loud knocking jolted me out of bed.

I pulled my jeans on and opened the door. Madelin Santos stood in the hallway, clearly distraught. I stepped aside and she rushed into the room.

"Hey, not bad, Uncle Mark!" said Patrick. "Gorgeous babes banging on your door to get in! My dad usually has them banging to get out!"

"Patrick, go back to sleep. Maddie, let's go talk in the bathroom." Maddie stared at Patrick in amazement. "Don't ask," I said.

I was mindful of the fact that Maddie was indeed quite attractive, and that Eileen would not appreciate her presence in my room at this hour of the night, if she were ever to learn about it. Something told me that Patrick was not a reliable chaperone.

But Madelin Santos obviously had more pressing problems on her mind. In order to speak privately, we had to use the bathroom as a makeshift conference room. I found myself perched on the bathtub rim, having gallantly offered the toilet seat to Maddie.

"What is it?"

"The police captain, DiCarlo, was waiting to talk to me when we broke for the night." It was a reflection of the seriousness of the moment that I didn't even think to ask Maddie how her chip stack was doing. "Mark, the police found my gun."

"You'd already told them it was missing, right?"

She stared at the tile floor.

"Maddie!"

She looked up at me. Her striking green eyes were brimming with tears. "Mark, I was afraid to! I mean, how would it look?"

"Not as bad as it looks now." I shifted my weight. The rim of the bathtub was not a comfortable roost. "Okay, calm down. Where did they find it? The gun, I mean."

"He wouldn't say. Somebody found it somewhere and turned it in, that's all I know."

"So you told him it had been missing?"

She examined the tiles some more. "Yeah. He asked me why I didn't report it sooner."

"Have they run a ballistics test? Do they know if it was used on Shooter?"

"He told me there were four shells missing from the chamber. They're running the tests. He said if the results showed my gun was involved, I'd want to think about getting a lawyer."

"Okay, don't panic. What about fingerprints? Did they find any?"

"He didn't say anything about that. Well, mine would be all over it anyway, wouldn't they? But maybe if there were somebody else's ..."

"I doubt it. If somebody used your gun and threw it away, they wouldn't have left any prints on it. If your prints are on the shooting grip, and nobody else's are, that would be bad. It would mean that nobody else had fired the gun after you. But if the gun is clean, then it could have been anybody. Including you."

"Mark, you don't think I had anything to do with it!" She grabbed a tissue and wiped at her eyes. This was a new Madelin Santos. Until now, my experience with Maddie had been either at a card table, where she was solid ice, or around a dinner table, where she was carefree and enchanting. Half of the regular poker players on the East Coast were infatuated with her.

Even here, sitting on a commode in the overlit bathroom of Room 824, with her face pale and overwrought, Maddie looked good. I was uncomfortably aware of her sexuality. She was wearing a cotton tank top with a scoop neck and a pair of shorts that left most of her long legs exposed. She was leaning forward from her awkward seat, her hands clasped between her knees, and the cleavage between her breasts was exaggerated by the position. It was difficult not to glance. I was also sitting with my weight forward, in order not to fall off the bathtub rim. This left my knees just inches from hers, and my hands within reaching distance. Our forward-leaning body English seemed to urge us toward each other. She was several years younger than I was, and mixed up in something she couldn't handle. She needed me.

What the hell are you thinking? I came back to myself. *What kind of a person are you?* My friend was in distress and I was drifting off

112

into sexual fantasyland. What is there about a vulnerable woman that can turn a normally decent guy into a predator? I abruptly sat upright and nearly fell backward into the empty tub. If she noticed, she didn't say anything.

"No, of course I don't. Except that you *are* involved now, like it or not. Listen, Maddie. They have a motive on you, and now maybe a weapon. If the ballistics test is bad news, then you will absolutely need to have a good solid alibi, *and* a credible theory of how somebody else could have taken your gun and used it. It doesn't take a genius to see what you're hiding—you were in your room with somebody, and you don't want to talk about it. Okay, fine, but you can't avoid talking to the police, and you have to tell them the truth."

"I did."

"Good." A silence hung between us until I spoke again. "And it wasn't Jack."

It was really a question, not an assertion. Jack Shea was utterly shameless, a terrible liar, a reckless gambler, and an occasional drunk, but I wanted to believe that in the end he was faithful to Brigid. If there was a tiny bit of jealousy in my asking, I would never have admitted that to myself.

"No! My God. You think I'd be stupid enough to get mixed up with a dickhead like Jack? Give me some credit."

"Sorry. It's just the way he talks about things, sometimes, I'm never too sure…" I trailed off awkwardly. Maddie looked at me wide-eyed and said nothing. The silence grew more uncomfortable, and I mumbled, "So, I'll see you tomorrow morning, then." I stood up and ushered Maddie out the door.

Before stepping into the hallway, she turned around, took my hand, and squeezed it between hers. "Mark, thanks so much for listening. It's good to know I can count on you."

After I closed the door behind Maddie, I looked at the clock on the nightstand. It was one-thirty a.m. and I was both exhausted and wide awake at the same time. I decided to follow up on DiCarlo's request to check out the voodoo symbol. It was a good time to do it; the person I needed to call considered one a.m. to be the middle of the day.

I could have used the phone in the bathroom, but I felt like getting out. I walked down the hall and around the corner to the stairwell and climbed down the eight flights of stairs to the casino level. Mild claustrophobia had afflicted me for as long as I could remember, and I avoided elevators when possible. This sometimes created a concern in a hotel-casino, where large amounts of cash could frequently be found in my pockets, but so far I had never had a problem.

I went to the bank of pay phones near the entrance to the casino and placed the call to Henri L'Ouverture, a former client. The name was pronounced in the French style—*Ahn-ree.* Henri was as weird as they come. I had represented him when he was arrested for holding a pizza delivery person against his will. Possibly to conduct bloody voodoo rituals, but more likely because the pizza had been cold. It was hard to tell with Henri. He habitually drank twelve beers every evening as his first meal of the day. "The beer turns into food when it gets to your stomach," he explained to me. What he needed more than anything was psychiatric attention, but the state of New York didn't have nearly enough money to deal with all the nut jobs that were running around on the streets.

Henri had gone through the legal system, served a little time, and was back living his upside-down life in a Brooklyn loft that looked like the set from *Indiana Jones and the Temple of Doom*.

In the course of representing Henri, I had learned a small amount about voodoo—enough to understand that it was based on an African religion called Vodun, which was neither bizarre nor sinister. But like all religions, there were those who practiced their own extreme forms of it.

"Mark, my very good friend, it is always a pleasure to hear from you."

"Always a pleasure to talk to you, Henri. Are you keeping yourself out of trouble?"

"Well, you see, the trouble seems to come and find me no matter where I hide. Just yesterday—"

"Listen, Henri, I'm sorry to interrupt, but I need to ask you something and I don't have a lot of time." I described the symbol of the drum with the knife sticking out of it, and Henri's voice rose in recognition.

"That is not a sacred sign. There are not any spirits who keep their dwelling in that sign."

I wasn't sure what that meant, but I pressed on. "If it isn't a sacred sign, does it mean anything?"

"Oh yes indeed, my friend, it means quite a great deal. You will have to talk with Queen Ezili if you want to learn more."

"Queen Ezili?"

"A very powerful spirit person. You will find her body in Miami."

"Her body? Is she dead?"

Henri laughed heartily. "No, my friend, she is anything but dead! I mean you will find her body in Miami, although you might find her spirit almost anywhere. Sometimes I talk to her here in my room. But if you want to talk to her, I suggest you go to Miami."

L'Ouverture began humming a tune that I didn't recognize. I tried to press him for an address, a phone number, or any other clues to exactly where in Miami Queen Ezili's corporeal manifestation could be found. But the limit of Henri's coherence had apparently been reached. I hung up.

By now it was almost two a.m., but I knew that I was too wired from all this weirdness to get to sleep. Across the casino floor I could see a waving croupier stick indicating a crap game in progress. It was that or TV Land, but the crap table was closer. I approached the table and placed a few small bets. A minute later I felt a familiar nudge.

"Where's Junior?" Jack Shea had appeared at my elbow.

"You bastard."

"Hey, sorry. I panicked. Let me know what I can do to help. Does the kid need his diapers changed or anything?"

"I think I have it under control." I had a thought. "Actually, you could do something for me. Let me have your cell phone, so if Patrick needs me tomorrow he can reach me."

"Why don't *you* have a cell phone? You're a big-shot lawyer."

"Because I hate them. Besides, have you ever met one of my clients? If I had a cell phone, they'd be calling me all the time."

"Well, I can't give you *my* phone. What if Brigid called and you answered? She knows you're here. I'd be toast."

"Okay, then I'm going to give Patrick your number, and if he's in trouble, he's going to call you."

"Deal. Now let me tell you about the day I had! Do you realize that I am number five in the chip count right now? I've got these

homophobic shitweasels completely on tilt. There's this one guy …"
Jack rambled on about his adventures in his usual comic fashion, but I was too preoccupied to enjoy it.

"Jack, I did something really stupid."

"Congratulations. You've finally joined the rest of us. Anything fatal?"

"I hope not. I represented Binh in his interview with the state police. He begged me to."

"*That's* what has your shorts in a bundle? C'mon. Lighten up, Francis. What does Binh have to do with Deukart, anyway?"

"I can't tell you that. But my gut says he's clean on the murder. He says he was in his room all Monday night."

"Hey, winner!" Jack suddenly shouted. "Nicely, nicely!" The shooter had rolled a five and made his point. Jack and I reached into the table to pick up our winnings, his being considerably larger than mine. He used most of his winning chips to double his bet on the Pass Line.

"You know what?" Jack said. "I don't think he *was* in his room."

"What? Who?"

"Binh. I remember seeing him getting into an elevator when I was coming into the casino. I tried to say hi, but he acted like he didn't hear me. Which was typical."

"What time was that?"

"I don't know, eleven, maybe."

"Are you sure of this?"

"Pretty sure, yeah."

Great. Perfect. Now I had another reason to doubt Binh's story. But I couldn't tell DiCarlo what I had learned, even if I'd wanted to. I still owed Binh a lawyer's privilege, even though I wasn't representing him anymore. So who was going to watch out for *me*?

"Damn!" Jack slapped his hand on the edge of the table as the shooter sevened out. The dealer swept up all of our bets. Jack had a lot more out there than I did.

"Hey, Jack," I said. "Do you know who told the police what I said to Shooter about his toothpick?"

"I think everybody told the police. It was all over the casino that day, along with a hundred other stupid stories that didn't mean anything. Why, what's the difference?"

"Shooter's body was found with a toothpick up its ass."

Jack looked surprised, just for a moment. Then he grinned. "Now I can believe there is poetry in the world," he said. "That is sheer poetry. They don't think that you …"

"No, I don't think so. But I'm not completely sure. The captain tells me things about the case, things a cop doesn't usually let out during an investigation. Confides in me, encourages my suggestions, which you wouldn't ordinarily expect from a cop to a defense lawyer. Makes me wonder if he's playing me a little bit."

"Like a strong poker hand calling down a weak one. Let the weak hand bet, and just call, call, call. Let the weaker hand dig himself into a hole."

"Yeah, something like that," I fretted.

"Know what I think?"

"What."

"I think you need to get laid. Hey, Anita!" he called down to Anita Wilson, who was dealing at the other end of the fifteen-foot table. "My friend Mark here has a guilty conscience. He needs some sweet honey to make him feel better."

She displayed a confident smile that caused every man within her field of vision to go weak in the knees. "Tell him to get himself a nice cup of hot tea. That always works for me. And you, Jack Shea, you go take a cold soak."

I looked at my shoes in embarrassment while the four other players around the table—all men—stared at Jack in awe. He dared to speak to the goddess! With such familiarity! Why hadn't a lightning bolt come down from the sky to strike him dead?

Jack ignored them. "Hey, I want you to do something for me."

Coming from Jack, this was a harbinger of trouble more often than not. "Yeah?" I asked in a wary tone.

"These hints that the cop captain is dropping on you. Can you let me in on any of them?"

"I shouldn't. What are you looking for? I'm sure you're not burning to avenge the death of Shooter Deukart."

"No, I can't say I've lost any sleep over it. Right now I'm thinking about a different obnoxious prick who needs to learn some manners."

"Gant? You're talking about goofing on Gant some more?" His silence meant yes. "Listen, you've already gone too far. This is serious business." I tried to maintain a stern look of disapproval, but despite myself, I felt a grin working at the corners of my mouth.

"C'mon!" he urged me. "This is the payback opportunity of a lifetime! Think what an asshole he is! Just tell me something, anything, the cops might be looking for. I swear to God I'll never tell anybody I got it from you."

"Oh, like they'd have trouble guessing." I made another effort at frowning. "I am an officer of the court. I can't get involved in practical jokes when there's a real live crime being investigated."

"Officer of the court, my ass. Listen, you just complained about how this cop is jerking you around. Isn't he an officer of the court? Here's a way for you to level the field a little."

He spread his hands in a questioning gesture and looked at me with his eyebrows raised in high anticipation. This was one of the worst ideas I'd ever heard, but Jack could see that I was going for it.

"Okay. I don't know what the importance is, but there's something to do with a symbol. A drum with a knife through it. And if anybody asks, you heard it from Zip Addison, not me."

Jack beamed. "Perfect. You're one hell of a guy, you know that?"

"One hell of an idiot, you mean."

"Same thing."

We didn't speak for a few minutes while the crap game occupied our full attention. Jack's full attention, anyway. I was busy kicking myself for aiding and abetting Jack's *Animal House* caper. I was also dying with curiosity to know what he had in mind. Eileen sometimes called Jack my "shoulder devil," referring to the cartoons in which the character had a good angel on one shoulder and a bad devil on the other. I definitely had the good angel part of it down—Jack did his best to provide balance.

"Here's a question," he said during a lull between rolls. He was looking reflectively into the distance. "If you could choose, would you rather get laid by Maddie Santos or win first place in this tournament?"

"Oh hell, Jack, don't ask me things like that."

"No, really. Which would you choose?"

"Well, both would be a lot of fun, obviously. But only one of them would make me hate myself the next day."

"Hmmph. Choirboy. You are definitely a bad influence on me, you know that?"

Jack was quiet again for a minute or so while he concentrated on the dice. "You know," he said during another pause in the action, "I have another problem."

"Oh, *you* have a problem. Yeah, let's talk about *your* problems for a while."

"Okay, here's my problem. I didn't plan on making it to the second day of the tournament, much less the third or the fourth. Brigid thinks I'm coming home tomorrow from Albany. I'm going to tell her that I developed a couple of hot sales prospects at the conference and that I'm going to stay in town to try to work them out."

"Sales? I thought you were in trading or analysis or something like that."

Jack shrugged. "Same thing. But Brigid isn't dumb, unfortunately, and I don't know how long I can pull this off. Damn, if I get to the fourth day, it will be just about impossible." His face suddenly went pale—a color that I saw only when the fear of Brigid's wrath was on him. "Oh my God, I just realized, the final table of this tournament is going to be on TV. If I keep winning at this rate, I'll be there. *Then* what do I do?"

"Such problems you have." I smirked. "You'll think of something. You always do."

16

Thursday, September 30

THE EIGHT A.M. WAKE-UP came as a jolt. I felt as though my head had just hit the pillow, which was almost true since it had been after four when I got back to the room. The casino at the Humpback was closed between four and eight a.m. This was unusual in the 24/7 world of gambling, but the elders of the Missequa Nation had apparently insisted on it as a gesture toward moderation. It was a good thing for people like Jack and me, who otherwise might never get any sleep at all. In my case, even the four a.m. curfew didn't help. It was almost six before I'd relaxed enough to nod off.

I sat up, my head feeling numb, and was momentarily confused by the lump in the other bed, until I remembered that I had a twelve-year-old nephew under my care. I dragged myself into the bathroom and splashed some water onto my face. Somewhere in my brain there was an absurd notion that splashing water on your face can make up for missing sleep three nights in a row. It didn't work.

Patrick and I went down to the breakfast buffet that was laid out for the players. It was a time to catch up on gossip and learn who was still in the tournament and who was not. Among the important players who had been knocked out the previous evening was Tran Le Binh. I wanted to talk with him but he wasn't in the room.

Patrick was being extraordinarily well-behaved. He listened to the conversations of the adults and spoke respectfully when they addressed him. His behavior reminded me a little bit of the obsequious Eddie Haskell from *Leave It to Beaver*. This caused a warning bell to ring somewhere in the back of my mind, but I willed myself to ignore it. I got him set up with a tray of food, and he settled down to eat while reading a *Calvin and Hobbes* book.

The other guy I really wanted to talk with was Willy Hopkins. Normally, he didn't eat breakfast from the buffet with the commoners, but this morning I found him with a heaping tray of pancakes and bacon.

"Kenneth, will you excuse us for a minute?" I asked. Kenneth didn't move until Willy dismissed him with a flip of his hand. I sat down.

"I learned the most amazing thing, and I thought you might be able to tell me something about it," I started. He smiled politely and raised his eyebrows. "Turns out Shooter Deukart was dead broke. Looks like some sort of loan-sharking outfit was into him balls-deep and he couldn't get away from them. Is that incredible?"

Willy shifted in his chair and carefully cut a piece of bacon. He had to be the only person in the room who ate bacon with a fork. "And why would that concern me?" he asked without looking up.

"Well, frankly, you seem to be in the middle of everybody's business around here. No offense. I mean that in a nice way. Also, to be honest, you kind of surprised me the other night when I found out you were setting up games for Spanish mob types."

He put down his silverware and wiped his mouth with his napkin. "As usual, Mark, your instincts are superb. I'm going to tell this to you, and you only. And I expect you to keep it to yourself."

I moved my chair closer.

"It came to my attention several months ago that Shooter Deukart was in a desperate situation. I took it upon myself to help. I am in the middle—*was* in the middle—of negotiations to buy out his loan and extricate him from his troubles, when he was killed. And yes,"—he held up his palm—"since you were about to ask anyway, our visitors from Spain were associates of my new—despicable—acquaintances. Nothing else would have induced me to deal with them. Now that Shooter is dead, I've washed my hands of it. And for obvious reasons I'd prefer the police not learn of my efforts on Shooter's behalf."

"So do you think these money guys had any reason to have him killed?"

"I can't imagine why they would. In their eyes, he was a valuable piece of property—nothing more, nothing less. They were certainly demanding an exorbitant amount to buy out his loan."

"That would mean they expected to keep making money from him for a long time."

"Presumably, yes."

"Who else around here is in the same kind of mess?"

"If I knew, I wouldn't tell you. Suffice it to say I have no intention of being involved any further."

"Tell me something, Willy. Why do this for Shooter? It's not like the two of you were particularly close. I once heard him call you a 'petrified piece of peckerwood' to your face."

"I had no fondness for him. But he was a great man in his own right, and I couldn't bear to sit by and do nothing. He earned whatever help I could give him."

———————

After breakfast, the poker resumed. With Patrick safely up in the hotel room and two cups of coffee surging through my system, I was hoping that the focus would come back into my game. The tables were reshuffled for the new day, and I found myself at Table Eight playing with five or six people whose games I was more or less familiar with. Unfortunately, one of them was Barracuda Gant. Not that I was concerned about playing against him; I just wasn't in the mood to listen to his bullshit.

The first big hand of the morning came when I limped into a pot in early position with a pair of sixes and hit a third six when the flop came out A♠ K♣ 6♣. Beautiful. The player on the button, who had also limped into the pot without raising, was my favorite guy, Barracuda Gant. If he had a king or an ace, I could hurt him pretty badly. I slow-played the hand, checking and allowing Gant to bet. He accommodated me with a small bet; the player in the big blind folded, and I called.

The turn came—eight of clubs—and this caused me a bit of concern. If Gant were playing a couple of clubs, he would have me beaten with a flush. On the other hand, if he had been drawing to a flush, he wouldn't have bet small on the previous card. He would either have checked, to see a free card, or would have raised big to try to win the pot right there. So I decided that I wasn't worried about Gant having a club flush. The biggest problem with the clubs on the board was that he might make *me* for a flush, which would spoil the surprise that I was planning with my set of sixes. I checked, hoping that he would bet so I could raise him. He checked.

The river card was a nightmare: the two of clubs. With four clubs on the board, anybody with a single club in his hand would have a flush. My sixes didn't mean much anymore. It was basically a contest of who had a higher club, and I had no club at all. I should have bet anyway, to show a flush, but I was too disgusted that I had missed my chance to bet on the turn and avoid this debacle. I checked. Gant fired out a big bet, and I didn't waste much time thinking about it. I tossed my monster set of sixes into the muck and said, "Take it."

Gant said, "Don't mind if I do," and showed his cards: a five and an eight, neither of them clubs. He'd had nothing at all. "Someday when you grow up you'll learn to play this game," he said to me with a smirk. "What did you say your name was?"

I didn't respond. *Prick.* What I did do was go on a minor tear and win several hands over the next two hours. None against Gant, unfortunately. But there were two super-satellite winners at the table whom I had marked as playing loose, passive games, and I got the cards I needed to take advantage of them.

When break time came, my stack was over $30,000 and I was feeling good about the world. Now I had some sleuthing to do. My intention was to feel out a few more players, try to see who else might be caught in the same trap that Shooter was in. I knew there were plenty of gamblers who had financial backers, and some of those backers were probably not fully accredited financial institutions.

But when I rose from the table, I found that I was mentally exhausted. I had to go back to my room to get a few minutes of rest. And check up on Patrick, whom I had managed to put out of my mind.

As usual, I took the stairs, despite being worn out from lack of sleep. I felt the exercise of climbing eight floors would do me good, and the last thing I needed right now was the added anxiety of an elevator ride.

Rounding a landing between the third and fourth floors, I sensed, before I saw, a figure waiting on the steps above me. I turned around instantly and began walking downstairs, looking for the quickest entrance back into the hotel. The $1,500 in craps money I carried in my wallet suddenly felt like quite a lot.

"Don't shit your pants, Newcomb. If I wanted to rob you, you'd be unconscious by now."

I stopped and turned to face the man coming toward me down the stairs. He appeared to be in his mid-fifties, of medium build, neatly dressed—casual slacks, button-down oxford shirt, and tasseled loafers. His hair was black and slicked back.

It was only when the man was standing level with me on the landing that I noticed his eyes. Lifeless, dangerous eyes that I had seen a dozen times before, sometimes in my own clients. Eyes of a person who considered taking a human life to be the moral equivalent of ordering a cheeseburger. In my office we even had a code to identify this type of indifferent criminal: "Would you like fries with that?"

"Martin Ennis," the man said with an arid smile, offering his hand.

I didn't take it. My mouth went clammy. "What do you want?" I managed to ask.

Ennis's smile disappeared. "Just a private conversation." He leaned further into my space. "I heard you don't like close places, Newcomb."

I waited. *How did he know that?* The stairwell was feeling closer all the time.

Ennis eased back a slight distance and gave me another icy smile. "The people I work for were not happy that Shooter Deukart got thumped. We had a sweet deal going with the old fucker. Eighty percent of everything he won belonged to us. The other 20 percent... also belonged to us. The person who killed him has to pay."

"So what does that have to do with me?" I made a show at sounding tough. It was probably the most transparent bluff I'd ever attempted.

"You told him you were gonna put a toothpick up his ass. That night Deukart is found dead, with a toothpick up his ass. Put it together, Perry Mason."

"Toothpick! How did you find out about that?"

"Connections."

"Look, I've already gone over this with the cops. There were hundreds of people who heard about that, and hundreds of people who could have done it. And I have an airtight alibi for the whole evening. So you've got the wrong guy."

"Hey. You don't get a trial where I come from. You're looking at the judge and the jury. And the executioner, when I need to be."

I fought to keep my composure. "Why don't you just tell me what it is that you want?"

"We want what's coming to us." Ennis surveyed me coldly. "Shooter Deukart belonged to my boss. You killed him. Now you belong to us. Only you're no Shooter Deukart, even at your best, are you? So we're still not even."

All things considered, I was beginning to feel that I would have preferred the elevator ride.

"We're going to be partners, you and me," he said. "I want you to think about that for a little while. Of course, you always have choices." He leaned forward into my space again. "You don't like elevators. How are you on boxes? Ever thought what it would feel like to, maybe, get buried alive in a pine box?"

It must have been my claustrophobia that caused it, but I had an extreme physical reaction to Ennis's threat. Just short of messing my pants, I guess, but my body literally shot sweat out of every pore. My shirt went from dry to soaked in a couple of seconds; my eyes stung from the salty sweat gushing down my forehead. I'd thought I was afraid out in the parking lot on Monday night, but that was nothing compared to this. Ennis smiled again, a genuine smile this time, gloating in his obvious success at getting into my head.

The smile pissed me off. With a supreme effort, I pulled myself together. "Look," I said, "I had nothing to do with Shooter getting killed, and I think you know that. You're running a bluff. Now I'm going up to my room, then I'm going back downstairs to play cards. Whatever it is you want from me, you can't get it if I'm dead." I paused for a breath and he didn't respond. "Although I have to admit, as attention-getters go, the coffin bit is working."

I felt that it was important for me to walk away without asking his permission. As I turned to move up the stairs, Ennis's hand fell lightly on my shoulder. "Hey, Newk, you're all right. I like you. I might just shoot you before I bury you. We'll speak again soon. But you need to know something, poker player." He smiled at me again with unnerving blankness. "I don't bluff."

17

I DIDN'T GO BACK to my room when I entered the hallway on the eighth floor. As soon as I had the stairwell door closed behind me, I leaned against it, closed my eyes, and breathed deeply for a full minute. If anybody walked past and noticed the strange sight of a soaking wet guy apparently meditating in the hallway, I didn't care.

I went straight for the nearest telephone, in an alcove next to an ice machine. As I reached for the receiver, a wave of nausea swept over me and, just in time, I stuck my face into a garbage bin and vomited. Afterward, I scooped some ice out of the machine and rubbed a handful of it over my forehead and across the back of my neck. When I felt sure of myself again, I placed a call.

"DiCarlo here."

"Frank, this is Mark Newcomb. I can personally confirm the theory that Deukart was mixed up with organized crime. I just had a very close and unpleasant encounter."

"You too, huh?"

"You mean I'm not the only one?"

"You and five or six others."

Vast relief. A suffocating weight was lifted off my chest. Of course, I shouldn't have been happy that some of my fellow poker players had also been terrorized. But if misery loves company, fear wants a whole party. So I was right; Ennis had been bluffing. The guy wasn't going to kill six or seven people just to prove a point. Was he?

"Who else has he been after?"

"That's not something you need to know."

"I think it is. I'd like to know who's in the same boat with me."

"It wouldn't mean anything. This guy Ennis is just blowing smoke. He's shaking a lot of trees and hoping something will fall out."

"He told me Shooter made a lot of money for his organization."

"We're in the process of pinning that down. Deukart was into somebody for a huge amount of money. With the interest piling up at something like 10 percent a week, he could play poker every night and barely keep up."

"I don't see how that's possible. Shooter had to be winning half a million, a million dollars a year, easy."

"You'd be surprised. He borrowed too much money, from the wrong guy, at the wrong time. And the cards didn't go right for him when he needed them to. You get in that deep and there's no digging out."

"He knows about the toothpick, by the way. Ennis, I mean."

"I was going to ask you about that. I thought I told you to keep that to yourself."

"I did! I told my wife, who's a New York City cop, and that's it." *Jack!* I swore at myself inwardly. *I told Jack last night.* The last thing I was going to do was bring up Jack's name with DiCarlo. Jack was perfectly capable of getting himself into trouble, without any extra help from his friends.

"Hmm. Well, this guy seems to know a lot of things that he shouldn't."

"I assume you're going to arrest him? I guarantee you at least an assault conviction based on my testimony alone." Though I was greatly relieved at what I'd learned from DiCarlo, I would still feel much better if Martin Ennis were in police custody.

"We will when we find him. He's dropped out of sight for now." DiCarlo spoke carefully. It occurred to me that DiCarlo's investigation might actually benefit from having a loose cannon like Ennis out there rattling people—like a hunting dog flushing game birds out of their cover.

"Well, he was right here in the Humpback as of five minutes ago. Hardly out of sight. I guess you'll want to bring the FBI into this, now that it's definitely a mob case?"

"The hell I will. I have a murderer to catch. The feds come in and they won't care about anything except using Ennis to get to his bosses. The most I'll do is ask them to track down a solid ID on our man. I can't imagine that Martin Ennis is his real name. You want my advice? Don't spend too much time worrying about this guy."

Easy for you to say.

"Another thing," he said. "I'd be very interested in anything you can learn about the private game that went on in the luxury suite Monday night. The joker that was registered in the suite is suspected of being involved in moving heroin into the U.S. If there's any connection with Ennis and the people he works for, I want to find it."

"I'll keep that in mind." *Why the hell did Willy let himself get mixed up with those guys?* I changed the subject. "Listen, Captain, Madelin Santos came and talked with me last night. She's very worried."

"She ought to be."

"I want you to know, she told me two days ago that her gun was missing from her room. The only reason she didn't go to you with that is because she was scared. For what it's worth, I'm very confident that Maddie Santos could not, and did not, kill anybody."

"I don't think she did, either."

"Oh?" I was surprised.

"But that doesn't mean she didn't shoot him."

Huh? "I don't understand."

"Whoever put the bullets into Deukart did it two hours after he was already dead."

I was silent for a moment while this new information soaked in. "So what are you telling me, that somebody killed Shooter and then a different person came by later and shot him? That's crazy. I can't imagine Maddie Santos just happened to be strolling around the parking lot with her gun in her hand, stumbled upon Shooter's dead body, and pumped a few slugs into him. Ridiculous. It had to be the killer who came back to create some red herrings. The bullets. The toothpick. Probably other things you haven't told me about."

"That's one theory. A theory that works pretty well for you, of course."

"So what *was* the cause of death?"

"Somebody was beating on him and he had a heart attack."

"Beating on him? But I didn't see any bruises on his face when we found him in the parking lot."

"You wouldn't have. Not on the face. His abdomen got worked over pretty good, though, and he had three broken ribs. If the heart attack hadn't killed him, internal bleeding probably would have."

"You must have plenty of forensic evidence then, if there was that kind of direct contact. Skin samples, blood, maybe some fabrics."

"Not much, actually. Somebody knew enough to wear gloves."

"Well, this is damn good news for Maddie. Can I tell her? So she can stop worrying?"

"Absolutely not. There's every reason to think she was mixed up in Deukart's death in some way. She's not in the clear by any means."

"I thought she told you everything she did on Monday night."

"Think again. There's something this lady is hiding."

Hmm. "Fingerprints on the gun?"

"Clean. More good news for your friend."

"She's a smart woman, you know. Way too smart to let her own gun get mixed up in a murder, if she had anything to do with it."

"I get your point, counselor. But until she comes clean with an alibi, I'm keeping my eye on her."

"Can I ask you something? Why are you telling me all these things?"

"Because you've got good ideas. And because I want your eyes and ears out there working for me."

Very little of this was making sense to me. But I didn't have time to figure it out. I had to get back to the tournament, and I had missed yet another opportunity for some rest.

"Oh, by the way, I learned a little bit about your mysterious voodoo symbol," I added.

"I'm listening."

"It isn't really a voodoo symbol, as far as I understand. More like a personal badge or something. It's associated with somebody named Queen Ezili whose body can be found in Miami."

"She's dead?"

I chuckled. "Don't be so square, Frank! Her body lives in Miami. Her spirit roams all around the universe. At least that's the way my informant described it to me."

"I see. Any details on which particular part of the universe we can reach her?"

"Just Miami. That's all I could get."

"Okay, well, thanks for the help."

I hung up and immediately dialed Zip Addison's cell phone.

"So who else besides me is on the loan shark's list?"

"Oh, the scary guy got to you too, did he? You still in one piece?"

"We just had a polite conversation, that's all."

"Well, you're lucky. He shoved Barracuda Gant's head into a toilet and flushed it three or four times."

"Did he really?" I should have been appalled, but I found myself smiling. Barracuda would never know that he had Jack Shea to thank for the phony tip that put him on the list of suspects.

"I'll tell you who else is on the Vegas list when you stop jerking my chain about Tran Le Binh. Love child, my fanny." *Did he just say "my fanny"?* "Tell me why the cops are talking to Binh and I'll tell you what I know."

"I can't do that."

"Okay, then. Bye." He hung up.

18

THERE WASN'T ANY TIME for the nap I was craving. As badly as I needed sleep, I needed a shower even worse. And a change of clothes, thanks to Martin Ennis.

As I pushed my key card into the door, I thought I heard the TV being turned off. Patrick was sitting on his bed, reading a comic book with an air of studied nonchalance. "Oh hi, Uncle Mark, how are the cards today?"

"I never complain about the cards, Patrick, no matter how terrible they might be. Why don't you order yourself some lunch. I can't stay here long, I just have to take a quick shower."

Patrick mumbled something under his breath. Whatever it was, or whatever he was up to, I didn't have the time or energy to deal with it.

Freshly deodorized, I hurried back to the Showroom. Jumping back and forth between a poker tournament and a murder investigation in a caffeine-supported haze was making my head spin. The encounter with my new bestest buddy Martin Ennis hadn't

138

helped matters. By any reasonable standard I should have been driving home to Brooklyn at about ninety-five miles per hour. Di-Carlo seemed to think that Ennis wasn't a serious threat, but then he hadn't stared into those merciless eyes.

Distracted and fatigued as I was, the thought of giving up never entered my mind. Instead I bellied up to the table, impatient and overwrought, and played poorly. I probably should have been eliminated from the tournament that afternoon, based on the overall incompetence of my game. But sometimes you just have to throw yourself on the mercy of the card gods.

The biggest hand of the day came when I was dealt 10♦ J♥ — marginal cards. Since I was in late position and nobody had raised the pot yet, I decided to call the blind bet of $1,000 to get a cheap look at the flop. Jim Huong in early position had called, and Joe Rudolph in the big blind checked after me, leaving three players in the pot.

My hunch turned out to be a good one, as the flop came out K♣ Q♦ 9♣ —a tremendous stroke of luck. I had a straight. It was, in fact, the "nut" straight, meaning that with the cards dealt so far, it was the best possible hand. Rudolph in the big blind checked, and Jim Huong bet the size of the pot, $3,500. I felt pretty sure that Rudolph would be folding. Now there was a decision to make. Should I make a big raise here, or should I slow-play the hand by simply calling, with the hope of enticing further bets from Huong? If a third club or a pair appeared on the turn, my straight wouldn't be the nuts anymore because I would be in danger of losing to a flush or a full house. I raised $6,000.

To my surprise, Joe Rudolph did not fold but instead announced, "All in." Huong tossed his cards into the muck. I had nothing at all to think about except to marvel at my good luck. "Call," I said calmly, careful not to sound too triumphant, and flipped over my nut straight. Rudolph's face fell. He turned over a pair of kings. His three kings had been a monster hand, but a monster will sometimes turn against its master.

There was still a 33 percent chance that Rudolph could make a full house or four of a kind. With almost all of my chips in the pot, I tried to look cool as I watched the dealer, with agonizing slowness, produce the turn and the river. For a few moments, Shooter Deukart and his toothpick had never existed. Frank DiCarlo and Martin Ennis were fleeting ghosts. Patrick could be entertaining the Swedish Bikini Team in my room for all I cared. In what seemed like super-slow motion, the dealer produced the five of clubs on the turn, and on the river … the ten of spades. Inside my mind, a *Beverly Hillbillies* celebratory square dance erupted. *Oooh, doggies!* My stack had just shot up from $45,000 to $78,000.

I shook hands with Rudolph and consoled him on his rotten luck, then I stood up to stretch and release the tension of the moment. Barracuda Gant was sneering at me with undisguised contempt. "Guy's running on pure luck," he muttered to his neighbor without trying too hard to lower his voice. I might have objected if it hadn't been so obviously true. Tough shit. I had the chips and he didn't, so there, Mr. Assahola.

I took the occasion to look around the room. Two tables over, Maddie Santos was concentrating on a hand; it looked as though she had a healthy stack of chips in front of her. Willy Hopkins was holding court over at Table Seventeen, still in the tournament. Kenneth, on duty behind Willy as usual, was staring intently at something—or somebody. I followed his gaze, which led in the direction of Maddie's table. In fact, I was pretty sure, he was looking straight at Maddie. *Why, Kenneth, you old hound dog,* I thought with a smile.

Next door, at Table Nine, the Jack Shea juggernaut seemed to be rolling right along. I did a double take at the size of his stack. He had to have well over $100,000. Jack was chattering away about something or other, and I could see at least two of the men at the table glowering at him with open hatred. As I returned to my seat, I heard a sudden, irritating, high-pitched giggle and a voice that could only be Jack's crying, "Oh b*ehave!*" I smiled to myself. Jack Shea's latest poker theory might have been ludicrous or it might have been working, but either way it was very entertaining.

Evelyn Gibbs wandered by with a tray of drinks for nobody in particular. "Are you catching any of the swishy act Jack is putting on?" she asked. "What's that all about?" She seemed put off.

"He's not making fun of anybody," I explained. "It's his latest theory on how to beat the game." She handed me a cup of coffee and I gave her a ten.

"Whoa! Thanks! You must be making out okay here."

"So far so good. Keep those coffees coming, all right? You're bringing me luck."

"You got it, sweetie. And tell your friend he's gonna start really pissing some people off pretty soon."

"Since when does Jack care if he pisses somebody off?"

Evelyn rolled her eyes. She moved to the next table with her tray, and I returned my attention to the cards.

That was when I made my best poker play of the tournament. Sitting in the big blind, I was dealt a pair of queens. A strong but dangerous hand. Queens can rapidly become unplayable if a king or ace appears on the flop, which happens nearly half the time. The only other player in the hand was Barracuda Gant, who had called the blinds from his middle position. I will say this for the young man, he was showing no signs that he'd been harassed by a mobster earlier in the day. Maybe Zip Addison was wrong again.

I decided to slow-play the queens, so I merely checked rather than raising the pot. The flop came 4♣ 8♥ Q♠. Incredible. My three queens were now in a dominant position and completely disguised. I turned to the business of milking the most possible money out of my friend Mr. Gant. I checked. Right now my cards were too good; I needed to give him a free card so he could have a chance to develop a hand. Gant made a small bet, $2,000—the sort of bet you would make to cause the big blind to drop out if he had nothing. I showed a moment's hesitation, looked probingly into Gant's face as if I actually gave a shit what his cards were, and called. The turn came: a king of spades. Perfect. I prayed silently that Gant had a king underneath, which would give him a very nice hand—and set me up to maybe get all of his chips.

I made a moderate bet, $6,000. I hoped he would conclude that I had a king with a small kicker. There was now over $12,500 in the pot, and Gant looked as though he had about $50,000 left in front of him.

He looked at me insolently and gestured with both hands toward the center of the table. "All in," he said. *Yes yes yes.* The word "Call" was on my lips, and in my mind I was drinking champagne in a bathtub filled with a million dollars in championship cash, when a tremor of doubt hit me. I looked at Gant. Barracuda had gone into poker-face mode and was staring at the pot with no expression. Here I was with the kind of hand you dream about. I had my victim just where I wanted him, and Assahola Gant of all people;

but something wasn't right. Was it possible that he was holding two kings in his hand and had me beat? Very unlikely. Or was it? Why had he only called before the flop? With a king-ace, wouldn't he have raised, and with lesser cards, wouldn't he have folded? Maybe he had tried to see a cheap flop with a king-queen or a king-eight suited and had lucked into two pair. Maybe he had two spades for a flush draw. What was I worried about? The last time I got into a hand with this guy he bluffed me out with nothing.

I sat and sat, watching Gant. Why had he made such an over-sized bet? If he had a monster hand, he would've made a smaller bet to induce a call from me. Wouldn't he? Unless. Unless he had a read on me and knew that I was holding a very big hand. *Stop it. Now you're getting paranoid.*

I couldn't reason my way to any conclusion other than calling the bet. But the evil vibe coming off of Gant was way too strong to be ignored. In the back of my mind, I could hear the voice of Shooter Deukart on that horrible night four months ago, as he raked in the last of my bankroll: "Never put your faith in a pair a queens, ol' buddy."

"I'm gonna let you have it," I said, flipping my queens face-up on the table. "I fold." Barracuda looked up, making no attempt to hide his disappointment, and stared at my queens in disbelief. Very slowly he said, "Nice lay-down," and showed his own cards—the king of clubs and king of diamonds.

"Wow!" somebody breathed, as Gant added the pot to his stack. Several players at the table applauded quietly. "Hell of a lay-down," somebody else said. "How did you have the balls to fold that hand?" I didn't look up or respond to the comments. I watched Gant stacking his modest winnings, and I knew then that I could play cards with anybody in the room. I hadn't felt so proud of myself since first grade, when I finally learned to ride a two-wheeler. I even felt the beginnings of warmth toward Barracuda Gant. He didn't have to show his cards after I folded. It was a gesture of sportsmanship.

The dinner break found me shaking my head in amazement. By all rights I should have been knocked out of the tournament by now. The card gods must have been looking out for me. I had played poorly most of the day, but I had managed to blunder my way to a $58,000 stack. And the one time it really mattered, with most of my chips on the line, I had come up with something great. There were maybe a hundred players still in the tournament, and the average stack would be about $38,000. I was ahead of the pack, and I hadn't really started to play yet.

19

Dinner break on Day Two of the tournament was only an hour and a half, but I intended to make the most of it by finally getting some rest. Buddha Brown nodded to me as the crowd shouldered its way out of the Showroom.

"Hey, Buddha," I asked, "how many hours would you say you spent playing cards with Shooter Deukart over the years?"

"God, I don't know. Too many."

"Do you remember ever seeing him wearing a wristwatch?"

Brown thought for a minute. "No, I guess not. In fact, I'm sure of it. I must have seen his broken arm show a hundred times. Why do you ask? It's a strange question."

"It's a strange world, Steve."

"I've noticed."

In the elevator up to the eighth floor—I had been temporarily cured of my stairwell habit by the encounter with Martin Ennis—I felt another wave of fatigue sweeping over me. If I didn't get a decent night's sleep tonight, I just couldn't see how I was going to get through another day of poker tomorrow. And there was still the evening session ahead of me. Hopefully, Patrick wouldn't be making too much noise and I could catch a quick nap.

I closed my eyes and breathed deeply, which was the best way for me to endure an elevator ride. Fortunately, the excellent musical taste of the Missequas' top honcho extended to elevator music as well, and a saxophone player that I didn't recognize was laying down a very smooth "Embraceable You," which got me up to the eighth floor in relative tranquility.

Just as I began to stick my card key into the door of Room 824, I felt somebody grab my arm from behind. Given what I had been through that day, it would have been natural for me to lash out with full force at whoever was there. It was a good thing that I didn't. What I encountered was a very small woman in a housekeeping uniform. She was irate and was scolding me severely in a language that I assumed was Spanish. I thought that I had a pretty fair command of Spanish, but I wasn't even close to keeping up with whatever was being hurled at me by the cleaning woman. Then I realized that she must be speaking Portuguese. *Yelling* Portuguese, actually. She was pointing repeatedly at my door, and I did pick up a few words: "boy," "bad," "very bad," "devil."

I disconnected myself from the housekeeper's grip, mumbled, "Obrigato, obrigato," and backed into the room, closing the door gently in her face as she continued to rage at me. I turned around.

It was not as messy as I expected it to be. There were several room-service trays lying around the room, each with a half-eaten meal on it. A few comic books were scattered on the floor, and naturally the clothes had not been folded away, but on the whole the room did not look much messier than I might have left it myself.

"Hi, Uncle Mark!" chirped Patrick, looking up from his hand-held video game. "How did the tournament go today?"

"Uh, good, Patrick, thanks," I answered. "How was your day? Were you bored?"

"Oh no, not really." There was a deliberate casualness in the child's voice that roused my suspicion. My mind went back a few hours to the last time I entered the room, and it hit me; I guessed what the housekeeper had been upset about.

"Patrick, what did you watch on TV today?"

"On TV?" Patrick responded brightly. "Not much. Some nature shows."

I strode across the room and dialed the front desk on the telephone. "Hello. This is Mark Newcomb in Room 824. Can I find out whether anybody watched any pay movies in my room today?... Uh-huh... Do you have the names of the movies there?... Uh-huh... Really... Oh... Listen, is there a way to put a block on the room or on the TV to prevent... Okay... Okay, thanks. Thanks very much."

Patrick's face was buried in concentration over his game. Having no children of my own and very little experience with babysitting, I didn't quite know how to manage the anger and exasperation that this twelve-year-old menace was generating inside my already spaced-out head. So I just yelled.

"*Spring Break Coeds Gone Wild?*" I stormed at him. "*American Booty? The Dominatrix Reloaded!?*"

"Excellent flicks," said Patrick without looking up, his fingers clicking away at the game.

I was simply not equipped to deal with this. Ordinarily, in a situation in which there was a question related to appropriate family behavior, I would turn to Eileen, my in-house expert. She had babysat—and had been nearly a parent to—cousins and younger brothers and sisters for most of her life. But I was not about to admit to her that I'd allowed a twelve-year-old boy to sit in my room and watch pornography.

"You know," Patrick said, still without looking up, "it was awful boring sitting around in here all day. After I had my massage, there wasn't anything else to do."

"Massage? You had a *massage*?" I was incredulous.

"Sure. Your friend Jack said it would be okay. I called him on his phone like you told me to. He thought it was a great idea. He told me if I tipped her extra she might even put out."

I was speechless, trying hard to swallow the notion that even a clown like Jack Shea could have said something so grotesquely inappropriate to a twelve-year-old boy.

"Some massage," continued Patrick, still rapping away at the controls of his game. "Guy named Oscar. Chopped me up like hamburger meat."

Oh, that's fantastic, I thought. *The kid that I'm responsible for was alone in my room with a massage guy named Oscar.* I picked up the telephone and tried to call Jack's cell phone. Maybe I didn't have the first clue how to handle a kid, but I sure had an earful for my jackass friend. There was no answer. He must have been playing craps; that was the only time he turned off his phone. Wheeling back on Patrick, I sputtered, completely at a loss for words.

"You broke our deal!" was all I could finally manage. "We had a deal!"

Patrick finally looked up from his game. He yelled right back. "I did not break the deal! I stayed in the room! Do you know how hard that was? My dad *never* makes me stay in the room. He lets me go wherever I want!"

Now that Patrick was arguing with me, I was on familiar ground and able to regroup. I knew how to argue. "First of all, I have no way of knowing if that's true," I said. "Second, it doesn't matter. I'm not your dad. Tomorrow you're going to the child-care center and that's all there is to it." I shuddered at the thought of it. I would have to leave a very large tip for the workers in the child-care center.

I expected a storm of protest from Patrick, but it didn't come. He bent over the Gameboy and didn't say a word, leaving me staring at the tousled strawberry-blond hair and wondering what was going on behind it. But if Patrick thought that the silent treatment was going to bother his uncle, he was way off the mark. Silence was worth about ten dollars a minute just then.

"Look," I said, "I have an hour to rest and I'm going to sleep." First I had to eat something. I picked up the food trays and finished off a couple of Patrick's meals while ordering a wake-up call from the hotel phone.

I lay down and tried to close my mind to the flood of thoughts that demanded my attention. Replay the mistakes I'd made at the poker table? Ponder the complexities of Shooter's murder case? Give myself over to raw fear at the thought of Martin Ennis? Worry about being arrested for neglecting my nephew?

Sleep wouldn't come. Resigned, I took the remote control and found TV Land. *The Honeymooners* was on.

20

THE SECOND DAY OF play ended at 12:18 a.m., when there were sixty players remaining in the tournament. The next day the sixty would be reduced to nine, who would play on Saturday at the final table. Of the sixty, thirty-seven would finish in the money.

I was still alive, with $65,000 in my stack, which was about average for the players remaining in the tournament. I made a beeline for Jack the moment play was suspended for the night.

"You told Patrick it was okay to get a massage in the room?"

"I'm starting to like that kid. C'mon, let's go shoot some dice. I need a few hours of a good heterosexual game to get my head right."

Somehow my resolve to be pissed off at Jack didn't last. I couldn't seem to stay mad at him. Eileen and I frequently asked ourselves how Brigid was able to put up with Jack's bullshit, but moments like this partly explained it. I found myself too distracted by his latest theory to remember that I was angry. "Craps is a heterosexual game?"

"Oh yeah, definitely! Look at the shape of the table. An oval-shaped opening, two feet deep. Very vaginal. You throw a pair of dice into it. Those are your nuts, of course. They're controlled by a long, slightly curved stick. And look at the names of the bets. The 'horn'? And you want to make the table 'come.' That's subtle.

"This is why," he continued, "it's very hard to win when there's a babe like Anita at the table. Saps all the mojo out of the players. Instead of thinking about making the point come in, they're thinking about getting into the babe's pants. All the good dice mojo gets sent in the wrong direction."

I shook my head. "You know what, I can't handle a new theory right now. I can't play craps right now, either. I still have Caligula up in my room, remember? Also I need sleep in the worst possible way."

"Sleep? At a time like this? C'mon, relax. This is the most fun we'll ever have! Hey, you and me, both still alive on Day Three. Isn't that awesome?"

I peered closely at my friend's face. "Jack, is that ... makeup?"

"Just a little bit. Do you think it works with my colors?"

"Listen, if you start wearing women's underwear, I'm telling Brigid."

"Newk, I've struck gold with this thing. There were a couple of guys at my table today who wouldn't look at me, wouldn't get in a hand with me no matter what. One guy, I must have stolen six or seven pots from him."

By habit, I opened my mouth to say something derisive. Then my eyes fell on the huge pile of chips in front of Jack's position—easily twice what I had. I hesitated, my mouth still open, and said nothing.

"There's only one problem," Jack said.

"Yeah, this murder case hanging over our heads," I muttered.

"Murder case? Who gives a damn about that? I'm talking about Brigid. I think she's catching on to me."

Jack went on to describe the elaborate measures that he was taking to maintain his ruse. He'd called a specialty chocolate shop in Albany and had a box of truffles delivered to Brigid by overnight express with a nice "I miss you" note attached. Naturally, Jack made sure that the words "Albany, New York" were prominently featured on the box. Then Brigid, moved by the gesture, had suggested that she come up to join him for the weekend. She was a classical music fan, and the Albany Symphony was playing an interesting concert. Jack had squirmed out of that one with a flimsy excuse, at further cost to his already meager credibility.

I didn't even bother telling Jack how I'd been threatened with a live burial earlier in the day. Somehow it didn't seem real, and Jack would certainly have shrugged it off as nothing to worry about.

Eileen, surprisingly, showed a similar lack of concern over my encounter with Ennis. "These small-time mob guys love to talk big, but they almost never kill people," she told me during our nightcap phone call. "Certainly not because they just *think* you might be involved. If you owed them a lot of money, that would be different."

I was a little annoyed, to put it mildly, by Eileen's nonchalant response. I had already decided that I wasn't going to worry about Ennis, but I sure as hell expected her to worry about me. I was also surprised when she didn't seem very enthused about my success in the tournament. "Does this mean you won't be back by tomorrow night?" she asked.

"I *hope* not," I answered. "I could get knocked out on the first hand in the morning, but with luck I'll be playing all day." *Why does she sound disappointed?*

"So, you're going to miss Freddie's bachelor party."

Ah, that explains it. "Well, yeah. I'm sure Freddie will understand, though, what with me playing for a million dollars and everything."

"I was really hoping you would be there."

Am I imagining this? "Eileen, it's a bachelor party. They'll just get drunk and go to a strip joint. You wouldn't want me doing that anyway, would you?"

"No. But I want you to go to my cousin's party more than I don't want you to go to a strip joint."

Somewhere in that sentence there may have been some logic, but I wasn't quite able to put it together. As often happened, I was flummoxed into silence by a twisted cord of reasoning that was unique to the Donnelly clan—or, I shuddered to contemplate, may have been common to all tightly knit extended families. The Donnelly Code always ruled that the guy who wanted to do something different was the selfish jerk.

It struck me that my wife was more worried that I would miss her cousin's bachelor party than she was worried that I might get whacked by a hit man. "Okay," I said with no attempt to hide my irritation, "let's summarize the situation. I'm one of sixty surviving players competing for a million-dollar prize in a tournament. I have a police captain playing cat and mouse with me in a real live murder case. I have friends who are active suspects who need my help. I have a twelve-year-old truant on my hands. I have a sociopathic killer threatening to bury me alive. And *your* greatest worry is that I'm going to miss your cousin's *party*?"

"Right. So what's your point?"

We both laughed at the same time. Laid out like that, the situation was so absurd that even Eileen had to give me a break. And I hadn't mentioned that I was helping Jack deceive her best friend, which, if Eileen ever found it out, would make being buried alive by Martin Ennis seem like a preferable alternative.

"Honey, it's not really about Freddie's bachelor party," Eileen said. "I *am* worried about this guy Eenis, or whatever his name is. Just a little bit. I wish you would lay it all down and come home. You're in over your head, but you won't admit it."

"Of course I'm in over my head, but here I am. You know how you can help? Have one of your friends on the Organized Crime Task Force check out Martin Ennis for me."

"Okay. But if I find out something really scary, you have to promise to stop playing cop and come home."

"Sure. As long as *I* get to define what 'really scary' means."

She made an exasperated sound. "My mother warned me not to marry a lawyer. All right. Have it your way. So are you at least getting any sleep in the middle of all this craziness?"

"Not much. Even when I have a chance to sleep, I'm too wired up. And all the coffee in my system isn't exactly a sedative."

"Okay," she said soothingly. "Here's what I want you to do. Stop worrying about Patrick. Tomorrow he's going into child care for the whole day and he'll be somebody else's problem. Everything else you can handle because you're a natural-born genius. Right? So make yourself a nice hot bath, have a good soak, then put on the lucky underwear that I got for you. Have you worn it yet?"

Eileen had snuck a pair of underpants into my bag. It was white underwear covered with pairs of lurid red dice. She was always doing stuff like this. Although I generally preferred boxer shorts, the dice underwear were skimpy briefs that would barely cover me. I had no intention of wearing them.

"Not yet. I was saving them for the final table if I got there."

"Well, don't save them. Put them on tonight. They're going to help you sleep, because I put a magic spell on them. Just trust me."

I had to trust somebody. It might as well be my wife. I followed her prescription exactly. I tucked Patrick into bed—eventually a twelve-year-old will get sleepy even if he is a lascivious maniac—and drew myself a bath. Twenty minutes in the tub and my racing brain had slowed down to a gentle walk. Whether it was the bath, or the magic underwear, or sheer exhaustion, I found that I was able to drift off to sleep without too much difficulty.

21

I HEARD THE SCREAMS through a muffling barrier of deep slumber, as though I were under ten feet of water. It took several seconds for my mind to break the surface into consciousness, slowly processing the fact that the screaming sounds were not part of a dream but were really happening in the room around me.

"Put me down! Let me go! Get your hands off me! Put me down!"

I bolted upright and looked around frantically for the source of the yelling. Still not fully awake, I was disoriented by something vaguely wrong about the lighting in the room. The other bed was empty, and the sheets and blankets were splayed all around.

"Let go of me!" The yelling sounded from nearby, and I became alert enough for the situation to come into focus. There was no light on in the room; the light was coming from the hallway through a half-opened door.

In one fluid motion, I leaped out of bed and shot through the open door. I turned left, then right. The hallway was empty. Too late, I spun back toward the door, which clicked shut in my face. *Patrick!* I grabbed at the handle in a futile effort, knowing it was locked from the inside.

"Patrick!" I called through the door. "Are you in there?"

"I thought you were supposed to be the smart one in the family." Patrick's voice came from the other side of the door. "You fell for that one like a sack of bricks."

"Open the door!"

"I can't, I'm not supposed to open the door for strangers."

I took a deep breath to calm down. It didn't work.

"I'm not a stranger, now *open the goddamn door!*" I pounded on the door with my fist.

"Not a stranger? You look like a pervert to me!"

I suddenly became aware that I was standing in the hallway of a hotel wearing nothing but a very tight-fitting pair of briefs covered with pictures of dice. I felt cold and naked, and my goosebumped skin was unnaturally whitish in the fluorescent lighting of the hallway. I glanced up and down the corridor. Thankfully, there was nobody else in sight.

I spoke urgently, in a subdued voice, through the door. "Patrick, you are in big trouble. Really big trouble. Now open the door this instant before it gets worse." With that effort, I exhausted my supply of child-care skills.

The door opened a crack, but Patrick had fastened the emergency chain. His elfin face appeared in the narrow opening.

"I told you I wasn't going to child care. Now here's the deal. I get to stay in the room tomorrow if I want. And I can go to the pool, and the arcade too."

Somewhere in the back of my mind I knew that it was wrong to negotiate a deal with a child who was misbehaving this badly. But once again, under duress, I retreated to familiar ground. Negotiating a plea bargain came naturally. "No pool. I'm not going to have you going through the locker rooms by yourself. And no dirty movies on the TV."

"Deal."

A pair of excited voices came toward me from the direction of the elevators. It was a familiar sound: two guys who had won money at the tables and were still on a nervous buzz over it. As they rounded the corner and were confronted by a pale, spindly pervert wearing nothing but bikini underwear, their chattering stopped dead.

My first instinct was to act nonchalant, as though I were perfectly comfortable standing in the hallway almost naked. This feeble attempt at dignity lasted only a moment, though, and I quickly realized that my only option was to turn toward the door and hide my face.

The two gamblers walked past without saying a word. I could feel their eyes glancing sideways at my barely covered alabaster buns. Meanwhile, the frontward contents of my bikini briefs were shriveling in mortification and trying their best to escape up into my abdominal cavity. As the gamblers rounded another corner and passed out of sight, they burst into laughter. "The Diceman cometh," cracked one of the voices, and the other cackled gleefully. Patrick released the chain, and what was left of me slinked back into the room.

"Patrick," I asked, with a quiet composure born of resignation, "do you happen to know when your dad is coming back from this business trip he's on?"

"*Business* trip? Man, Uncle Mark, you really are a dope. My dad's out in California watching the Red Sox play the Angels. He'll be back when the series is over."

I closed my eyes and stood as if in silent prayer. *One of these days, Eileen,* I thought. *One of these days.*

22

Friday, October 1

THE RINGING OF THE telephone hit me like a croquet mallet on the side of the head. I turned over and peered at the clock. Six-thirty? I'd asked for a wake-up at eight! Even the hotel switchboard had it in for me.

It was not the hotel switchboard, though.

"Yeah?" I answered through a slumberous fog.

"DiCarlo here. Hope I didn't wake you up."

"Uh, no, no problem at all. What's on your mind, Frank?"

"When is the last time you saw Tran Le Binh?"

I had to exert myself to concentrate. I wasn't sure I was alert enough to have a conversation more complicated than ordering breakfast. "Frank, can you hold on a minute? I have to take the call in the bathroom, I don't want to wake up my nephew."

Patrick was half-sitting up in bed, rubbing his eyes. "Go back to sleep, Patrick," I mumbled. I shuffled into the bathroom and took the receiver next to the toilet off its base. I had stayed in hotels with phones in the bathroom for most of my adult life, and I'd never understood why they were there in the first place. Now I knew why—in case you got a call from a police detective in the middle of the night and didn't want to wake up your deranged nephew. I shambled back into the bedroom, still unable to hold my head straight, and hung up the first phone. Then I returned, at what could almost be described as a normal walk, back into the bathroom, where the other receiver was waiting off the hook.

The movement was getting my blood flowing and rousing me into something resembling full consciousness. There was a coffeemaker on the bathroom counter. I looked longingly at it and considered preparing a pot, but decided I shouldn't make DiCarlo wait any longer. Instead I grabbed the foil bag of coffee, tore it open, stuck my nose inside and inhaled deeply. *I'm pathetic*, said a small voice in my head.

"You aren't alone in your room?" asked DiCarlo. Good cops are always nosy.

"It's a long story. In the middle of all this, I have to take care of my twelve-year-old nephew for a couple of days. Can you believe it?"

DiCarlo did not display any sympathy for my plight. I wondered vaguely whether I had just handed the officer a weapon. *If he doesn't get me for murder, he can always get me for child neglect.*

But Frank DiCarlo had more pressing things on his mind. "Tran Le Binh. Can you tell me when you last saw him?"

This time I was alert enough to understand what he was asking. I thought for a few seconds. "Last time I talked with him was during the afternoon break on Wednesday. I gave him the name of a lawyer in Boston. I'm pretty sure I didn't see him after that. I know he got knocked out of the tournament sometime later that day. No surprise, with everything he's got on his mind." I was silent for a moment. DiCarlo waited. "You should talk with Boley & Huff in Boston," I continued. "I think they might be his lawyers by now."

Finally, the importance of DiCarlo's question dawned on me. "Why are you asking? Did he blow out of town?"

"We don't know. Nobody has been able to locate him since Wednesday night."

"Is his room cleaned out?"

"Suitcase empty, clothes in the drawers."

"So if he bolted, he was in a big hurry." Now was the time to tell DiCarlo what I knew—that Binh was hiding something, that he had been lying when he said he was in his room on the night of the murder. But I couldn't tell him any of it. "Maybe he just had to get away from the hotel for a little while after losing in the tournament. Maybe he went to Boston to meet with his lawyer and then decided to stay the night."

"Maybe. Boston isn't very far, though, and he agreed with me that he would stay in town. We'll certainly check with Boley & Huff. There is another possibility, though …"

DiCarlo was probing me, for some reason. Did he always wake people at six-thirty in the morning, or only when he was trying to trip somebody up? "I'm out of guesses," I said. "What are you driving at?"

"Several of the players in the tournament have come to us after being harassed by Martin Ennis. Binh is not one of them. It's possible Ennis just hasn't caught up with him yet. Or maybe he has."

"What are you saying? That Ennis has done something to Binh?"

"It's a possibility. Maybe he was poking too close to Binh and Binh poked back. Or he might be making an example for the rest of you."

"Did Ennis know about Binh? About his history?"

"I don't see how he could. But then I don't see how he could know a lot of the things he knows. You might have told him."

"Or you might have a leak on your team."

From the other end of the phone, I could almost hear the steam coming out of DiCarlo's ears. Apparently, a nerve had been struck. "I'll worry about my team. Let me know if you hear anything." He hung up.

I had to face the real possibility that Tran Le Binh, the guy I'd stuck my neck out for, had taken off to Canada. Or some other "whereabouts unknown" type of place. Because he actually did kill Shooter Deukart? Then who else was he working with? He couldn't have done it himself. Or was Binh running for some other reason?

I turned off the light in the bathroom and crawled back into bed. I lay on my right side and tried to shut off my brain. *Binh is missing. Martin Ennis is at large. Maddie's gun was used after the killing. I'm still at some risk of going down in history as the Toothpick Killer.* I turned over onto my left side. *I'm heading into Day Three of a major tournament. I'm a better-than-even shot to finish in the money.* I definitely preferred the left side.

––––––––––

Minutes later, I was prodded out of a deep dream state by what felt like a series of electric shocks being applied to the back of my skull. I lay semiconscious and helpless, wishing the shocks would stop, but instead they grew worse. Louder. *How could shocks be getting louder?* As my mental acuity progressed from that of a mollusk to something approaching human, I became vaguely aware that it was just the telephone ringing. Again.

"Uncle Mark, aren't you going to get that?"

"Wha … ? Who?"

The ringing ended. Somebody was talking. "Hello? … Yes, thank you." The phone clicked in its cradle, and the voice I now recognized as Patrick's said, "That was your wake-up call." He made the ringing stop. My hero.

I lay in bed, incapacitated, like a castaway tossed up onto a rocky shore. My mind was a fuzzy half-blank. The clamor of the phone had been replaced by a steady buzz in both ears, and my frontal lobes were in the grip of a tight, low-level pain. Four nights with hardly any rest, and the little teaser sleep after DiCarlo's call had been the final insult. My central nervous system was in open revolt.

Rescue was just steps away—the coffeemaker in the bathroom—but it might as well have been on the moon, because I wasn't getting out of bed on my own. The world was a bleak, hopeless place, and an easy slide back into unconsciousness was the only sensible course of action. Just for a few hours …

The tournament! "Patrick. Do you know how to work the coffeemaker?"

He was sitting cross-legged in bed, playing his Gameboy. "Sure. It's easy."

"Would you … please … make me a cup of coffee? With a little sugar?"

Patrick didn't look up. He continued tapping away at the keys on his game. "What's it worth to you?" he asked.

You have to be kidding me. "Patrick, just get me some coffee, please."

"No, really," he said. "Make me an offer."

This was more than I could handle. "Okay, here's an offer. You make me a cup of coffee, and I won't come over there and strangle your little smart-ass neck until your head snaps off." Did I really say that?

Patrick's eyes widened, and he stood up. Apparently, I had stumbled onto an effective management strategy. "Ah, yes, well," Patrick said in mock seriousness, doing a fair impression of John Cleese. "One cup of coffee it will be, milord." He strode into the bathroom, posture erect like a high-class butler.

Soon I was sitting up in bed, with a warm cup in my hands, feeling the coffee do its miraculous work. The buzzing in my head quieted, the pressure that had gripped my skull eased off, and the gray desolation of a coffeeless world gave way, sip by sip, to the full-color possibilities of normal human existence. *How does anybody manage to live without this stuff?* I wondered.

After a second cup I was mostly rehabilitated. Not 100 percent, but fit enough to get back into the fray. I showered, shaved, and made my first important decision of the day. I would wear the lucky underwear. *The Diceman rides into battle.*

23

I FINISHED DRESSING IN my jeans and flannel shirt. Patrick and I headed down for breakfast. Once again I chose the safety of the elevator, closing my eyes and breathing deeply to counteract the effects of claustrophobia.

"What's the matter, Uncle Mark?" asked Patrick.

"Nothing. Just a little pre-poker ritual of mine." I wasn't about to admit a weakness to Patrick and place another weapon into the kid's already formidable arsenal.

As we entered the players' buffet, Patrick started off on his own. "You are not to leave this area," I commanded. "In exactly forty-five minutes I'm going to take you back up to the room." Patrick snapped to attention with an exaggerated salute, turned, and vanished into the crowd. I shook my head and sighed wearily.

I poured myself another cup of coffee from the tureen and piled a plate full of bacon, eggs, and pancakes. I hoped if I packed enough calories and caffeine into my system I could somehow offset the deadening effects of sleep deprivation.

There was an empty seat next to Jack, and I sat myself down. "Called Brigid yet this morning? How's the weather over there in Albany?"

He did not respond to the jibe. "Here, look at this." He reached into a bag and pulled out a baseball cap.

"Yeah?"

"Look at it." He handed it to me.

I glanced at the cap and did a double take. On the front of the cap there was an insignia. A drum with a knife sticking through it.

"Where the hell did you get this?"

He smiled. "These long breaks they're giving us are just an invitation for troubled youths like myself to fall into wrongdoing. I went to a T-shirt shop in town and had them make this up for me."

With everything I'd gone through in the past day, I'd forgotten giving Jack the information about the symbol. Another thing to fret over. "Jack, this thing is really becoming pretty serious. I don't think there's a lot of room left for screwing around." I described what Zip Addison had said about Gant getting the swirly treatment from Martin Ennis.

His eyes lit up. "It's my birthday! Oh, this is going to be *perfect*!"

I shook my head. I wondered what it felt like to be Jack.

"So, anyway, did you hear?" he asked.

"Hear what?"

"Anita Wilson's in trouble. She wasn't working her shift last night. It's all over the craps pit. The cops have been talking to her. Apparently, she's got an aunt or something, some big voodoo weirdo down in Miami. I think it might have something to do with the murder."

Holy shit. Anita Wilson! I decided to share what I knew with Jack. "Okay. This symbol that you now have on this cap? It's linked to

167

a woman down in Miami. Anita's aunt, apparently. DiCarlo hasn't told me in so many words, but I'm pretty sure it was found on the body along with the toothpick."

Jack looked at me with mock surprise. "Newk, I had no idea you were a practitioner of the dark arts as well as being an anal toothpick insertion specialist."

"Stop joking. Don't you ever get serious?"

"Hell. Get me to that final table tomorrow and you'll see me serious as shit. I want to run my hands through that million in cash."

"Jack. Has Maddie talked to you at all? About this case?"

His eyebrows shot up in genuine surprise. "Maddie? No, not really. She told me her gun was missing. I said big deal. Don't tell me her gun is mixed up in this?"

I didn't answer. I was thinking. If Anita were involved in the shooting, how could she have gotten access to Maddie's gun?

"Jack." I grabbed my friend's arm. "You had dinner with Maddie Monday night, right?"

"Yeah."

"And you walked her to her room. What happened then?"

Jack could see that I was serious but couldn't imagine what it was about. "Nothing happened. As usual, we joked around about me coming inside. Mark, hey. You know I wouldn't do anything like that. I mean, you know I'm—"

"No, I know. This isn't about you. Did you get a sense that there might have been somebody else in her room? Waiting for her, maybe? Was she hiding the view from the door? Was she in a hurry to get rid of you?"

"I don't think so. She might have been in a little bit of a hurry to get rid of me." Then Jack saw where I was headed. "Wait a minute. You're telling me that Anita was mixed up in the killing because of some bizarre voodoo shit, and somehow she took the gun out of Maddie's room and used it? And how would Anita get the gun out of Maddie's room? She would have to—"

I interrupted. "Only if Anita was in Maddie's room with her that evening. Or earlier in the day. Or both."

If I'd stopped to think about it, I would have admitted to myself that this was a very slender line of reasoning to support a conclusion that Maddie and Anita were lovers. I also would've admitted that this particular subject has a tendency to overstimulate the creative thinking of many males, including, apparently, myself. On the other hand, it is not uncommon to stumble onto the right answer for all the wrong reasons.

Jack shook his head in disbelief. "If Anita Wilson and Maddie Santos are going girl on girl, then I want to get hold of Maddie's gun. I'll use it to shoot myself."

"Oh, c'mon," I said. "It wouldn't be the end of the world if they were. Just don't think about it."

"Don't *think* about it? The question is whether I'll ever be able to *stop* thinking about it! And why I would *want* to?"

"Well, it's just a possibility, anyway. Crazy, probably. Have you ever seen them together?"

"Never. Maddie doesn't shoot craps. And Anita doesn't let me follow her around after hours. Not that I haven't tried."

"You're a dog, you know that?"

I stopped talking and sniffed the air. I looked around. There was nobody else nearby. I sniffed again.

"Jack. Please tell me you're not wearing perfume?"

"Do you think it's a little strong for this time of the morning? I have to tell you, I'm getting nervous. We're down to sixty now, and these are some pretty tough players. I don't know how much longer my plan is going to keep working."

"I won't argue with that," I said. My attention swung back to the tournament. The field of sixty that remained in the game was extraordinarily tough by any standard of measurement. I was feeling outclassed. Jack was in *way* over his head. Of the remaining people that I knew personally, all were players I considered to be my equals or better, with the possible exception of Willy Hopkins. Although Willy had the knowledge and skill that were needed to get to the final table, he could pretty much be counted on to throw all his chips into the pot in a losing effort at some point during the day. Maddie Santos was still in the game, along with four other women. One of the chip leaders, in fact, was Sandy Baker, the dean of the women on the poker circuit. Some of the male players cruelly called her "Cincinnati" behind her back, because of her unfortunate resemblance to Steve McQueen. "More like Pete Rose, I'd say," Jack snorted. Of the rest of the surviving field, most were professional players or very skilled amateurs, and only a small handful of $50 super-satellite winners remained.

"You know, Jack," I said, "these hombres are so tough you might need a dress and a pair of falsies to throw them off their game."

"I know," Jack said glumly. "I've got other problems too."

By now I knew that when Jack complained of a problem, it could only mean one thing.

"If I get to the final table tomorrow, it'll wind up on TV, even though it won't be aired for a month or two. Brigid wouldn't be tuning in, of course. But somebody is bound to watch the show and tell her about it. If Jack Shea turns up on TV playing in the Northeast Open, then Jack Shea could not have been in Albany nailing down a new account. And even if she didn't make the connection to this week, she'd be wondering how I managed to avoid telling her that I'd made the final table of a big tournament."

"That's not good. What are you going to do about it?"

"I don't know. I have an idea, though." Jack spotted the tournament director on the far side of the room. "Yo, Bob!" he called, and rushed off.

I grinned as I watched him hurrying away. Jack's intense focus on his own small problems somehow made my real problems seem more manageable. Buddha Brown came wandering by holding a tray of food. I gestured toward the empty seat. Brown set down his tray, which held oatmeal, a bowl of fruit, and yogurt. No bacon for the Buddha.

"Hey, Buddha, I hope we're sitting at the same table today. I could use a little calm. Do you have any idea what's been happening to me these past couple of days?"

Brown smiled. "You know, the cops have been talking to just about everybody here. Most people had some kind of nasty history with Shooter, so there's plenty of paranoia going around. I think it's affected everybody's play, not just yours. Everybody's rattled. It evens out."

Yeah, but how many have been threatened with a live burial? I wondered, with a little bit of self-pity.

"Hey, Mark, tell me something, if you can. Is this story about the toothpick true?"

"Yeah. I wasn't supposed to talk about it, but it's all over the place by now. Whoever killed Shooter stuck a toothpick up his ass.

Funny joke. You can imagine how hard I laughed when the cops hit me with *that* tidbit."

"Uh-huh, that's tough. Nobody's going to think you had anything to do with it, of course."

Nobody except maybe the police detective on the case. And maybe the sociopathic mob killer.

"Well, I know you're not laughing," said Brown. "But a lot of other guys are. Talk about karma. I mean, it's perfect."

"You know, what the hell *is* karma, anyway? Some sort of good vibration or something? I think I want to buy some."

Buddha grinned. "Don't be so sure. A lot of people think karma is a kind of good luck, but that's a pretty severe misunderstanding of the concept. Karma is more like justice. Poetic justice. 'What goes around, comes around' describes it pretty well. For Shooter, getting a toothpick up his ass was pretty fair karma, considering what a douchebag he was most of the time, but it wasn't exactly good luck for him. Of course, in the long run, any form of justice is good for you. If you believe in reincarnation, that is."

This was the problem trying to talk with Buddha Brown. You had to be ready to go pretty deep.

"I've got enough to keep me busy in *this* life right now, thanks," I said. "I'll tell you what, after the tournament is over we'll sit down with a couple of beers and you can explain to me all the mysteries of life."

"I wish I understood them myself," he said with a smile.

I cleaned the last scraps of pancake off of my plate. "You know, Steve, you and Jack Shea probably have more in common than I realized. When I told him about the toothpick, he said it was pure poetry. Sort of like karma, I guess. Have you checked out his latest theory of poker?"

"I heard a couple of guys talking about it, but I haven't seen him in action yet. I think it's brilliant, actually. I've often had the same thoughts, but I would never have the balls to pull off an act like the one he's been using. Now that people are expecting it, though, I don't think it will get him anywhere."

As the crowd in the room thinned, I saw Madelin Santos at a table in a corner of the room. I gathered my tray and rose from my chair. "Steve, there's somebody I have to talk with. Good luck today."

"You too, Mark."

Maddie was alone. Although she had a newspaper spread out on her table, I could see that she wasn't reading it. She seemed lost in thought. "Mind if I sit down?" I asked.

"Please." She looked across the table at me. Most of her breakfast was undisturbed. A pile of shredded napkins lay under her nervous fingers. "Mark, I don't know how I got this far in the tournament—I'm a nervous wreck. I can't play poker like this."

"You and me both. Maddie, listen. I can't tell you why I know this, but I really think you have less to worry about than you realize."

She peered at me. "What makes you say that?"

"I can't tell you. I'm sorry. But trust me, you aren't high up on DiCarlo's suspect list. I shouldn't even be telling you this much, but you looked so damn miserable."

"Well, that's the best thing I've heard in a couple of days. Even if I don't know what the hell you're talking about."

"Just trust me. Hey . . . I don't want to make things any worse, but I have a question I need to ask you."

Maddie frowned. "Everybody has questions for me. Go ahead."

"You know," I started, "I don't want to pry into your personal affairs. And you should know that I am totally modern in my attitudes about sexuality."

This surprised her. She blushed and showed me a disarming smile. "So, what is this big question that you're afraid to ask me?"

"Maddie, I have to know this. Is the person that you shared your room with on Monday night, by any chance ... not a man?"

Maddie's blush disappeared. So did her smile. She got busy folding up her newspaper and spoke in a flat voice. "You know, Mark, I appreciate your trying to help me, and I know that I came to you in the first place, but I really think I can handle things by myself now. I want you to know that I'm not offended by your question. Just please don't ask me anything more about it."

"Okay, I won't. But I'll tell you something, for your own safety. If that person was Anita Wilson, then she has dragged you into a whole lot of trouble."

Maddie had her poker face on now. From the empty gaze she was showing me, it was impossible to know whether my guess had been on the mark. I opened my mouth to speak when a familiar and annoying voice interrupted me.

"Hey, Uncle Mark! Forty-five minutes, just like I promised!" piped Patrick. I forced myself to smile at the boy.

"Patrick, this is Madelin Santos. Maddie, this is my nephew Patrick. I am lucky enough to have him staying with me for a few days."

Patrick dropped his façade of polite respect and leered at Maddie. "Hey, I know you! You're the babe who banged on our door two nights ago. Not bad, Uncle Mark, not bad!"

Maddie looked at Patrick in disbelief. "Wow, Mark, I thought *I* had problems," she said.

I sighed and rolled my eyes. "Just ignore him. This afternoon I'm taking him to the vet to have him neutered." I got up to go. I had a sinking feeling that someday a very inaccurate picture of all this was going to get back to my wife.

24

Day Three found me sitting at Table Five with $65,000 in my stack. There were only six tables left at this point. They were arranged on the main stage of the Showroom. I was pleased to find Willy Hopkins also at Table Five, along with eight other players. Six or seven I knew either by sight or by name.

Willy was attended by the astonishing Britta. Kenneth must have had the day off, I thought. As usual, Willy's pencil-thin mustache was perfectly trimmed. He was wearing an alpaca cardigan that must have cost at least a thousand dollars. His natty appearance was in stark contrast with the grubby jeans, T-shirts, and unshaven faces of most of the other gamblers. A poker room was the one place where I was never underdressed. Britta, looming behind Willy like a monument to libido, could have worn a burlap sack and still looked fabulous. I was trying not to notice, with limited success.

The atmosphere at the start of Day Three was much looser than it had been on Day One, even though the stakes were higher.

Everybody who had made it this far had proven themselves. The fear of a disgraceful early exit was gone. Small talk flowed freely.

A few minutes before play began, Willy gestured to me to come around to his end of the table. Britta pulled Willy's wheelchair back from the table and pushed him to a quiet spot several feet from any of the other players. I pulled up a chair and Willy spoke to me in a subdued voice.

"It's come to my attention that this fellow Ennis, who claims to represent an ownership interest in Shooter Deukart, has been harassing several of the players in this tournament. Well, I won't have it."

Willy looked very pleased with himself. "I want you to know, I've given Kenneth instructions to seek the man out and obtain a guarantee that he will leave you all alone. Kenneth is, shall we say, rather adept at that sort of thing. That should put the matter to rest. The last thing any of us needs to be worrying about. Now, go back to your seat, so we can start kicking each other in the behind. Figuratively speaking, of course. I don't have much of a kick, and you don't have much of a behind."

"You know what, Willy? That's the nicest thing anybody has said to me all week. But listen, I have to warn you, the state police are trying to link Ennis with those Spanish wiseguys from the game Monday night. It's only a matter of time before they put you in the middle of it."

Willy smiled. He reached over and patted my knee. "Not to worry, dear boy, not to worry. I've done absolutely nothing wrong or illegal."

"I know that. Just be careful, that's all I'm saying."

I was really very fond of Willy Hopkins. Even though the man was a bit of a caricature, he took good care of his friends. And every gambler was his friend. This made it more ironic that, like everyone else at the table, I would be waiting for my chance to pounce on Willy in a big hand, because that was where the man was most vulnerable. A card player has to be cold-blooded. Given the opportunity, I would gladly take all of Willy's chips—and crush his dream of winning a big tournament—without the slightest compunction. Afterward, of course, I would feel bad about it. Just a little.

I might have been tempted to cash in my $65,000 in chips, if it were allowed, but tournaments don't work that way. The chips could only be used to move ahead. Thirty-seven of the remaining sixty players would finish in the money. The person who finished thirty-eighth would go home with exactly the same amount as the person who was first knocked out of the tournament: nothing.

Around my table, there were three players with much larger stacks and several with smaller. The blinds at this point were $2,000 and $4,000, and they would be increasing every ninety minutes throughout the day. Those with short stacks would be forced to gamble. Those with large stacks would try to take advantage of them.

I was in less familiar territory now. I had been to the final table of several smaller tournaments, but only twice before had I survived this far into a tournament with a million-dollar first prize.

One strategy at this point could be to play only the best hands, take no risks, pay the blinds, and hope that twenty-three other players got knocked out before I ran out of chips. This might be the best plan if my goal were simply to finish in the money, which would be worth about $19,000. But a conservative approach at this point would make it almost impossible to get to the final table. I hadn't come this far just to limp into the money and earn a measly profit of $9,000. So I would be gambling.

The gambling started almost right away. Sitting in fifth position, I looked at 5♦ 7♣—a garbage hand that would have been an automatic fold earlier in the tournament. When the early position players had all folded, I raised the pot with a bet of $10,000. *No big deal, just $10,000. Petty cash.* Anybody who knew my normally tight style would have to assume that I was betting from a strong hand in this position, so I was bluffing with the fervent hope that they would all fold and let me have the blinds. I mentally held my breath while forcing my body to breathe normally. Tim Deaton, to my immediate left with a short stack of less than $30,000, called. *Shit!* The rest of the table folded.

I knew Deaton to be a steady, cautious player. I also knew that it generally takes better cards to call than it takes to raise. So I assumed that I wasn't going to be able to bluff him out of this hand, and I was a dead duck unless I got some sort of miracle on the flop.

The flop came out K♥ J♠ 6♦. Absolutely nothing for me, and three cards that might have strengthened Deaton's hand. I checked, prepared to fold. Deaton also checked, allowing me to see the next card for free. The turn was dealt: 5♣. Okay, a small pair, which was probably worse than nothing because it was going to tempt me to play the hand more aggressively. I checked, again prepared to fold if he bet any substantial amount. Deaton checked again. The river card was a two of diamonds, almost certainly providing no help to anybody.

Now I felt uncertain. Did we have two weak hands here, and anybody with the guts to make a bet would push the other guy off the pot? Or was he just patiently lying in wait for me? It sucked to have to go first. My pair of fives might be the best hand, but if

I checked and he bet, I'd have to throw them away. If I made a bet of $20,000, I would put Deaton all in. Was Tim holding cards that were worth the risk of getting knocked out of the tournament? There was only one way to find out. Of course, one of my rules was never, ever to make a bet because "there's only one way to find out." If that was the reason for betting, it would be a foolish play. I bet $20,000 anyway.

I didn't have to wait long. Tim Deaton tossed his cards into the muck with a bitter expression. "Medium pair?" I guessed. "Or missed your ace-queen?" Deaton did not respond. He kept his head down, stacking and restacking his dwindling pile of chips, as if by fondling them he could make the stack grow bigger. *Another one for Jack's theory*, I thought. "You should have bet me. I would have folded," I said. I knew that I was rubbing salt into an open wound, which was not the sort of thing I would normally do. But the person to your left is your most important adversary in a poker game, and if you can get into his head, you can take his money. I was up to $81,000. *Hey, this is easy.*

Twenty uneventful minutes later, I felt a hand on my shoulder.

"Excuse me, Mr. Newcomb?" I turned to see a uniformed hotel security guard.

"Yes?"

"Sir, could I have a word with you?"

"Well, I'm in the middle of something pretty important here, as you can see."

"It involves your nephew."

Oh shit. Horrible visions of kidnapping and molestation flashed through my mind, and the bottom fell out of my stomach. *What the hell was I thinking, leaving him alone?* I rose shakily from my chair and followed the guard to a corner of the stage. It was a huge relief to see Patrick standing there, safe and sound—in the custody of another guard. It took about two seconds for my relief to turn into anger because he had obviously been in trouble again.

"Sir, we found him in the women's spa area. Apparently, he was pretending to be a towel boy, trying to sneak peeks at some of the guests."

Patrick smirked.

"And he had this," said the guard, handing me a palm-sized electronic device.

I took it. As a person who didn't even own a cell phone, I had no clue what the device was.

"It's a small video camera," said the guard. "He had it hidden in a pile of towels, trying to get pictures of the guests. Sir, we're going to have to ask you to take this boy into control from now on. He really can't be left by himself."

"What about the child-care center? Can you take him there for me?"

"Sir, we've already talked to the child-care center. They're familiar with the boy and they say they can't handle him. We know you're playing in the tournament, but we really can't do any more for you."

I looked over my shoulder to Table Five, where a hand had already been dealt and folded. This wasn't like Wednesday, where I missed a few hands that were probably meaningless. This was Day Three, and every hand could potentially mean the difference between winning a million dollars and going home with nothing.

Across the stage, I saw Evelyn Gibbs leaning idly against a chair, talking with another cocktail waitress. I had an inspiration.

"Evelyn!" I called. I grabbed Patrick's hand and speed-walked across the stage, half-dragging the child in my wake. "Evey, you don't look too busy."

"Nah, they put four of us on this shift but these uptight poker players aren't drinking much. Bottle of water, maybe a cup of coffee." Evelyn tugged at the seam of her skimpy uniform where it was riding up the left cheek of her rear end.

"How much do you make an hour at this?"

She seemed surprised at the question. "Depends on tips. Sometimes ten, sometimes twenty or thirty. Not much today."

Another hand had been dealt at Table Five. My poker life was being drained away. "If you can get off work, I'll pay you thirty bucks an hour to watch my nephew Patrick here until the tournament is over."

I pulled Patrick forward by the hand. The boy leered at Evelyn. "All right! An experienced woman! Uncle Mark, you are my man!"

"Tell you what, I'll make it forty," I added hastily. I looked over in time to see my cards being folded by the dealer.

Evelyn smiled at Patrick. "It's a deal. He's just about the same age as my grandson in Phoenix. I know all kinds of fun things we can do. And you don't have to pay me that much, really. Unless you finish in the money, of course."

My shoulders sagged in relief. "Thank you, thank you, thank you. Look, you can see I don't have much time to talk. You can bring him back to Room 824 anytime. He has a key. I'll see you later on. Oh, Evey... I should warn you. He's a bit of a handful."

She grinned. "I can see that. Thanks for the advice, rookie. I think I can manage him."

Without looking back, I dashed to my seat and nearly knocked Tim Deaton over in my panic to get back into my chair. A fresh hand had just been dealt; I eagerly peeked at my cards. Ten of spades and seven of diamonds. Fold. What kind of hands had I missed? I would never know.

25

I PLAYED SLOW, JUST treading water, until the lunch break. Fourteen players had been knocked out, including Tim Deaton and Buddha Brown. Nine more and I would be in the money. Willy Hopkins had been playing masterful poker all morning, stealing small hands here and there, pushing weaker players off of pots, bailing out when he needed to. He had built his stack to nearly $100,000. Jack wasn't doing so well. Nobody was falling for his effeminate routine, and he'd lost two big hands with cards that weren't quite good enough. His stack was smaller than mine now, around $50,000.

On the other hand, Jack's bid for induction into the Practical Joke Hall of Fame was growing stronger. As the players drifted off to get lunch, I watched Jack sidle over to Barracuda Gant. I couldn't resist the temptation to wander past and eavesdrop.

"Cuda, you a Red Sox fan?" Jack opened, with a gesture toward the backward-facing Sox cap that Gant was wearing.

"Hey, if it isn't Jack Squat. Nah, not really. This is a collector's item, though. Got it at an auction. It was worn by one of the outfielders on the day they broke the Curse."

"Wow, I'm impressed." Jack reached up and absentmindedly scratched his ear, drawing attention to the cap on his own head.

Though Barracuda was highly adept at reading faces in a card game, his interpersonal skills away from the poker table were practically nonexistent. He fell into Jack's trap almost willingly.

"So what's that thing *you're* wearing?"

"This? Oh, not as cool as your Sox cap, by a mile. But it's kind of interesting. You ever heard of the Colombos?"

"No." Since the conversation had stopped being about himself, Barracuda was rapidly losing interest.

"Real tough street gang down in Miami. Serious dudes. This cap is part of their colors."

"Huh. So how did *you* get it?"

"Bought it off a guy. He was happy to get rid of it, actually. Colombos catch you wearing this and you're a dead man."

"Really." Gant was sniffing at the bait. Jack just had to jiggle it a little bit.

"Yeah, I sure as hell won't wear it if I'm anywhere near Miami. Actually, I don't know if I'll have the balls to wear it if I get to the final table. Somebody might see it on TV and come after me."

Gant snorted. "Oh yeah, like you're going to make it to the final table. Tell you what. When *I* get to the final table, I'll wear the cap. If one of those Colombo dudes wants to come after me, they know where to find me."

The Barracuda had taken the bait. Jack set the hook.

"No, I don't think so. I'm pretty attached to this thing. Brings me luck. You don't think I made it this far in the tournament on *skill*, do you?"

"Tell you what. I'll make you an even trade for it." Gant removed the Red Sox cap from his head and offered it to Jack.

"What, are you kidding me? I'm a Yankee fan. I wear that thing in the City, it'd be more dangerous than wearing the Colombo cap in Miami."

"C'mon, this thing is worth some money." Gant spoke lower, into Jack's ear. "Incredible pussy magnet at the bars in Boston too."

"Well, when you put it that way ... Deal." Jack removed his cap and executed the swap. Gant walked away looking pleased with himself.

Jack strolled over to me. "In the words of Darth Vader, that was all too easy."

I shook my head. Unfortunately, I had to tear myself away from Jack's playtime world and take care of serious business. I went to find a quiet pay phone where I could call Eileen. As I walked through the casino, a familiar-looking person standing behind a blackjack table caught my eye. Too late, I realized that it was one of the men who had passed me in the hallway the previous night.

"Hey, Diceman, how's it going?" grinned the stranger. I pretended not to hear him and hurried on.

I called Eileen's office and was put through to her. In the artificial world of a casino, it was easy to forget the days of the week. Back in the real world, it was Friday and people were still working. Eileen was in the middle of eating her lunch.

"Mark, I've been waiting for you to call. When the hell are you going to get a cell phone?"

"Nice greeting. How about, 'Hi, darling, how's the tournament going?'"

"Because I don't give a damn about the stupid tournament. Listen, I checked out this Martin Ennis guy, and he is serious material. His real name is Martin Paisley. Also goes by the name of Andrew Starr. He's basically a high-priced collection agent, used to work for two or three of the Vegas casinos before they cleaned up their act. Now he works for a big loan-shark operation, the place the addicted gamblers go to when the casinos cut off their credit. Nice guys. He's been questioned in connection with several deaths and disappearances."

"Sounds like a tough character."

"He is. Heavy-duty stuff only. Not a break-your-kneecap kind of guy. More like a bullet-through-your-skull kind of guy."

"Oh, well, that makes me feel a whole lot better."

"So are you going to come home now, where it's safe?"

"Well, I was kind of thinking I would stick around to see if I could win a million dollars. Sweetheart, you know I can't come home now. This Ennis guy is just blowing smoke. Besides, if he wants to find me, he's gonna find me. At least up here the place is crawling with cops and security guards."

"Our apartment is crawling with cops too. One cop, anyway, crawling the walls worrying about her husband." There was silence for a few seconds while I tried to think how to explain that there was no way, no how, that I was going to drop out of this tournament. "Maybe you're right," she finally said. "But I'm still worried about you."

"Now you know how I feel every single *day*, Detective Donnelly."

This was a low blow. The fact that Eileen had chosen a dangerous profession was a continual sore spot between us.

"Hey, I thought you *wanted* me to be worried about you," she protested.

"Well, sure, but not to the point of making me quit playing. C'mon, it'll be okay. Listen, for a woman who makes her living busting heavily armed crack-addled dope dealers, you're getting awfully worked up about one harmless little hit man."

"That's because *I* know what the hell I'm *doing*. You're always talking about these dead money players who don't have a chance at the poker table, right? I just think you're into a different game with this murder business, and *you're* the dead money player."

Ouch. This time Eileen had landed the low blow. My silence told her that I wasn't backing down, and we had reached another of our stalemates.

She sighed and gave up. "So how's our little nephew Patrick?"

"Oh my God. You're not going to believe this, Eileen. The kid is lucky to be alive." I was more than glad to change the subject. In the back of my mind, I knew Eileen was right, but I also knew that I wasn't leaving this tournament other than feet first or at the losing end of a pair of wired aces.

I told Eileen at great length about Patrick's escapades, his towel-boy stunt, and how he had locked me out of the room. I gave her the details all the way down to the Diceman comments. Eventually, she was laughing so hard she snorted; I could hear the Dr. Pepper spraying out of her nostrils.

When she calmed down, she managed to say, "Where is he right now? Is he safe?"

"Is *he* safe? I'm a lot more worried about the other people in the hotel. But I found somebody good who can take care of him."

"Someday you're going to thank me for this."

"Yeah, right. Listen, I've gotta go. Wish me luck."

"Good luck, darlin'. And promise me you'll be careful. Stay around bunches of people where you'll be safe."

"I will. I love you."

"I love you too."

My next call was to DiCarlo. I assumed that the captain already had the information on Martin Ennis, but I wanted to make sure. DiCarlo did not answer his desk phone or his cell phone. I called his office again and waited through many rings until somebody picked it up. Captain DiCarlo, I was told, was not available. He was handling an emerging situation out at the Humpback.

26

I WALKED QUICKLY AROUND the casino to the guest office suite that DiCarlo had commandeered as his temporary headquarters. I entered the corridor that I'd first seen on Tuesday morning when I had my interview with DiCarlo. The captain wasn't there. A uniformed trooper told me I could find him out in the parking lot.

"Any idea which one? There must be half a dozen separate parking lots out there."

"You know, the place where the first body was found. That's where he is."

"Thanks," I said, and turned to go. I was halfway out the door before it hit me. "The *first* body?" I asked.

The trooper looked at me. "I think you should just go find the captain, sir."

It wasn't a long walk out to the parking lot, but the crime scene was at the far edge. I hadn't been out there since Monday night, and it gave me a creepy flashback feeling to walk through the lot, even in the daylight.

I was walking fast already, but when I saw the ambulance I quickened my pace to a near-run. A circle under the R25 sign was sealed off with yellow police tape, and a small crowd of curious onlookers had gathered. I knew there was a very limited range of things that these gamblers would find more fascinating than a slot machine. Either somebody was hosting a live sex show out there, or somebody had been murdered.

Hustling back and forth between the taped area and a cluster of vehicles were uniformed officers, people in plain clothes, a photographer, and paramedics. I arrived just a couple of minutes before they covered Binh's face. There was a single red hole in the center of his forehead. I stood and stared.

"No blood on the scene," DiCarlo said from behind me. "Whoever killed him brought the body here."

I didn't have anything to say. I had conducted several murder trials, had examined forensic evidence, had argued over the relevance of gruesome photographs. But until this week I had never seen a murdered person in the flesh. Now I was looking at my second in four days.

The captain showed no sympathy. It was plain that he had a low opinion of defense lawyers who waxed eloquent about constitutional rights of defendants but had never experienced the horror of a victim at a crime scene. Not that this one was so terrible. If it weren't for the hole in Binh's forehead, you wouldn't know there was anything wrong with him.

"You were looking for me," he said. "You have anything I need to know?"

"Two days ago I was sitting in a cab with him," I mumbled. "We talked about the foliage." I couldn't take my eyes off Binh's face.

DiCarlo walked away, clucking contemptuously.

A few moments later I forced myself to look away from Binh, and I approached DiCarlo where he stood next to a patrol car. "How long has he been dead?"

"We don't know yet. Not more than a few hours, I'd guess."

"Any weird markings or anything like that?"

"Or signature toothpicks, you mean?" I hoped he was at least half-joking. "We won't know for sure until the coroner is finished. But it looks like a perfectly clean body except for the head wound. Different killer, then, maybe."

"So somebody dumped his body in the same place where Shooter was found. What does that mean?"

"You're the genius lawyer. You tell me."

"Martin Ennis, you think? Figured that Binh killed Shooter, and this is his payback? Or could be he's sending a warning to the rest of us. Pay up or end up like this."

DiCarlo took a clipboard from a uniformed officer, glanced at it, and signed his name. "Maybe he was leaning on Binh the way he leaned on you, except Binh had the balls to fight back and got himself killed."

I chose to ignore the implication that I had no balls. I thought I had plenty of balls.

"Captain, you need to know something. I have reason to believe that Binh was lying when he said he spent Monday night in his room." Technically, Binh's death didn't relieve me of the duty to protect his privilege, so I shouldn't have been telling this to DiCarlo. But I hadn't exactly been going by the book this week.

"I know he was lying. I also know where he was—got a break this morning. Binh spent the entire evening in the penthouse suite of the Humpback playing poker."

Oh. I leaned against the patrol car and thought for a moment. It made sense. So Binh was in the bar, waiting for the game to start. And talking to Shooter, who expected to be in the same game. "If he had such a good alibi, why did he have to lie about it?"

"I'm not sure," said DiCarlo. "I guess he figured Immigration wouldn't be too happy to learn he was consorting with international drug runners. Remember, he was in this country on a provisional basis."

Of course. Now I felt awful. I had been working myself up to thinking that Binh was a killer, when really he was just trapped and scared. And now dead. But why should *I* feel guilty? All I had done was follow the evidence. Binh was the one who'd behaved recklessly, for a guy who needed to keep a low profile. He couldn't keep himself away from the biggest games he could find. But still I felt rotten that I had suspected him. *I'd make a terrible cop*, I thought.

I followed DiCarlo as he walked toward the forensics van. "So that leaves us with Ennis, right?" I asked. "Prime suspect now in both killings, I would think."

He stopped. "Right now all I have is a body. I don't have anything solid on Ennis. Just menacing a few poker players. I'll sure as hell never find the gun that fired this shot. And right now we have no idea where Ennis was the night that Deukart got killed. When we find him, we'll hold him. But without more evidence we won't be able to keep him for long."

"I assume you already have this, but my friends in the NYPD dug up some bio on him." I made a point of saying "my friends" rather than "my wife's friends." At the moment I felt the need to shore up my credentials with DiCarlo. *No balls.*

"Martin Paisley, I know. The Vegas cops are running down his connections out there for us. Still doesn't give us a reason to arrest him for *this* crime."

"I guess not. What about the FBI? With another body and a potential mob connection, I doubt you'll be able to keep them out of this case now."

"Watch me."

I shook my head. Ego and turf protection. "So what do we do now? I mean those of us who are on Ennis's 'special friends' list. Can you give us protection?"

DiCarlo looked at me. "I don't have the bodies for that," he said. "Just be smart. Don't go anywhere alone. Stay out of stairwells, for Chrissakes." DiCarlo had plainly had enough of this conversation. He walked away without saying goodbye.

27

BACK IN THE SHOWROOM there was quiet panic as Bob Herr and the people from the cable TV network tried to decide how to react to the escalating body count. It soon became clear that any attempt to proceed immediately with the tournament as scheduled would meet with a rebellion from many of the players. Binh had not had any close friends in the group, but he was well respected. Even the coldest of cold-blooded gamblers couldn't just shuffle up and deal after something like this. Eventually, Herr decided that the tournament would be postponed for five hours. It would resume at six o'clock and would continue that night until it was down to nine players, but the increases in the blinds would be accelerated. The final table would go on the next day as planned.

Maddie Santos approached me as I was sitting with Jack. She seemed to be deeply distressed. Since she was barely acquainted with Binh, it couldn't have been personal loss that was bothering her. The strain of the week, I thought, looking at her with sympathy. Maddie asked Jack if she could speak privately with me for a minute.

"God, this is awful," she said when we were alone. "But at least we know my gun wasn't used this time. Does that put me in the clear?"

"Not exactly. There could have been two different killers." I hesitated, then plunged ahead. "Look, Maddie, I shouldn't be telling you this. Shooter Deukart was in deep with some organized-crime people who owned all of his action. Binh's killer might be a guy who works for them. Maybe they killed Shooter in the first place. The police don't think that you did it. But if I say anything more, I'm gonna get myself into deep trouble with the police captain, and that's not a place I want to be."

Maddie smiled, placed a hand on each of my shoulders, and squeezed. "Thanks, Mark. That means so much to me." She held on to me a few seconds longer than she needed to. Then, abruptly, she stood up. "You know what? I wanna get the hell out of this place for a little while." I nodded my agreement. "In Yarmouth they have boats that leave every hour, just cruise around the bay," she said. "Let's take one."

This was a really bad idea, but I went for it without hesitation. Maybe I should have asked myself why I was leaving the safety of the hotel to go off on a boat ride with a beautiful young murder suspect ... or maybe that's a question that answers itself.

I asked Jack if he wanted to come with us, but he begged off. A cruise would be nice, he said, but there were no crap tables on those boats. I looked around. I had a strong sense that this event required a chaperone. Buddha Brown was across the room talking with another player. I invited him along, but he also passed.

Well, I tried. This would just have to go into that small drawerful of innocent little iniquities that Eileen would never hear about.

Also, I wasn't going to tell Eileen what had happened to Binh. She'd probably send up a police escort to forcibly bring me home.

I offered to drive, but Maddie wanted to take a cab. During the ride into town, she tried several times to bring up the subject of the murders, but I made it plain that I wasn't in the mood to talk about it.

The cab slowed as it entered the downtown area of Yarmouth. "Let's walk a little bit," suggested Maddie. We strolled down the busy main street, and Maddie occasionally stopped to look into a store window. Window-shopping was close to the bottom of my list of favored leisure activities, but it felt so good to be outdoors that I wasn't complaining. When we came to an antique shop that had a collection of old furniture and assorted useless junk out on the sidewalk, Maddie had to stop and check everything out. Becoming bored, I looked into the mirror of a bedroom bureau and was startled to see, across the street, an unmistakable face looking straight at me.

When I turned around to face him directly, he was gone.

"Hey, was that ...?"

"What?" Maddie turned away from her examination of an old saddle.

"I could swear I just saw Kenneth looking at us."

"Kenneth?"

"You know, Willy's attendant. The big guy with the busted-up nose."

She squinted at me. "Willy's wheelchair flunky? Well, I guess he must get a day off every once in a while. So what?"

"It's just that he's supposed to be ... never mind."

Maddie shrugged and returned her attention to the saddle, plainly uninterested in the subject of what Kenneth did with his free time.

"He has a crush on you, you know."

She looked up sharply. "Who does?"

"Kenneth."

Maddie rolled her eyes. "Great. Another one. Now you understand why I keep a gun." She took my arm and steered me down the sidewalk. "Maybe we should go catch our boat," she said. I felt a little uncomfortable with her holding my arm like that, but it would have been rude to pull it away. We walked two blocks to the Bay Cruise dock, paid ten dollars each, and climbed up a gangway onto the seventy-foot vessel.

The day was spectacular, and the cruise was everything it had promised to be. Swells of one or two feet rocked the boat gently. The sun had the kind of soft autumnal brilliance that invites you to stretch out, close your eyes, and revel in the warmth on your face. I sprawled on a deck chair and looked up at the sky. Maddie said, "Is this what the doctor ordered, or what?"

"This is exactly what the doctor ordered," I agreed. We were silent for a while. The sunlight reflecting off the water and the soft motion of the boat were working on me like a sleeping drug. I was happily giving in, but then I glanced at Maddie and noticed that her forehead had drawn itself into a frown.

"What are you thinking about?" I asked.

"What you told me before, about Shooter. We always thought it must have happened that way."

I sat up. "How's that?"

"Dad lost so much to Shooter—the dealership and everything—but that wasn't enough to explain why he vanished. He owed Shooter his marker for seventy thousand, but he could've worked his way out of it in time. If criminals were holding the marker, though—vicious criminals, from the way you describe it—that would be different."

"Your family never heard from him?"

"Not a thing."

"That's the worst kind of torture I can imagine. I hate to say this, but you would think, if your dad were alive—"

"Oh, he's not alive. After a few months went by, we were sure. Otherwise he would have gotten in touch with us. I don't have any doubt about that."

"Tell me about him."

"Dad was my hero. Came to this country with nothing, worked honest and hard his whole life. He loved us—his family, I mean. The only thing he did that was a little out of line was his gambling. I thought it was really cool when I was a kid—the gambling—but it was only later we learned how out of control it was. He just couldn't handle that walk on the razor's edge that makes it so exciting for the rest of us."

"Can I ask you something? How did you wind up a gambler? I mean, after it cost your family so much."

"I guess at first I wanted to beat the game that beat my dad, you know? But after a while I started to realize that I just love it. I don't have any problem controlling myself. And I'm good."

"Tell me about it. You're on your way to becoming a legend. So does this change the way you feel about Shooter, knowing that he didn't have many choices?"

"Not even a little. I think it makes me hate him even more. I mean, I really, really hate that scumbag."

"Shooter is dead, Maddie."

"Not dad enough for me. Not yet."

That was a conversation stopper. I chose not to point out Maddie's Freudian slip, and we resumed our silent contemplation of the ocean. After a couple of minutes her face brightened and she favored me with an easy smile.

"Sorry for the downer," she said. "I guess I need to learn to be more philosophical. Like Buddha. Did you hear about the bad beat he took today? Some donkey called down a big raise on the turn with nothing but a gutshot draw. The donk hit the straight, knocked him out, and Buddha just laughed about it." She pushed a strand of windblown hair off of her face. "I remember one time he told me I could control my feelings by thinking about a seagull resting on the water. You know, how the waves just pass under the bird and it floats over them…"

I missed the end of Maddie's story. The sun, the gentle motion of the swells, and my massive sleep deficit all caught up with me at the same time. I made like a seagull and floated off into a blissful, sun-drenched sleep.

An hour later I was awakened by the ship's horn as the boat approached the dock. It hadn't been a whole lot of rest, but it felt great. Maddie smiled at me as I groggily looked around. "You were out cold there," she said with affection in her voice. "You looked so cute."

"I hope I wasn't drooling," I said, feeling a little sheepish. Peering at the watch on Maddie's wrist, I couldn't help noticing that the soft, light hairs on her forearm set off very nicely against her tawny skin. I stretched, and with a shock I discovered a physical situation that was far more embarrassing than drool. Straining awkwardly against the denim of my jeans was a full-scale hard-on.

Now, as we all learned in seventh-grade health class, this is a natural phenomenon that occurs to normal adult males while they sleep. It doesn't mean anything, and it's nothing to be ashamed of. *Right.*

I sat up like a shot, crossed my legs, and folded my hands over my lap. Had she noticed? How could she not have noticed—I was stretched out on full display. *Oh, man.* But what was that glimmer in Maddie's eye? Amusement? Pity? Something else? Whatever it was, she didn't seem upset.

"Time to go," said Maddie, extending a hand to help me up. Now she was tormenting me on purpose. I had to stall, had to give Mister Woodrow a minute or two to make himself scarce. It would have been helpful if I could've thought of something clever to say, which I utterly failed to do.

"You know, I think it would be great to just sit here for a while longer."

Maddie's pursed lips looked as though they were suppressing a grin. "Okay. I'm going to find a ladies' room. Why don't I meet you down on the dock."

28

A COUPLE OF MINUTES later I was able to walk down to the pier, where I found Maddie waiting for me. There was enough time for a light dinner before we had to get back to the tournament, and we seated ourselves at a table in a busy, touristy café. Small talk smoothed over any awkwardness that might have been caused by the untimely showcasing of my masculinity. I ordered a lobster roll and Maddie ordered a vegetarian whole-wheat wrap. We had never shared a meal alone together.

When the food arrived, Maddie brought the small talk to an abrupt end. "Mark, I don't think I'll get a night of sleep until they catch this killer," she said.

"I know what you mean."

"I feel badly, though. Here I was, coming to you in a panic about my gun, and I had no idea they were after you about the weirdo toothpick."

"Naw, they haven't been after me."

She took a bite of her wrap and chewed thoughtfully for a minute. "So do you think it's for sure that the same person killed Shooter and Binh?" she asked. "This mob guy? If he did, then there's no way my gun was part of it."

"Well, it's logical, in a way. Hard to put a motive on why they would want to kill Shooter, though, when he was making so much money for them. Maybe the Vegas cops will come up with something." I was aching to tell her what I knew—that her gun could not possibly have been used to kill Shooter—but I held true to my promise to DiCarlo.

I took a few stabs at exploring the question of Anita Wilson, but she deflected me each time I tried to introduce the subject. It was clear that each of us had secrets we weren't able to share, so the conversation moved on to other topics.

Maddie was very curious about my work as a criminal lawyer. I had more than enough stories to keep her entertained, and her green eyes looked particularly striking as she listened with her chin resting on her hands. When she laughed at my description of a bizarre courtroom scene involving a juror and an illicit hot dog, I reflected that I was definitely taking more pleasure in this meal than I was authorized to do, under a strict interpretation of my wedding vows.

We were toying with the idea of ordering dessert when a waiter approached and handed me a note. "Excuse me, sir, a gentleman asked me to give this to you." I looked around but didn't see anybody that I recognized. I opened the note. It read, "Too bad your friend Binh couldn't join you on the cruise. Ennis."

I shot up from my chair and scanned the café, but I still didn't see anybody. "What! What is it?" cried Maddie. Then I saw him.

He was outside on the sidewalk in front of the café, staring in at us through the plate-glass window. Ennis gazed blankly at me and turned, disappearing into the bustling crowd.

I knew there would be no point in trying to follow him. I sat back down. *What the hell!* Kenneth was supposed to be after this guy. If he was, he wasn't doing much of a job of it.

Maddie had picked up the note and was reading it. "Oh my God," she said. She kept reading, and suddenly blushed. She folded the note and dropped it on the table, looking away.

I reached out and picked up the note. "I'll need to give this to DiCarlo," I said. I opened it to look at it again, and then I understood why Maddie had blushed. Underneath the message, in small print, Ennis had written, "If I were you, I would bang her. You never know when it might be your last chance."

29

THE CAB RIDE BACK to the Humpback would have been awkward if we were normal people. Normal people, of course, would not be able to lay aside murder, death threats, and sexual suggestion to concentrate on a card game.

Okay, so I'm not normal. Maddie and I were both focused on the poker action that lay ahead of us that evening. Not that I wasn't fazed by the new threat from Ennis, but it was shoved into the back of my mind with everything else that didn't involve cards and chips. At the café, I'd used Maddie's cell phone to call DiCarlo. After scolding me for being a stupid ass, he strongly advised us both to stay within the safe confines of the casino.

Neither of us had any plans on going anywhere else. Our thoughts right now were all on poker. We exchanged impressions of the habits and tendencies of various players who remained in the tournament. Maddie's stack was bigger than mine at this point. She had over $160,000 and was one of the leaders. I managed to suppress my stack envy by reflecting on the fact that by the end of the night, when only nine players would remain, it would take $400,000 just to be average.

The cab deposited us at the entrance of the Humpback. As we walked into the lobby, a barrier began to rise between us. The casual intimacy created by the shared experiences of the afternoon was gone. Although we wished each other luck, either of us would have been happy to take the other apart at the table, given the chance.

I should have known better, of course, but I was once again surprised when Zip Addison launched an ambush from his favorite hiding spot behind the whaling boat.

"Hey, be careful, Maddie," he said. "People who hang around with this guy are always getting themselves killed." He seemed positively delighted by Binh's death. "So, Mark, now you can tell me everything you *really* know about Tran Le Binh."

I stopped to face him. Maddie kept walking without saying hello. And without saying goodbye to me, for that matter. I didn't try to maintain a friendly façade with Addison. With everything else that was happening, I really had no patience for this guy. "No, I can't. Confidentiality doesn't expire with a former client's death. But even if I *could* tell you, I wouldn't."

"Not fair. I gave you a good warning about the Vegas goon. And guess what else I know." He shifted his eyes back and forth to make sure the coast was clear and lowered his voice to its deepest conspiratorial tone. "Captain DiCarlo has made a connection between Ennis's bosses, and Deukart, and one of the people involved in the poker tournament."

Willy Hopkins, most likely, I thought. "Interesting. Who and what?"

"I'm still working on it. So come on, tell me about Binh. Or … I'll bet Mrs. Newcomb would love reading about you going out on the town with the captivating Maddie Santos."

If I were more the macho type, I would have decked him for that. Instead, I ran a bluff at him. "First of all, my wife's name is Donnelly. Second, you can print whatever you want, because my wife and I don't keep any secrets from each other." Not big secrets, anyway.

"Oh, c'mon, I was kidding around. Listen, I'll make you a deal. Tell me the juicy stuff about Binh and you'll be the first person to know when I find out what the cops have on this card player who's working with Ennis's bosses."

I had a sudden inspiration. "Okay." I reduced my voice to a whisper to match his secretive tone. I bent my head down, and he lowered his into mine, until the two of us looked as though we were doing some sort of Vulcan mind meld right there in the lobby of the Humpback. "What would you say if I told you that Tran Le Binh had actually been a prison guard in the POW camp where Shooter was held?"

Addison straightened up and sneered at me. "I'd say you're the worst liar I know. That's right up there with the love child story. Why don't you let me know when you want to get serious."

I shrugged. "Hey, you asked me," I said, and walked away.

Addison didn't have much credibility, but I was concerned enough to check out what he had told me. I called DiCarlo's number.

"You again?" he asked. "Don't tell me you went for another cruise."

"No, I'm safe and sound here in the lobby of the Humpback."

"I have some good news for you," DiCarlo said. "We found the screamer from the parking lot."

"Really. Well, that *is* good news."

"Woman from New Hampshire was down for a night of gambling, playing hooky from her family. We took your advice, traced her through the security cameras and the player's card she used in a slot machine. Turns out they don't have cameras covering the lobby of the hotel, but they do film everybody going in and out of the casino. She did pretty much what you imagined. She got a little off track looking for her car, saw Deukart's body, and lost her nerve. All of a sudden she had no trouble finding her car. Now she's scared shitless that we'll arrest her for something."

"Can I get a look at her statement? Or talk to her myself? Obviously, it's important to me."

"No need. Her story corroborates yours just fine."

Okay, I guess I'll just have to trust you on that one. DiCarlo didn't miss too many chances to show who was boss.

"But that wasn't why you called me," DiCarlo said.

"No, it wasn't. I heard there's a new development in the case. Another one of my fellow gamblers is mixed up with Shooter's loan shark?"

DiCarlo was silent for a moment. "Where did you hear that?"

"My sources are strictly confidential."

"That prick Addison again." DiCarlo was plainly seething. I would be too, if somebody who worked for me was leaking information to the press.

"I think it's time you started keeping your nose out of this. You don't want to wind up like Tran Le Binh."

"No, I don't, which is precisely why I'm going to keep my nose *in* this until it's settled."

"Go play cards. Just let the professionals do their work." Di-Carlo hung up.

30

THERE WERE A COUPLE of minutes to spare when I walked into the Showroom. Willy Hopkins was already taking his place at the card table. I walked over and told Willy about the encounter with Ennis that afternoon. Plainly, Kenneth had not delivered as expected. Willy frowned. "To be honest with you, I haven't heard from Kenneth all day. Not to worry, though. He is more than capable of taking care of himself, and I'm sure he'll catch up with this Ennis eventually." I had a mental image of Kenneth hunting down Martin Ennis and engaging him in titanic combat, like Godzilla and Megalon.

"Willy, I assume you've already talked with DiCarlo. He is really focused on that private game that Kenneth helped with."

Willy gave me a face. "Would you please stop with this tiresome business? We have more important concerns right now."

He was right. The instant the first cards came flying across the table, Martin Ennis was a distant memory. He disappeared into the vanishing point that swallows everything not directly relevant to the game.

Thanks to the providential nap on the boat, I felt more alert than I had for days. But everything in this tournament seemed to be happening upside down. When I was debilitated with fatigue, I'd managed to stumble into some big hands. Now, when I felt sharp, nothing went right.

I couldn't catch any cards to play, nothing at all. A few times I made position bluffs, just to keep my hand in the game, but each time I was promptly raised by the player to my immediate left, Terrance McCarthy. McCarthy was a rising young pro who had grown up in East New York, one of the tougher neighborhoods in Brooklyn. In a poker world full of wannabe cool guys, McCarthy was the genuine article. Behind his shades and earphones, he was a complete cipher. I couldn't get the slightest read on him, and I never knew when he was going to come storming over the top of my feeble attempts to bet. Sitting on my left with a huge stack, he had the power to slap down any of my efforts at getting something going with a bluff. With Willy Hopkins now sitting two to my left, also with a big stack, it was extremely difficult for me to make something happen with weak cards.

The blinds, now up to $4,000 and $8,000, were eating away at me. The temptation to throw all my chips into the pot on a wild-ass bluff—and just get it all over with—was becoming hard to resist. *Patience,* I told myself. *Patience.*

At the same time, other players in even more desperate trouble were dropping out of the tournament. Each time a dealer intoned, "Player down, Table Three" or "Player down, Table One," I drew one step closer to finishing in the money. With my stack down to a meager $39,000, a dealer called, "Player down, Table Two," which was followed by a burst of applause from the handful of onlookers. The tournament was down to thirty-seven players. I was in the money.

Now I could afford to gamble a little more. Realistically, I didn't have much choice. Three more times around, paying the blinds and antes, would reduce me to nothing.

The button was three to my right. I was sitting in first position. The next hand, I would be in the big blind and would be forced to bet another $8,000 of my precious chips on what would undoubtedly be another unplayable hand like 2♥ 7♣. I peeked at my cards and, when I saw them, hoped that I looked just as listless and frustrated as I had all evening while picking up dreck. A♥ K♣. Finally, a premium hand. Position was lousy, but I'd have to make the best of it. I hoped that nobody noticed the slight quickening of my pulse. But then again, I reminded myself, if anybody could read me from the way I looked at my cards, I didn't belong in this tournament in the first place.

I opened with a small raise, to $15,000. I didn't have the cash to bet more without committing myself completely to the pot. I was eager to put all my chips in, but I wanted to lure McCarthy or Willy into re-raising me, which they'd been doing all night. If I put it all in right away, chances were I would pick up nothing but the blinds. McCarthy folded. Two to my left, Willy Hopkins called the bet. I had to resist the urge to look sharply at him. In that position, calling a small raise from the first bettor was a sign of a strong hand. With lesser cards, the normal play for Willy would have been to raise me and force me to fold or go all in.

Everybody passed around to Jeff Robinson in the big blind, a solid player I remembered from a marathon game in Las Vegas a couple of years earlier. Robinson also called, but this could have meant anything. Since Robinson already had $8,000 in the pot, he only had to add $7,000 to see the flop.

The flop came out. I was aching to see an ace or king, but instead it came up rags—10♣ 4♠ 3♠. *Shit. Now what.* In the big blind, Robinson checked. *Decision time for Newcomb.* The $53,000 in the pot would go a long way toward keeping me alive. On the other hand, I basically had nothing. A pair of deuces would beat me right now. Even with two more cards coming, anybody holding a pair would be an 80 percent favorite to beat my ace-king. And I didn't have enough chips left to launch a powerful bluff. If I bet, and lost, the tournament was over for me. Robinson probably didn't have much. Willy was the threat.

"I'll bet. All in," I said. I pushed my chips toward the center of the table with what I hoped was neither an aggressive air, indicating an obvious bluff, nor a fearful air, indicating the truth.

Willy peered into my face for a few seconds. I smiled back, calmly. He knew that I knew that my $24,000 was not enough to bluff with. Logically, then, he should conclude that I had a big hand. Or that's what I hoped.

With Willy hesitating even a few seconds, I strongly suspected that he held a medium pair—eights or nines. Not that I had anything to gain from figuring out Willy's hand at this point, since I had no more chips to bet with and no more decisions to make. After an eternity of ten or twelve seconds, Willy heaved a sigh and said, "Call."

In all probability, I knew, I had just lost the tournament. Despite this realization, I had to be careful to show absolutely nothing, because Jeff Robinson still had a decision to make. Apparently, it wasn't much of a decision, because he immediately threw his cards away.

"Turn 'em up," said the dealer. I turned my ace-king up on the table. Willy showed a pair of nines. So at least I had the consolation of having figured him correctly. Whoopee. One of the next two cards had to be an ace or a king to save me. Or a jack-queen combination, which was extremely unlikely.

My tournament life could now be measured in the six seconds that it would take for the dealer to produce the turn and the river. The turn was no help—six of spades—and the river... a sublime ace of diamonds.

I sagged back into my chair while the tide of relief washed over me. I turned to Willy to offer polite condolences but was startled that Willy's usually gracious demeanor had dissolved into a look of murderous anger.

"You made the right call there," I offered.

"You're goddamn right I did," muttered Willy, bringing himself into control. "I sure the hell did."

The lucky beat gave me a surge of energy, and I now felt revived, as if I had just had ten hours of sleep. I was all over my game. Four hands later, holding nothing at all, I pounced on a medium-stacked player to my right who had made a tentative raise. I fired out a big re-raise and he folded up. My stack was now over a hundred thousand. Not a dominant position, but definitely in the game. The very next hand, I picked up a pair of jacks. Next to ace-queen, this was possibly the most dangerous hand to have in the game of Hold'em, and it needed to be handled like a poisonous snake. I played the jacks perfectly and took another medium-sized pot.

"Hey, somebody pull the alarm. Grab a hose. This guy's on fire," said Terrance McCarthy.

"I volunteer to direct the nozzle," grumbled Willy Hopkins.

"Careful what you say, Willy," I said. "If they find me dead with a fire hose up my ass, you'll be the number one suspect." It's easy to joke around when things are going good.

I stayed on my rush. Jeff Robinson, down to his last desperate chance, made a raise at the pot holding not much. I was lucky enough to have an ace-ten to call him with; I knocked him out of the tournament and took his chips.

With the blinds now up to $6,000 and $12,000, chip count meant everything. The small stacks were forced to gamble, and the big stacks could pick them off at their leisure while avoiding direct combat with each other. The rich got richer and the poor went broke. The few remaining in the middle had to try to stay away from the big dogs while jumping on the little dogs every time they got a chance. This was a stage where you had to choose your battles very carefully.

By ten p.m. it was down to eighteen players, who had been consolidated into two tables. Madelin Santos joined my table. I exchanged glances with her, and the understanding was immediate. Our afternoon together, and the shared trauma of the past few days, didn't mean a thing. Right now we were nothing but a couple of wolves on the hunt, and if I exposed my neck to her, she would be glad to rip it open.

Around ten-thirty the room shook with an explosion of sound from Table One. It was Jack, leaping out of his chair and pumping his fist into the air, shouting, "Yes! Yes!" I stood up to see what it was about.

Jack hurried over to me and grabbed me by my shoulders. "Got into a hand with Gant," he exclaimed. "Semi-bluffed a flush draw, wound up all in. Made the flush on the turn."

Some say that the key to winning a tournament is surviving long enough to get lucky. Jack and I had both done that. Barracuda Gant had played a big hand perfectly, precisely as the mathematics dictated, and lost. He was still sitting, looking with disgust at the fatal cards that had knocked the props out from under the natural order of things. So much for the strong devouring the weak.

Gant's rotten luck didn't end with the bad beat that Jack had put on him. One of DiCarlo's investigators—Schmidt, I thought it was—heard the shouting and trained a curious eye on the table. I saw him do a double take, then peer closely in the direction of Gant. Obviously, he had just noticed the symbol on the cap. He pulled out a phone and began punching at the buttons.

Before midnight, it was over for the day, and the Open was down to the final nine. Jack Shea, Madelin Santos, Willy Hopkins, and I were all still alive.

As the surviving players milled around, pinching themselves to make sure this was real, Britta pushed Willy Hopkins to where Jack and I were talking. "Would you two gents like to join me for a nightcap?" he asked. "Personally, I think I need to unwind a bit before I try to sleep." We instantly agreed. "Fine. There's an establishment on the other side of the hotel called Thar She Blows! A name that conjures up a number of images, none of which I care to contemplate at the moment. Please do join us there in a few minutes." He gestured to Britta and rolled away. Only Willy Hopkins could make a simple thing like meeting for a drink sound like the opening scene of a Sydney Greenstreet movie.

Jack cajoled Maddie into joining us, and then Jack and I headed into the men's room to wash up. He said, "I have to take care of something. Do me a favor? Make sure nobody comes in here and flushes anything for a while." Jack was always asking things like that. He disappeared into a toilet stall. A few seconds later I heard him speaking. "Brigid? Hey, honey, it's me. Did I wake you up? . . . Sorry, just got back to my room. Another big night out on the town with the most boring senior account manager in the history of the technology industry . . . Yeah . . . Really?" They chatted for a few minutes. "No, tomorrow. Definitely. Guaranteed, I'll be home . . . When does it start? Nine? That's perfect. Count on me. Okay . . . I love you too. G'night."

Jack emerged from the stall looking worried. "She smells something, Mark."

"Well, considering where you made the call from, that would figure."

"I need you to do me a favor."

I started to say, "Anything," but stopped short, knowing from experience that Jack might ask for something I couldn't do. My eyes narrowed slightly.

"Okay," said Jack. "I've been saving this one up, hoping I wouldn't have to use it. But now my back is really against the wall, and I need a big one."

A stranger who had come in to use the bathroom was obviously intrigued by the conversation. Jack waited for him to wash his hands and leave.

217

"Here's what I want you to do. You call Brigid. You're all excited about being at the final table. You want to tell me about it, but you don't know where I am and you lost my cell phone number. So you want Brigid to give you my number. That way, you see, she'll figure *you're* at the tournament, and *you* don't know where *I* am, so obviously *I'm* not at the tournament, so I must really be in Albany. See?"

I protested. "Jack, I'm already out on a limb with Eileen for not ratting you out in the first place. Now you want me to be an active part of the lie?" Although I did not live in mortal terror of Eileen the way Jack feared Brigid, I did have a healthy respect for my wife's occasional outbursts of high Irish temper. That plus the fact that Eileen and I genuinely trusted each other, and I wanted things to continue that way.

"Listen, Mark," Jack pleaded. "Look at where we are! We're at the final table of a giant goddamn poker tournament! This will never happen again to either one of us, let alone both of us. It's not even once in a lifetime. It's once in a *hundred* lifetimes. It's *never* in a lifetime. Just do this for me. I swear I'll never ask for anything like this again."

I sighed. Friendship could be a heavy burden sometimes. I went to a pay phone to make the call. "Don't forget to apologize for waking her up," nagged Jack. "Otherwise she'll know you just talked to me. She's very smart about things like that."

I spoke with Brigid for a couple of minutes. Jack confronted me eagerly as soon as I had hung up the phone. "How'd it go? What'd she say? Did she go for it? Whaddaya think?" I smiled. I never owned a puppy, but I guessed that having Jack Shea as a friend was the next best thing.

"I think it went fine," I said. "She didn't say much. Gave me your number, wished me luck. She seemed more interested in the murder case, asked me a few questions about that. She told me she was glad you're not here, said you'd probably get yourself killed."

"She did? She said that? That's good! That's good! You think that's good?"

I made a quick call to Eileen, waking her up, and gave her the news about making the final table. I left out a few minor details about my day, like the fact that Tran Le Binh had been shot in the head. Or that the guy who probably did it was stalking me. Or that I had shared a chummy afternoon with a young woman who could easily have made the cover of the *Sports Illustrated* swimsuit issue. The good angel on my right shoulder was giving me an earful, but I wasn't paying attention. Jack and I headed off for the bar.

Thar She Blows! could have contended for the title of Tackiest Bar on the East Coast. The interior designer who had tried to combine a whaling theme with a modern discotheque was, hopefully, pursuing a different line of work by now. It didn't matter. We were a happy group. The least that any of us would walk away with, the ninth place award, was $68,000. We were all on a gambler's high, at a level that was new to us. Or almost new. One time, when I was in college, I'd scraped together $100 and caught a bus for Atlantic City. I got hot at a blackjack table and came home with $1,600. The elation I now felt was comparable to that. Many high-stakes gamblers looked down their noses at the people playing quarter slots and two-dollar keno tickets. But I knew, from experience, that the thrill of winning was relative to the size of your bankroll, not the size of your bet. Sometimes it made me feel a little sorry for Willy Hopkins. The money wasn't part of it for him. He could buy and sell a hundred of these tournaments. I couldn't help but wonder, what was it that drove him?

Conversation around the table was subdued; we were just soaking it all in. It was notable how much better Willy treated Britta than he treated Kenneth. He actually invited her to sit down and join us, an amenity that he had never afforded to Kenneth. I guessed that her "hands that could melt steel" might have had something to do with it.

Jack was meeting Britta for the first time. Predictably, he monopolized her, falling all over himself to impress her. Maddie made it a point to ask Jack how Brigid, his *girlfriend*, was doing. He mumbled something in reply.

"Hey, Jack," I asked. "What are you going to do about the TV coverage tomorrow?"

"It's all worked out," he answered. "I talked with Bob Herr earlier today. He needed a little persuading, but I've got it all set."

"Yeah?"

Jack only smiled. "You'll see tomorrow."

Maddie was more quiet than the others. She apparently found it harder than I did to shake off the events of the day. "I think we ought to drink a toast to Tran Le Binh," she said.

"Absolutely," I agreed. We raised our glasses. None of us had known him well. I was tempted to tell the amazing story that I had learned two days earlier, but I held back.

"Are we going to drink to Shooter Deukart?" I asked.

Jack raised his glass into the air. "To hell with him," he said.

"Bastard," added Maddie, taking a sip.

Gamblers are not known for being reverent, but I thought this was taking it a little far. I decided to call it a night. "That's it for me. I've got to go check in on Hell-boy."

"How is the little rascal?" asked Jack. "What's he up to tonight, a tour of the local strip bars?"

"He's lucky to be alive," I answered. "I've got Evey watching him for me. I hope she's hanging on to her sanity, but at least now I'll be able to give her a good payday. You wouldn't believe the stuff this kid gets himself into." Suddenly, I realized that I had been carrying Patrick's mini-camcorder in my shirt pocket since the morning. I'd probably violated some tournament rule against electronic recording devices. Oh well, no harm.

"Good night, all," I said as I rose. "Tomorrow we'll be at each other's throats. So I'll wish you good luck now, and no hard feelings when one of us is holding the cash." In keeping with tradition, the Open would pay the winner in cash, right at the table. I turned to walk away, but stopped to listen as Jack spoke to Maddie.

"Hey, Santos, I wonder if two people who are about to play at a final table have ever spent the night having wild sex with each other. D'you think?"

"What you and Mark do on your own time is none of my business," Maddie retorted with a straight face. "But I've gotta tell you, Jack, the makeup and perfume are not a turn-on for me."

I thought about Anita Wilson and wondered whether makeup and perfume might not be a turn-on for Maddie after all. As I walked back to the elevators, I laughed out loud as I realized that Jack had been trying to impress Britta this whole time, oblivious that he was wearing eye liner and smelled like Passion.

31

FOR SAFETY'S SAKE, I loitered around the elevator bank until I was able to get a ride up with two other people. Though I was beyond exhaustion and very anxious to get to sleep, I could spare a few minutes if it meant avoiding another confrontation with Martin Ennis. DiCarlo seemed to think that there was no danger inside the hotel, but I would play it safe anyway.

I put my card key into the door of Room 824, waited for the green light, and pushed the door open as quietly as I could. I was amazed at the sense of peace and calm that pervaded the room. Evelyn was sitting in an armchair, reading a book. Patrick was fast asleep, a gentle smile curling at the corners of his mouth. With his tousled mop of hair, he looked like an angel. Evelyn smiled and closed her book as I came into the room.

"How'd it go?" I asked.

"Just fine!" she answered. "He's a fun little guy!"

I looked closely at Patrick to make sure she didn't have the wrong child. Apparently, there was an art to handling kids—an art that I did not yet possess.

"How did you manage?" I asked. "What did you two do all day?"

"Oh, I was able to keep him busy. I'll let Patrick tell you about it."

"But wasn't he rude? Crass? Obscene?"

"Well, yes, there is a little bit to work on there," she admitted. "But basically he's a good kid. So how 'bout you? What's the news?"

I had been looking doubtfully at Patrick, but at the question I turned my full attention to Evelyn and smiled. "Well," I said, "the good news is, I'm in the money."

"That's great!" Her eyes lit up. "How exciting! What position did you finish in?"

I grinned broadly. "The better news is that I'm not finished yet. I'm at the final table. Jack is too."

"Oh, wow!" She seemed genuinely pleased for me. My weariness probably contributed to it, but I suddenly felt very emotional— deeply awash in affection and gratitude to Evelyn.

"Evey," I said, "I can't thank you enough for this. You saved my life today. You can do it again tomorrow, right? Around quarter after nine?"

"Of course," she smiled. She hitched her bag onto her shoulder and opened the door. We stepped out into the hallway to avoid waking Patrick. For the first time I noticed that, freed from the ludicrous cocktail waitress outfit, wearing a pair of jeans and a sweater, Evelyn was really a very nice-looking fifty-five-year-old woman. She would make a great catch for an older man.

"Hey, Evey," I joked. "We've gotta be careful about meeting like this. People might start to talk."

As luck would have it, at that moment two young men rounded a corner of the hall and approached us. It was the same two guys who had passed me in the hall the night before. Their eyes lit up when they recognized me.

"Yo, Diceman!" said the taller of the two. "Go for it, babe!"

"Hey, lady," said the other, "I'd check out his drawers before I went any further with this guy." They laughed and passed down the hall.

"What the hell was that about?" asked Evelyn.

"It's a long story," I muttered. "I'll tell you later. G'night, Evey. See you in the morning."

Back in the room, I washed up and climbed into bed, still wearing the lucky underwear Eileen had given me. No way was I taking these off until the tournament was over. I picked up the phone, hit zero for the operator, and asked for an eight-forty-five wake-up call. The final table would be starting an hour later than the previous days' events, and I would make grateful use of those extra sixty minutes. I closed my eyes and fell almost immediately into a deep sleep, which was soon interrupted, once again, by a frenzied banging on the door.

32

WHAT THE HELL! THIS cannot be happening again! I was getting really, really tired of this. I looked at the clock on the nightstand. It was 2:14.

The banging continued, accompanied by sounds of raucous laughter. "What the hell," I repeated, aloud this time, as I forced myself out of bed and pulled on a pair of jeans. Out in the hallway I could hear rowdy voices shouting, "Marco! Polo! Marco! Polo!" They sounded somehow familiar. *Is this real?* I thought groggily. *Is this a bad dream? Am I in some sort of weird Italian movie or something?*

I opened the door and was immediately blitzed by three or four large men who surged into the room and almost knocked me to the floor. They were laughing hysterically. A familiar voice called, "Marco! What up, bro!" In a flash, it hit me. These were Eileen's cousins. It was Freddie's bachelor party.

I stood and gaped as they continued to pour into the room. Somebody turned on a light. There were ten or twelve guys. Half were dragging six-packs or fragments of six-packs. All were clearly drunk and at various stages of incoherence. Most of them were either talking or laughing, all at the same time. Patrick was sitting straight up in his bed, his eyes wide with excitement.

Eileen's brother Kevin stuck a beer into my hand. "You couldn't come to the bachelor party, so the party came to you!" he crowed. Several of the revelers were watching me absorb the news, waiting for my face to light up, waiting for a joyous affirmation of the heroic gesture of loyalty and kinsmanship they had made.

With what may have been my best acting job of the week, I showed them the excitement and gratitude they deserved to see. "You guys are the *greatest!*" I exclaimed, holding my beer up in the air. "Whoo-hoo!"

Inside, of course, I was groaning. *I cannot believe this is happening to me! Do these lunatics have any idea how much tomorrow means? How badly I need some sleep?* I had to decide quickly whether to join the party or send them on their way, which is what I desperately wanted to do, but it wasn't much of a decision. I knew I had already lost. These guys had come all the way up from New York just for me, to show that I was part of the family. If I politely explained that I needed sleep and sent them off, it would be beyond bad manners. It would be interpreted as an act of severance—a declaration that I wanted nothing to do with the family. And since Eileen and her family were inseparable, she would take it the same way. In the end, it came down to a simple analysis. What did I value more highly: a once-in-a-lifetime shot at winning a big tournament, or my marriage with Eileen? I didn't even have to think about it.

"Guys," I said. "Let me put some clothes on. We'll go out."

There was a general roar of assent from those who were cogent enough to follow the conversation.

"So where are we going?" I asked.

"Casino, man!" shouted Freddie. He was barely able to stand. "You're gonna show us how, dude! You're the boss! You're the king!"

"Hey, whadda we do with the little dude?" somebody asked, indicating Patrick.

"Bring 'im along! We need a mascot!" called another in a slurred voice.

"All ... *RIGHT!!*" shouted Patrick. He was already fully clothed.

"Uh, guys? That's not too practical. Patrick isn't going to be allowed ..." I trailed off. The logic of my position would be totally lost on these gents, who were flying at a different altitude than I was. That's when I saw my out.

"Okay, let's go, guys," I said, and led the charge to the elevators. A couple of minutes later, we hit the casino and descended on the crap tables. I did my best to play host, trying to teach the basics to those who had never played before. This was hopeless, since most of them wouldn't have been able to tie their own shoes at this point.

It took only a very short time before one of the pit bosses noticed Patrick. "Who's in charge of that kid?" he asked. "You have to get him out of here, I mean right now."

This was the excuse I was waiting for. I started to make my apologies, and explain why I had to get back to the room with Patrick, but nobody was paying any attention to me anyway. The revelers were all too busy playing craps, or ogling cocktail waitresses, or trying not to throw up. I left them to the tender mercies of the crap dealers and led the protesting Patrick back to the room. Once tucked in, the boy went straight to sleep. I looked at the clock—3:28—and slid into bed for the second time that night. "The hell," I muttered to myself. "What could possibly happen next?"

33

I WAS DREAMING. I was inside an episode of *The West Wing*. In the dream, of course, it wasn't a TV show; it was fully real. Although the characters were the White House staff from the TV show, the location of the dream was not the West Wing but rather a series of elegant rooms in the Waldorf-Astoria Hotel in New York City.

Leo McGarry, the president's chief of staff, was on a killing spree. I was the only person who realized what was happening. Leo was moving from one room to another in a series of private conferences, and at the conclusion of each talk, he dispatched the person he was meeting with. He slipped poison into the teacup of the secretary of state and laughed as the secretary convulsed in agony on the floor. He jabbed a hypodermic needle full of strychnine into the thigh of a senator from Pennsylvania. On and on it went.

I was somehow accompanying Leo through these meetings but was powerless to say or do anything to prevent the killings. To make matters worse, each room was progressively smaller and more cramped than the last. Claustrophobic anxiety, combined with the dread of the deaths that I was impotent to stop, increased to the point of being intolerable.

Leo was wrapping up his meeting with a representative from the League of Women Voters, and I watched helplessly as he casually picked up a throw pillow, obviously intending to clamp it over the face of the seventy-three-year-old woman and smother her to death. The walls were closing in on me. Leo's face showed sly delight as he anticipated the moment when he would launch himself onto the unsuspecting septuagenarian. The sheer horror of it woke me up, sweating and gasping for breath.

What the hell is the matter with me? I wondered, when I had recovered myself into consciousness. *I must be going nuts.* I didn't look at the clock because I didn't want to know what time it was. I lay still and stared at the ceiling for a few minutes, until sleep overtook me again.

A few hours later the telephone rang with what must have been my wake-up call. But I was too weary to do anything except pick up the phone and drop it back into its cradle. Anything to stop the ringing. I immediately fell back to sleep.

34

Saturday, October 2

THE NEXT THING I knew, the phone was ringing again. I sat up and forced my eyes half-open. Patrick, on his side of the room, was pulling the covers up over his head. I squinted at the clock on the nightstand. 9:22. *9:22! Cards would be dealt at ten! What the*—

I picked up the phone. "Hello?"

"Mark, are you okay in there?"

"Who's this?"

"It's Evelyn. I knocked on the door and nobody answered. I'm just outside calling you from my cell phone."

"Oh, Evey, thank God for you. I guess I slept through my wake-up." I leaped out of bed—the threat of being late for the final table was working like a dozen cups of coffee—put a towel around my waist, and opened the door.

"I'm going to jump in the shower real fast. Can you get Patrick up?"

Eight minutes later I came out of the bathroom. I was showered and dressed, but I hadn't taken the time to shave. "Listen, Evey. I have to get downstairs and try to grab some breakfast. Whatever you guys want to do today, I'll pay for it. Sky's the limit. Fly him to Paris, whatever. Patrick's dad left me a message—he's coming back this afternoon. He'll meet you here at the room sometime between three and four. Okay?"

"Don't worry about a thing. We're going to have fun."

"I can't thank you enough for this, Evey. Patrick, be good."

Both Evelyn and Patrick wished me luck. As I walked alone down the hallway to the elevators to begin my day at the final table, the enormity of the occasion suddenly hit me. Butterflies were roiling in my stomach. I wasn't headed downstairs for a nice game of 10-20 Pot Limit or to while away a couple of hours shooting craps. This was *It*.

There was nobody else waiting for an elevator, and when a downward-bound car stopped, I had a brief moment of panic. I'd already taken more elevators in the last two days than I would normally take in a month, and the added specter of Martin Ennis possibly lurking behind every corner didn't help my anxiety at all. The elevator was empty. I got in it, pushed the large "C" button for the casino, and breathed deeply all the way down.

The elevator disgorged me into a chaotic scene. The press had gotten hold of the murder story now in a big way, and they were milling around all over the gallery that separated the elevator bank from the Showroom entrance. Normally, there is a small media contingent at a major poker tournament, consisting of some of the specialty gambling magazines and maybe two or three local news outfits. The Humpback Murders, as they were now being called, had attracted network news organizations and major papers from across the country. Camera crews with wires trailing all around, photographers, and reporters sticking microphones into people's faces all combined to create an atmosphere of pandemonium.

The Showroom itself, I knew, would be something of a sanctuary, because only the cable TV channel would be allowed to have cameras or microphones inside. Even inside the Showroom, though, there would be reporters desperate to get interviews with any of the nine remaining players. And fighting through the crowd to get to the Showroom would be a feat all in itself.

I wanted to think about nothing right now except cards. The last thing I was looking for was to bandy words with a reporter who would probably misquote me and get me into serious trouble. *The Toothpick Killer Speaks.* I was pretty sure that all of the other players would feel the same way. One thing we had going for us was that none of the national reporters had any idea what the nine players looked like. Although Zip Addison would not be above taking cash in exchange for pointing us out.

In the middle of the turmoil appeared an improbable, showstopping figure. A medium-set man stepped out of an elevator into the gallery, clad in an oversized jacket with a long hood pulled up over his head. Underneath the hood, little could be seen of his face other than a crisply shaven chin and a large pair of sunglasses. The jacket was not the tattered sweatshirt or casino-logo jacket that one would expect to see at a poker game. It was a brightly colored red, white, and blue jamboree of a jacket, spangled with stars and stripes. There was also something unusual about the shades. They reflected images of the American flag in a way that changed the image with the angle, so that if the wearer moved his head back and forth, the flags appeared to be waving. Even more arresting than the outfit, the man carried himself with a swagger that commanded the attention of everybody in the room.

The amazed crowd fell almost silent. The apparition walked through the gallery toward the entrance to the Showroom, and the throng parted before him as it would for a presidential motorcade. He made a slight detour in my direction. "Say hello to Kid America," Jack murmured out of the side of his mouth as he passed me and swept imperiously through the doors into the Showroom.

35

Up on the stage of the Showroom, we all settled into our seats. Jack asked that as long as there were cameras or microphones present, he be addressed only as "Kid America." He offered no explanation. The other players were only too glad to oblige his weird request. They considered Jack to be dead money at this table, and anything that kept him happy was okay with them.

The blinds were starting at $10,000 and $20,000, and I was beginning the day with exactly $273,000 in chips. The average stack at the table was around $400,000. Maddie Santos and Willy Hopkins were well above that number. Jack—Kid America—was beneath it. One of the finalists, Jeff Ford, had played his way into the tournament through a $50 super-satellite. Adding to the media interest in the event, the chip leader as play began was Sandy Baker, who was making a solid run at being the first woman ever to win a million-dollar tournament.

There was a surreal quality to the atmosphere around the table, simply because there was nothing unusual about it. It was so normal it seemed unnatural. There should have been more pomp and ceremony, I thought, like the spotlighted introductions at an NBA game. But the cards were shuffled and dealt just as they would have been for a Tuesday-night $100 buy-in event at anybody's local card club. The only thing that was really out of the ordinary was Jack's absurd costume.

My butterflies vanished the instant the first deal came shooshing across the felt. I cupped my hands over the cards and peeked at them. Eight of clubs and four of diamonds, an automatic fold. Good. I never liked playing the first deal of the day.

For two hours, the play was slow and tentative, very uncharacteristic for a final table. There was a great deal of ducking and dodging, with no solid blows being landed. It was apparent to me that everybody was biding their time, waiting to get into a big hand with Willy Hopkins. But Willy was playing as cool as could be—calmly, patiently, getting maximum value from each hand and slowly increasing the size of his stack. Meanwhile, I was picking up a lot of nothing—two-seven, jack-four, king-three. Because of the overall tightness of the table, though, I was able to steal enough blinds to remain in business.

When the first break came, not a whole lot had changed. Two players, Bill Lane and Jeff Ford, were dangerously low on chips. Sandy Baker's lead had slipped when she lost a good-sized pot to Frank Levey, a pro from the Midwest who I'd never played with before. The rest of us had increased our positions, but nobody had made a big move other than Levey. When play resumed, the blinds would be up to $20,000 and $40,000 and it would be impossible to avoid major confrontations.

The thirty-minute break presented a dilemma. After two hours of intense concentration, it was imperative to get out of the Showroom for a few minutes. But on the other side of the doors we would face a pandemonium of pesky microphones and cameras.

"Just follow me," Kid America said. He breezed up the aisle of the Showroom and into the crowded gallery, ignoring the desperate pleas of the reporters. They tried to shove microphones into his face, but somehow they didn't dare to block his path. Maddie and I stayed close. The three of us swept through the gallery into the elevator bank and ducked into the first upward-bound car. Before the doors closed, Jack turned to face the reporters, holding up his hands palm outward, and regally announced, "Kid America will answer questions at the conclusion of the tournament."

As the elevator doors closed behind us, Jack peeled off his hood and glasses and laughed out loud. "Damn! This is fun, isn't it?"

I laughed with him. "So this is your strategy for staying out of the limelight?"

"Oldest trick in the book, my friend. The best place to hide is right out in the open."

"Really? What book would that be?"

"Oh, you know. The book."

Jack and I were loose, having fun. Maddie was quiet. We got off on the eighth floor and walked to Room 824. Assuming that Patrick had not thoroughly pillaged the mini-bar, there ought to be some soft drinks and crackers in there. We entered the empty room and I was going for the snacks when Maddie stopped me.

"Mark," she said, "I know this is a terrible time to bring this up. But I have to talk to you about something."

I felt instantly deflated. "Oh no, Maddie, can't it wait?"

"Captain DiCarlo called me this morning and told me the ballistics report confirmed it was bullets from my gun that shot Deukart."

"Bastard!" Jack snarled. "Why couldn't that wait until after today?"

I agreed. That was uncalled for. I decided that my promise to DiCarlo was no longer binding, and it was time to tell Maddie everything I knew. "Okay, Maddie, listen to me carefully," I began. I was interrupted by the sound of a card key and the opening of the door. It was Evelyn and Patrick.

"Oh! Sorry!" exclaimed Evelyn. "I didn't expect to find you guys here." Patrick looked white as a ghost and very unhappy. "Patrick isn't feeling very well. He bet me he could eat fifty sour balls for breakfast. I won the bet—he only made it to forty-five."

"Well, I guess that's one way to keep him out of trouble," I said. "We'll be gone in a little bit. You can let Patrick go to bed. Listen," I said, turning back to Maddie, "come into my office so we can talk." I walked into the bathroom, which by now I considered to be a sort of adjunct conference room. She followed me, and Jack squeezed in behind her.

"I want to be a part of this too," he said.

"Look, Maddie," I began again, "here's what I learned from DiCarlo. The bullets from your gun did not kill Shooter Deukart. He was beaten to death. It was two hours later before anybody put the bullets into him. Two hours later." I watched her to make sure this was sinking in, then continued.

"Okay? So you have a good solid alibi for the first part of the evening, right? You were having dinner with Jack." We both looked up at Jack, standing proudly in his Kid America uniform. "Well, maybe 'solid' is overstating it a little. But the worst thing you might have done is pump four bullets into a dead body. That's not much of a crime.

"More important, even if they wanted to get you for *that*, they *wouldn't*. No prosecutor is going to go to a jury with a muddled-up murder case where one defendant is the killer and an unrelated defendant did something to the body a few hours later. That would create way too much confusion and make it very easy for a jury to find reasonable doubt.

"So they *want* to believe that you had nothing to do with this. They want you to be the innocent person who just had a gun taken from her room. But like it or not, you're involved. So you're gonna have to give them an alibi they can confirm, embarrassing or not."

Maddie was shifting on the edge of the tub and taking this all in. We heard a knock outside the bathroom, on the door to my room. "I'll get it," came Evelyn's voice.

I started to say, "Evey, I don't think you—" Then I heard a sharp gasp coming from Evelyn. A moment later the bathroom door opened. The first thing that I saw was the gun, which seemed to occupy my entire field of vision for a moment or two. Then my look flashed up from the gun to the eyes of Martin Ennis.

36

ENNIS WASN'T WASTING ANY time. He ordered the three of us out of the bathroom. With his free hand, he grasped the bathroom telephone and ripped the cord out of the wall. He pointed Evelyn and Patrick into the bathroom. "You two wait in there," he commanded. "The three of you, sit at the end of that bed with your hands on your knees." We all obeyed. Madelin, Jack, and I sat at the foot of one of the beds and looked up at Ennis, who stood in front of us with his back to the TV console.

Ennis was wearing his usual incongruous preppie attire: an open-necked button-down shirt, blazer, and chinos. There was a press pass hanging from his lapel; apparently, it didn't take much of a disguise to get past the crack security guards at the Humpback. He pulled a set of papers from inside his jacket pocket.

"All right, here's the deal," he said. "Since I haven't decided which one of you destroyed our property, you all are going to pay for the damage." He looked directly at Maddie. "I got a look at that ballistics report. You and Toothpick Boy here are in some deep shit with the cops. That's why we're going to get our money out of you fast. So each one of you owes me $500,000, payable with the proceeds from today's tournament. If you earn less than that, we'll consider the balance to be a loan. At our standard rate of 10 percent a week. I have contracts here that spell it out very clearly. So now I want your signatures." He gestured at Jack. "You too."

"Me? What've *I* got to do with this?" Jack protested.

Ennis shrugged. "I don't like you, that's what."

"This is ridiculous," I said. "These contracts wouldn't be legally binding."

Ennis smirked at me. "That'll make a nice inscription on your headstone. These contracts are good enough for the people I work for. And that's all that matters to me."

"This is *bullshit!*" Jack shouted. "Listen, asshole, you don't just come in here waving that thing around. You don't do that to *me*, and you don't do that to my *friends*." Jack jumped up from the bed and squared off with Ennis. He seemed totally unafraid, as if his Kid America jacket had given him super crime-fighting powers.

"Jack! Be careful! This guy isn't joking around!" I warned.

"Don't worry. I know how to handle punks like this," muttered Jack through his teeth, his eyes locked with Ennis's.

"You *do*?"

"Yeah. You get right up in their grille and let 'em know you ain't giving up an inch of territory," answered Jack, still staring into Ennis's face.

Without a change of expression, Ennis abruptly dropped back a half step while bringing his right fist up into Jack's stomach. Not only had he done this with extraordinary speed, but he seemed to have used a very precise amount of force. He'd made his point to

Jack without seriously hurting him. Jack doubled over and fought for his breath for a few seconds, but that was the extent of the damage. He stepped back a pace, a safe distance from Ennis's fist, then resumed his seat at the foot of the bed.

"See what I mean, Mark?" he managed to wheeze. "Show 'em you mean business."

I was amazed by the complete lack of fear that Jack seemed to be showing. For my own part, I had to fight to keep a quaver out of my voice. "This *is* bullshit," I said. "You know perfectly well that none of us killed Shooter Deukart."

"Yeah? How would that be?" Ennis asked.

"Because you killed him yourself. An accident, probably, but dead just the same."

Ennis raised his eyebrows in mock curiosity.

"I'm guessing you were having a disciplinary session with Shooter and his heart gave out on him. You can't admit to your bosses that you fucked up, so you have to pretend that one of us did it. Then you killed Binh to send us all a message. But it isn't going to work. You don't have a plan, you're just freewheeling. If I were you, I'd be on a plane to South America right now, or some other place where your boss will never find you."

"You're wrong about Deukart," Ennis said simply. "I did off the riceball, though. Fuckin' Charlie." As he spoke, he was casually attaching a noise suppressor to the barrel of his revolver. "So here's what's going to happen. I get three signatures in the next sixty seconds or I open that bathroom door and I put a bullet into the broad's head. Sixty seconds after that I put one into the kid."

Although the predicament was extremely urgent, a childish corner of my brain was feeling peeved. Here I had confronted the killer with my brilliant theory, and he practically ignored me. It never happened that way in the movies, except to dunderhead detectives like Inspector Clouseau.

After a second or two, the gravity of our situation reasserted itself, and I shoved my wounded ego aside. I had little doubt that Ennis would carry out his threat without the slightest compunction. But I also knew there was a chance he might be bluffing. I had to buy some time. "I want to read the contract first," I said.

"Better read fast, lawyer." Ennis thrust the papers into my hands. "You've got fifty seconds."

Because I couldn't think of anything better to do, I began to read the documents. At that moment, a harsh, staccato rapping sounded at the door. It wasn't Evelyn in the bathroom; somebody in the hallway was knocking.

"Ignore it," ordered Ennis.

The rapping did not let up. It increased to an insistent pounding. "Open this goddamn door!" sounded a woman's voice from outside.

Ennis walked over and took a quick look out the peephole. He gestured to me with the gun. "Whoever it is, get rid of her. Say the wrong word and I won't be choosy about who gets shot."

I rose and approached the door. Jack, who had not been the least bit intimidated by the gun-wielding enforcer, had now gone pale as a sheet. I didn't have to look to know who was outside. And there would be no getting rid of her. I opened the door and got out of the way.

Brigid Corrigan stormed into the room. She paused just long enough to give me a painful punch on my left bicep. "You lying prick, I'll fix you later," she snarled.

Jack was on his feet again, backing into a corner between the bed and the wall, his hands raised in a defensive position. I noticed that Ennis had placed the gun inside his jacket. With the silencer still attached, it made a distinct bulge.

For the first few seconds, Brigid's fury was beyond words. She ripped and wheeled around the room like a Tasmanian devil, finally stopping six inches in front of Jack, her index finger stabbing into his chest bone. She yelled every obscenity in the book. Jack tried to stammer out a few words in his own defense, but he might as well have been shooting a squirt gun into a hurricane.

I looked at Ennis. The killer was obviously not happy that he had temporarily lost control of the situation. This was a very dangerous moment. Ennis was likely to resolve things with brutal violence at any time.

"Brigid," I pleaded, "why don't you go cool off somewhere, and we'll talk about this later."

She wheeled and stormed on me, shaking her finger in my face. "You! You sonofabitch, you don't get to talk about *anything!*" Ennis was about a foot away from her. I felt that it was a matter of seconds before he did something lethal. I had to get Brigid out of there.

For the first time, she seemed to notice Maddie Santos sitting on the bed. "And who is *this* floozy?" she ranted.

"*Floozy?*" Maddie shot back. "Listen, who do you think—"

She didn't get a chance to finish. With the speed of a striking cobra, Brigid ripped into Martin Ennis. He had at least ten inches and eighty pounds on her, but he never knew what hit him. Before anybody in the room understood what was happening, Ennis was face-down on the floor, Brigid's knee drilling into his spine, his left arm twisted behind his back in a position that threatened to pull his shoulder out of its socket.

"You wanna tell me what you're doing in my friend's room with a silenced gun in your pocket, asshole?"

Ennis grimaced in pain and disbelief. Maddie, Jack, and I looked on, dumbfounded and awed. The violence had been so unexpected and electrifying that it was several seconds before I could process a thought. "Careful, Brigid, he's very dangerous," I finally warned.

She shot me a withering look. "I figured that out by myself," she said. "Do something for me. Get on the phone, get me some backup. Not hotel security, real cops." She looked at Maddie. "Sorry about the floozy comment. I need you to come down here and help me disarm this guy." Finally, she said to Jack, "You. Worthless jackass. Do something useful for a change. I want you to come over here and sit on this guy's head."

"Sit on his head?"

"That's right. Don't put all your weight on him, though. He has to breathe."

Jack tiptoed around the bodies on the floor and lowered himself gingerly onto Ennis's head. He was careful to avoid eye contact. "What if he bites?" he asked.

"That's the whole idea of it," Brigid muttered through clenched teeth. "I'm hoping he will."

I dialed DiCarlo's number; he answered on the first ring. For a few seconds, there was quiet in the room except for the sound of me urgently explaining the situation to the captain, who told me to sit tight and wait for his men to arrive. Madelin searched underneath Ennis and carefully extracted his gun. Finally, Jack spoke from his perch on Ennis's head.

"Bridge, how did you know we were in trouble in here?"

"I had no idea. I was hunting for *you*, jerkoff. I didn't notice the guy's gun until I calmed down a little bit."

"You calmed down? I must have missed that part."

"Shut up."

Jack shut up. A few moments later, he spoke again. "So what took you so long, anyway?"

"I thought I'd give him a couple of minutes. I was hoping maybe he'd shoot you."

"No, not with him. I mean what took you so long to figure out that I was here at the Humpback?"

"You know what? I didn't have a clue. I was experimenting with *trusting* you. Until dickweed over there made that bogus phone call last night. Took me about two seconds to see through *that* bullshit."

Jack put his face into his hands. "I've outfinessed myself," he murmured.

"We'll talk about that later," Brigid said. It was clear that her rage was still simmering just beneath the surface, but she had more important things to attend to at the moment. "Who is this guy, Mark? Is he your killer?"

"I think so," I answered. "I've got him on tape admitting to at least one murder, and threatening to do more." I picked up Patrick's mini-recorder from the nightstand. During the initial confusion when Ennis had herded us out of the bathroom and into the bedroom, I had discreetly turned it on.

The bathroom door opened a crack. A tiny voice said, "Uncle Mark? Can we come out now?" Brigid shook her head vehemently at me. I hurried over to the bathroom door. Inside, Evelyn looked as though she were going to be sick. Patrick actually had been sick, though fortunately he had made it to the toilet on time.

"I want you to know that we're all safe," I said. "There's a police officer here who has the bad guy under control, okay? But until some more police come, it would be safest if you just stayed right in here. Okay?" Patrick looked unconvinced. "I'll tell you what. I'll stand right here outside this door to make sure nobody else can come in. All right?" Patrick nodded. At that moment, he seemed like a very small and innocent child.

"Evey? Are you all right?" I asked softly.

"I guess so. If you say we're safe." She also looked unconvinced. "Mark, what is all this about?"

"We have the guy who killed Shooter Deukart and Tran Le Binh in here. We have his gun and he's under control. I'm sorry you got mixed up in this, I really am."

Fortunately, DiCarlo already had several men present in the hotel. Inside of three minutes, there were two uniformed state troopers helping Brigid to secure the prisoner. The click of the handcuffs was the most comforting sound I had ever heard, and I suddenly remembered that I was still in the middle of the biggest poker game of my life. I looked at the clock on the nightstand. There were five minutes left in the break.

"Hey, uh, guys? We have to get back downstairs," I said. I turned to one of the troopers. "Officer, can you wait to take our statements? We need to get back down to the tournament."

The trooper frowned. "Captain DiCarlo is on his way here. We really ought to wait for him." He seemed uncertain.

"Can you get him on the phone? I'd like to talk to him."

A flurry of phone calls between me, DiCarlo, and Bob Herr added an extra thirty minutes to the break. I felt like we could have used an extra thirty hours, but it was better than nothing. I opened the mini-bar and passed out soda and candy bars. Evelyn volunteered to run down and get us all sandwiches. I looked at her in astonishment. "After what you just went through? You're amazing."

Evelyn shrugged. "Stay busy, I always say. Look out for Patrick till I get back, okay?"

Jack was being careful to keep himself on the opposite side of the room from Brigid, who in any event was too busy talking with the state troopers to pay much attention to him. Jack had a hangdog look that was in stark contrast with his usual animated appearance.

A few minutes later, DiCarlo arrived. He took each of us, in turn, into the bathroom and recorded our statements. I handed over the camcorder that contained Ennis's incriminating words.

"Thank you for your help on this," said DiCarlo. "Turning on that recorder was a heads-up move. I'm sorry you had to go through it. And I'm really sorry for the kid. Do you want us to do anything with him until his dad gets back? Maybe we can find a counselor or something…"

"No thanks. He's in good hands with Evelyn Gibbs. Whatever you can do for her, though, I'd appreciate. Anything to make sure she feels safe."

"Will do."

"So, this pretty much wraps it up, right?"

He spoke carefully. "I think it wraps it up as far as you and your friend Santos are concerned. I'm quite certain at this point that neither one of you is involved in any crimes." He paused and looked at me as if he were considering saying something more. Whatever it was, he apparently thought better of it. At that point I really didn't care. He stuck out his hand. "I'll see you again very soon. Good luck with the poker."

"Thanks." I shook DiCarlo's hand. It was something I didn't often have a chance to do with police officers—not in my line of work.

Evelyn appeared with sandwiches, and we wolfed them down. "I've gotta warn you, it's a real zoo down there," she said. "The press knows there's something going on up here. But the hotel security won't let anybody into the elevator or the stairwells unless they're a registered guest. So now you've got a mob of press waiting around the elevators and the gallery, and another mob waiting at the front desk to register, so they can get into the elevators."

"This looks like a job for Kid America," I said.

Jack shook his head sadly. "I'm afraid Kid America's crime-fighting days are over. I don't need the outfit anymore. Remember? My cover got blown." He looked at me. "Nice job acting on the phone last night, by the way. Some poker player. She read you in about two seconds."

"Hey, don't get on *me* about that! It wasn't my idea."

"Yeah, I know, I know." Jack was used to feeling in command of every situation. Now he felt lost. His greatest day ever was in danger of turning into his worst.

"Well, we'd better get going," Maddie announced.

Maddie and I started for the door. We paused as Jack timidly approached Brigid. She scowled at him. "Bridge?" he said in a low voice. "I'm sorry. I went way over the line. If you want me to, I'll forfeit the tournament. Just say the word."

Her scowl softened, just a bit. She considered him for a minute. "Just go win," she said. "We'll talk about it later."

Jack went away with a slight bounce in his step. If she had said, "Just go play," it would have been a putdown, as in, "Go play your child's game." But she had said, "Go win," and now he had a mission. It occurred to me that Eileen had never once told me to "Go win." It also occurred to me, for the first time since Brigid exploded into the room, that Jack wasn't the only guy who had been busted. I would be in deep shit with Eileen for my role in Jack's caper. Not quite as deep as Jack, but there would be hell to pay for sure.

"Hey, Brigid?" I asked. "Would you do me a favor and give Eileen a call for me? Tell her I'm all right. I'll call her as soon as I get the chance."

Brigid could have frozen me on the spot with a scornful response, but she showed mercy for the time being. "Sure thing. Just go play, all right? Good luck."

37

WHEN THE THREE OF us got into the elevator, we were once again alone. "Well, that was a relaxing little break," said Maddie. We laughed together. The murder case, and all the complications and threats that went with it, had now simply disappeared. It was as if I had been walking headfirst into a shrieking windstorm for the last four days and everything had instantly gone still and calm. The relief was palpable. I could feel the muscles in my chest moving more freely. I looked at Jack and Maddie with affection. They made a handsome pair.

The elevator opened onto a mob scene that was even worse than it had been earlier in the day. By this time, though, Bob Herr had his act together, and there were security officers available to escort us into the relative calm of the Showroom.

Back at the table, everybody wanted to hear the story. Jack took the lead in describing what had happened, displaying obvious pride in the heroic role of Brigid, and only slightly embellishing his own contribution. He said nothing about the disappearance of Kid America.

Willy Hopkins was still accompanied by Britta. I didn't ask him whether there was any news from Kenneth. Willy had a tremendous number of questions, which he directed at Maddie and me, ignoring what he assumed would be an unreliable recounting from Jack. I protested that I'd rather talk about it later. I needed to get my head back to the card table. Willy was persistent. Finally, I had to be short with him.

"Look, Willy, not now. We'll talk about this later."

The cards were dealt. According to every poker book or article ever written, Jack, Maddie, and I should have had no chance, given our mental states at the time. But nothing was going by the book anymore. In my case at least, the cards themselves seemed to be in control.

On the second hand, Bill Lane pushed his remaining $65,000 forward. In the small blind, I peeked at my cards and saw A♣ Q♣. If Lane had a small pair, I would be a slight underdog. I thought it was just as likely that Lane merely had one or two high cards and was desperately trying to improve his position by stealing the blinds. I raised, and Jack in the big blind folded. I had guessed right. Lane turned over Q♦ J♦. He needed a jack, or a bunch of diamonds. He didn't get either, and he was gone.

It went on that way for a while. Jeff Ford was eliminated shortly after Bill Lane. This time Jack was the beneficiary of a desperation bet. Maddie took a large pot from Sandy Baker. The blinds went up to $30,000 and $60,000, and there was no margin for error anymore. Entering a pot meant being prepared to risk all of your chips. Harvey Bangert, a legendary old pro from West Texas, was knocked out when Willy Hopkins paired his ace on the flop to beat Bangert's pocket tens. He left the table to a sustained round of applause from everybody in the Showroom.

I was surviving, but living from hand to hand. With $380,000, my stack was now second lowest. Sandy Baker's lead had been overtaken by Willy Hopkins, with Maddie at a close third, holding around $700,000.

I needed to make something happen soon. Sitting on the button, I found myself looking at another pair of queens. Queens had been my undoing more often than not, but I was happy to see them now. Willy Hopkins, in first position, opened with a raise to $150,000. *This is it.* I didn't have much to think about. If Willy had kings or aces, my queens would be a big underdog. If he held ace-king, I would be a very slight favorite. Any other cards in Willy's hand would leave me in charge. It was most likely that he held something less than queens. A big raise right now would probably take the pot, and might even lure Willy into calling me. So far in the tournament, he had played under control; I was hoping that now he would finally succumb to temptation.

I raised, going all in with my $380,000, and fixed a vacant smile on my friend Willy. *This is it*, I repeated to myself. Somewhere deep inside me there were nerves twanging all over the place, but I showed nothing. I hoped.

Willy's eyes lit up. Despite himself, a smile came over his face. With a sick feeling, I knew that my queens were overmatched, and my tournament was probably over.

There were three other players who hadn't acted yet, and Willy should've waited for them before he let his emotions show. If any of them had had any thoughts of calling the bet, they were abandoned when they saw the look of obvious delight playing on Willy's features. Jack tossed his cards into the muck pile. Maddie and Sandy followed.

With a triumphant air, Willy prepared to push his chips forward to call when a hand appeared on his shoulder. I had been so attentive to the game that I hadn't noticed Frank DiCarlo approaching from the other side of the table. Willy looked over his shoulder in surprise.

"Wilson Hopkins," spoke DiCarlo, "you are under arrest in connection with the death of Warren Deukart. You have the right to remain silent. You have the right…" The recitation of Willy's Miranda rights was swallowed up by the tumult that erupted all around him.

38

WHAT HAPPENED THEN WAS something of a blur. A moment of shocked stillness was followed by bedlam. The other players around the table were flabbergasted, and they all began talking at once. Willy Hopkins was enraged. He shouted furiously at DiCarlo and yelled at Britta to wheel him around so he could square off with the captain. Bob Herr came running onto the stage, fluttering his arms around out of sheer perplexity. Several reporters, ignoring the velvet ropes that cordoned off the playing area, charged the stage in an effort to record the moment firsthand. Security guards went after them.

Amidst the tumult, only Jack Shea kept his mind on the card game. He spread both hands out over the table and said to the dealer, "Watch those chips. If Hopkins doesn't say, 'Call,' his hand has to be folded. Right now those chips belong to Mark Newcomb." While chaos raged all around them, Jack and the dealer watched carefully to be sure that the arrangement of chips and cards was not disturbed.

With the obvious exception of Willy, nobody was more provoked by this new development than I was. For the moment I forgot the poker game, and my defense lawyer's instincts kicked in. I felt that I needed to be a part of whatever was happening between Willy and Frank DiCarlo.

Abandoning my pair of queens, I sprung out of my chair and rushed around to the other side of the table. At the same time, Sandy Baker pushed her chair backward and I tripped over one of the legs. Sprawled on the floor, I was lucky not to be trampled.

I scrambled to my feet in time to see Willy being wheeled off the stage by a uniformed trooper, Britta following dutifully behind. Two other troopers barricaded the backstage door through which they had gone. I recognized one of them and begged to be allowed through the door, to no avail. I pulled a business card from my wallet and scribbled a note across the back: "Must talk to you ASAP."

"Would you give this to the captain?" I asked.

"First chance I get, sir," responded the trooper. At the moment, though, he clearly had his hands full holding back the reporters.

I returned to the table. Bob Herr was frantically trying to restore order. The security guards' attempts at herding the reporters back off the stage were having little success until Maddie Santos hauled off and punched the reporter from the *Chicago Tribune* squarely in the mouth. That seemed to get the message across, and the rest of the reporters went more or less quietly back to their designated area. And every gambler in the room who wasn't already smitten with Maddie became so.

"Uh, thank you…for that, Maddie…I guess," said Herr when things were quiet enough for him to speak. "Listen, this is a big shock for all of us. We're going to take a twenty-minute break while we sort this thing out."

The table erupted with sound again as the other players started talking all at once. "Whose pot is this?" "What happens to Willy's chips?" "Who has the official rules?" "Split 'em up, gotta split 'em up." "No way, they just get blinded off." "That's Mark's pot! That's Mark's pot!" Jack's voice rose over the din.

I didn't say anything. I sat with my eyes on the two cards that Willy Hopkins had left lying on the table. They were face-down, but I didn't need to see them to know that they were either kings or aces. Unless the top of the deck contained another queen, Willy would have had all of my chips. I would be out, and Willy would have a commanding lead. *All he really wanted was to win one of these things,* I thought to myself. *What the hell is Frank DiCarlo thinking?*

Finally, things cooled down enough for Bob Herr to assert himself. Now he showed why they paid him the big bucks. "Okay," he said, "the rules here are clear. If Hopkins doesn't respond to Newcomb's bet, he folds the hand. All subsequent hands will be dealt to his position and folded if he's not at the table. His chips will be used to pay his blinds every time it's his turn, whether he's here or not.

"But before we go that way, I'm going to freeze the action until I get some word from the state police about the likelihood of Hopkins being able to resume playing in a reasonable time."

Sandy Baker tried to argue that there should be no delay. Apparently, she couldn't wait to start feasting on Willy's chips. Herr wasn't having any of it. "This is a highly unusual situation," he said, "and the rules of the federation give me extraordinary powers in the event of an emergency at the table."

"Dean Wormer invokes Double Secret Probation," Jack muttered under his breath—an allusion that nobody seemed to catch except me. Despite the gravity of the situation, I almost laughed out loud, and I had to choke it back with a cough.

Herr continued. "So sit tight. I'll be back as soon as I can. The cards and chips on the table are not to be disturbed."

We sat. What had been pandemonium a few minutes ago was now awkward silence. I stared at Willy's chips and tried to imagine what could have led DiCarlo to arrest him.

I'd warned Willy that DiCarlo was connecting him to Shooter's mob problem. But it never occurred to me that it would be anything more than an embarrassment to Willy. Obviously, DiCarlo wasn't buying the theory that Ennis had done both of the killings on his own. But what could he have on Willy other than a vague connection?

And Willy had been at dinner that night with a table full of witnesses. But no Kenneth. Kenneth hadn't been there; he was off setting up a card game—a game that Shooter Deukart expected to play in. Kenneth had to be the wild card. I should have been paying more attention to him from the beginning. Dammit.

Bob Herr returned. "Okay, I talked to the captain. It looks as though we're going to have to assume that Willy Hopkins will not be returning for the duration of this tournament. That means that his cards will be folded by the dealer, including this hand, and he will continue to pay the blinds when his turn comes around. If he's able to return at any time, he can resume playing with whatever chips he has remaining."

The dealer reached for Willy's cards to sweep them into the pile. "Hey, show the cards!" Maddie exclaimed, though she knew better.

"The hand was folded. We don't turn them over," said the dealer.

"We don't need to see the cards," I said. "Everybody knows what he had."

The dealer pushed Willy's $150,000 bet, along with the blinds and antes, over to me. Combined with the $380,000 I'd had, I was back to a respectable level.

Willy's chips were now up for grabs. Once every six hands, the big blind came around to his position, and the dealer took $60,000 from his stack and put it into the pot. On the next hand, it was the small blind, and $30,000 went into the pot. Because Willy wasn't there to defend his bets, the rest of the players were free to scrap for them. What followed was later written up by poker writers as "The Battle for Willy's Blinds."

I'm not proud to admit this, but once again the poker action blew all other thoughts from my mind. Willy Hopkins could have been sitting in the electric chair with the copper bowl on his shaved skull and the leather straps tightened around his arms. At that moment, I just wanted to be winning his chips.

Which I wasn't. The Battle for Willy's Blinds wasn't going my way. Without strong cards, I tried limping into the pot a couple of times, hoping that everybody else would fold and I could pick up the blinds on the cheap. But that was weak, foolish play. Each time I was pushed off by another player with a larger stack.

At last, sitting in first position with $480,000 in front of me, I found myself looking at A ♥ 8 ♣. With only five players in the game, this was a legitimate hand, though far from powerful. I counted out $150,000 and placed it onto the table in three stacks of ten $5,000 chips, casually spreading one of the stacks so the dealer could easily count them. I wanted everybody to fold so I could win the blinds.

Two to my left, on the button, Maddie Santos called. *Uh-oh.* Sandy Baker, in the small blind, called the remaining $120,000. *Double uh-oh.* I had hoped to pick up the blinds without a contest, but now I had the disturbing feeling that I might be stuck in a three-way knife fight holding a plastic spatula. I was going to need a hell of a flop to go any further with this one.

The flop was a puzzle—10 ♥ 9 ♠ 8 ♦. A pair for me, but with dangerous possibilities for Maddie or Sandy. Either of them could easily have a higher pair with ace-nine or ace-ten, in which case I was screwed unless I bet very aggressively and scared them off the pot. Not that either of these birds was the scaring type. I thought it unlikely that either of them would have called my raise with a queen-jack, so I wasn't too worried that one of them had flopped a straight. But it was possible that one of them could have queen-queen or jack-jack and have me beaten—or, worse, pocket nines or tens for three of a kind, in which case I was completely dead. All things considered, this didn't look like the moment for my heroic last stand.

I checked. Maddie and Sandy both checked behind me. Maybe they had nothing, and my eights were the best hand. Or maybe not. It wasn't going to change the way I played the hand, because I had already decided not to fight this one out.

The turn card was dealt—a three of diamonds, no help for anybody. I checked, and Maddie wasted little time firing out a big bet.

"Four hundred thousand." It was enough to put me all in if I called it. *Well, I'm out of this hand*, I thought.

Then something very unusual happened.

Sandy Baker, sitting to Maddie's immediate left and next to act, laughed resignedly and said, "Dammit, girl, you've got me again." Maddie smiled and flashed Sandy one of her cards.

Jack, sitting to my left, almost jumped out of his chair. "Show one, show all," he called out.

"What!?" Maddie looked at him in disbelief.

"You flashed a card. Now everybody gets to see it. Including Mark."

"Bullshit!" Maddie snarled. "You don't know what you're talking about. Sandy folded. She's out of the hand already." If a casual observer had been told that Maddie and Jack were friends who had shared dinner and drinks several times in the past few days, he never would have believed it. The two of them were glowering at each other like jackals squaring off over a kill.

Jack looked at the dealer. "I'm right, aren't I?" According to tournament rules, if any player shows a card to another player at the table, then everybody at the table is entitled to see it: "Show one, show all." But if the player who is shown the card has already folded, then the card doesn't need to be shown to the remaining players until after the hand is finished.

"Well, as far as I'm concerned, I already folded," Sandy Baker said as she tossed her cards into the center of the table. The dealer looked at her uncertainly, then at Maddie. He plainly wasn't going to take responsibility for this one. Bob Herr strode over. "What's this about?" he demanded.

"Maddie showed a card to Sandy before Sandy folded her cards. So she has to show it to Mark," Jack declared. I suppose I should have been advocating on my own behalf at this point, but Jack seemed to be taking my part with plenty of enthusiasm. Besides, the way Maddie was looking at Jack, I don't know if I would've had the guts to get in the way of all that loathing.

"That's a crock of shit," Maddie said fiercely. "Sandy folded, and I showed her a card. I'll show it to the table after the hand is over."

"Did Ms. Baker fold her hand?" Herr asked the dealer calmly.

The dealer, a nice-looking guy with a name tag that read "William," tried his best to look like he was sure of himself. "Well . . . ," he said slowly, "she made a comment like she wasn't happy, but she didn't say, 'Fold,' and she didn't muck her cards."

"That's the way I saw it too," Herr said. William was visibly relieved. Herr considered for less than five seconds. "Well, the rules are pretty clear here. Sandy didn't fold her hand, so Maddie has to show the card to the whole table."

"That is bullshit! *Bullshit!*" If Willy Hopkins had been there, he might have called it "codswallop" or "humbug," but what Maddie lacked in vocabulary she was making up for in fury. I had seen a lot of new things this week, but Maddie Santos's beautiful face twisted into an ugly purple rage may have been the most disturbing.

She looked around the table for help, but everybody including me was busy studying their chips, or the felt on the table, or their fingernails. Everybody except Jack, who looked steadily at Maddie and said, "It's a game, Maddie. You have to follow the rules."

I didn't think she could get any scarier, but the look she gave Jack just then would have knocked the horns off a bull. Jack never flinched.

Maddie could see that she wasn't going to get any help on this, so she reached for her card to show it. It briefly occurred to me that I could do something gallant—maybe cover my eyes, or turn my head away. Like a nobleman in a duel who shoots his pistol straight up into the air. It would be ten out of ten for style, that's for sure. But it turned out I wasn't all that gallant or stylish after all, because I just looked greedily at the card.

A jack of spades.

Ah, so. Maddie is on a straight draw. Her big bet was a semi-bluff, meaning that she had only four cards to a straight. She hoped to bluff everybody out of the hand, but if somebody called her, she still had a 22 percent chance of making the straight or a pair of jacks on the river.

So what was her other card? Most likely an ace, which would leave my pair of eights with a three-to-one advantage over her jack. But what if she had a jack-queen and her straight was already made? Or a pair of jacks, for that matter? In either case, I would be hugely behind. But that didn't make sense. She didn't show Sandy her made hand; she showed her only the one jack, because that was the card that revealed her holding. And otherwise, why would she have been so upset about having to show me the card? She was bluffing on a straight draw. I had her nailed. It was that simple.

"I don't suppose you want to show me the other one too?" I asked. From the glare that she shot back, I could see that my feeble attempt at breaking the tension had not had the desired effect. Maddie Santos was going to hate me and Jack forever now, that was plain.

Too bad.

"I'll call," I said. I turned over my cards. "Eights."

Maddie's features went blank and she looked at me for a very long moment with her remaining card face-down on the table. There was not an iota of expression on her face as she flipped it over. Jack of diamonds. She had a pair of jacks, and I had a puny pair of eights, with all of my chips in the pot.

To everybody else in the Showroom, this was a drama of Shakespearean proportions—Sophoclean, even, for those who remembered their high school literature lessons. Ambition, pride, and a startling turn of events, culminating in tragedy. To me, though, it was much more basic than that. Just a double-barreled blast that tore my gut open.

I suppose I had some vague hope that the remaining card would be an eight or an ace. But to be honest, I don't even remember watching William deal the card. Whatever it was, it wasn't what I needed. Maddie had all of my chips and I was out of the tournament.

39

HERE IS A SORROWFUL truth about gambling: the pain of losing is more intense than the pleasure of winning. Sometimes a lot more. At that moment, the fact that I had finished sixth and won $123,000 wasn't real. What was real was the aching, hollow pit that filled the space where my brain, lungs, and stomach used to be.

I was too stunned to understand that Maddie had snookered me. Later it would dawn on me that she had wanted to show me the jack all along, that she had put on an Oscar-worthy performance. But right then I couldn't think about anything except how awful it felt to be out of the game.

I stood near the table, watching the remaining players, and pining. I felt like a wet dog stuck outside during a rainstorm, looking through a window, whining to be let inside. Jack pulled an amazing play out of nowhere: slow-playing a monster hand, checking all the way to the river, inducing a big bet from Sandy Baker, then pouncing on it. It should have been me. I would have fed Jack piece by piece to Martin Ennis's meaner brother for a chance to get back into the game. Jack Shea and Madelin Santos were now the two dominant chip leaders. Who would ever have guessed it?

I heard a *pssst! pssst!* from the direction of the gallery. Zip Addison was trying to get my attention. I must have given him a very evil look, because his face blanched even paler than usual and he buried it in his notebook.

A few minutes later, Trooper Schmidt walked up and tapped me on the shoulder. "Mr. Newcomb? Captain DiCarlo would like to talk with you now."

This was a timely distraction. As I had done four days ago, I followed Trooper Schmidt through the gallery and down the corridor to the office suite that was being used by the state police. The further we walked from the Showroom, the better I was able to shake off the feeling of doom that had been on me since the jack of diamonds hit the table. It occurred to me that things could be worse. It occurred to me that my friend Willy Hopkins was under arrest for a crime I felt sure he had nothing to do with.

I found Frank DiCarlo sitting at a writing desk. He gestured to a chair and put down his pen and paper.

I began, "Unless there's something I don't know, a viable theory has Martin Ennis killing Shooter Deukart—"

"There's plenty you don't know," DiCarlo cut me off. "For starters, Ennis was in Las Vegas Monday night while Deukart was killed." He gave me a second to absorb this. "The second thing you don't know is that two weeks ago, Wilson Hopkins had a meeting in Las Vegas with one Phillip Shubert. The purpose of that meeting was to discuss buying out Deukart's loan, which Shubert was holding."

"Nothing illegal about that."

DiCarlo ignored my comment. "Hopkins had learned about the distressed situation that Deukart was in. Apparently, he had a notion about buying out the contract and letting Deukart pay off his loan at no interest. All he wanted was one thing. He wanted Deukart to take a dive every once in a while. Throw a tournament his way, if he had a chance to. Occasionally entertain some of Hopkins's business cronies by allowing them to beat the great Shooter Deukart. Generally be Hopkins's little poker lapdog."

"C'mon, Frank, do you really—"

He interrupted me again. "Deukart, amazingly, wouldn't go along with this. Apparently, he valued the integrity of the game more than he did his own freedom. Navy man. So Hopkins told Conway to talk some sense to him."

"Conway?"

"Kenneth Conway. Hopkins's attendant. Guy's had a tough life. Kicked around all over the place."

DiCarlo was holding two pieces of paper. "Is that his rap sheet?" I asked.

He nodded. "And some bio we took from his statement."

"Can I see it?"

DiCarlo held out the papers across the desk.

"Funny," I said as I took them. "I never thought of Kenneth as having a last name." I scanned the pages. "A lot of penny-ante stuff here. Odometer tampering? C'mon . . . No serious convictions . . . Hmm . . . Looks like he spent a few years in Phoenix before he connected with Willy."

"Does that mean something to you?" asked DiCarlo.

"Huh?" I shook my head, handing the sheets back. "No, I guess not."

DiCarlo continued. "Hopkins ordered his man to work Deukart over, show him the price of ingratitude. So Conway told Deukart that the location of the Spaniards' card game was changed, that he would drive him there. Got him out in the parking lot and laid into him. Conway got carried away, and Deukart's heart gave out. Conway didn't know what to do, went back to Hopkins. Instead of calling an ambulance and facing up to what he'd done, Hopkins took the weasel's way out. Gave Conway instructions to go back to the body and mess with it."

"This is all according to Kenneth Conway," I interjected.

DiCarlo looked annoyed. "According to his freely given confession, that's right." He paused, as if expecting more argument from me, then went on. "Hopkins knew Santos kept a gun in her room, and Conway knew how to get a hotel door open. So he thought he could get away with it by throwing out a lot of red herrings. What he didn't count on was Shubert's guy Martin Ennis being so obvious. He sent Conway to chase Ennis off, but it was too late.

"When the Vegas cops tracked down Ennis's connections for us, we found out that Hopkins had been talking with them. I pulled Conway in and he told the whole story. Signed a statement this morning."

"And you'll recommend the judge goes easy on Kenneth, in exchange for his testimony."

"That's right. Involuntary manslaughter, something like that. He'll do some time, a couple of years or so. Hopkins will face more serious charges, but we haven't worked those out with the DA yet."

"What about Anita Wilson? How is Willy Hopkins connected to her?"

"Dead end," DiCarlo shrugged. "Absolutely nothing checks out on her. As far as we can tell, she's just a law-abiding citizen who happens to have a freaky aunt in Miami. Apparently, there's some history there with Hopkins, but we haven't got that sorted out yet."

"You're sure about all of this."

"We have Conway's statement admitting the entire thing. We have four different people telling us that Conway disappeared from the Spaniards' suite the night of the killing. And we have blood in the trunk of Hopkins's car. The DNA test will seal the deal. Then there's Ennis. He isn't talking yet, but when he finds out that his Vegas pals aren't sending him any high-priced lawyers, he'll start to see us as his best chance. We'll get corroborating evidence from him too."

"In exchange for not bringing Murder One charges against him for killing Binh."

"Something like that. Murder One is a tough case to make anyway. You know that."

"You couldn't have arrested Willy during a break? You had to humiliate him like that?"

"I had planned to arrest him during the break, but your escapade with Martin Ennis interrupted me. By the time I had that sorted out, the game was back on. And I wasn't about to sit there and let him win the tournament. So I moved in."

Something was seriously wrong here. DiCarlo had what he needed to close the case. I just didn't believe he had the truth. "Where is Conway right now?" I asked.

"In the process of making bail. He's being extremely cooperative, and we want to keep him that way."

That was when the light bulb finally went on inside my deeply fatigued, caffeine-riddled, gambled-out brain. I sat silently for a minute. DiCarlo looked at me. "Something else on your mind?" he asked.

I started to speak, but thought better of it. I stood up, and DiCarlo offered his hand. "I want you to know I appreciate the help you gave me with this case," he said. "And congratulations on doing so well with the poker. How the hell you could concentrate on a game with all the crap flying around this week, I'll never understand."

I shook his hand, but without the warmth of our parting a few hours ago. I walked out of the office, down the corridor, into the gallery, and out of the hotel.

40

I sat in my car, parked across the street from the Falmouth County Jail. DiCarlo had made it clear that the police would support Kenneth's bail application, and I was going to be there when he got out.

The case against Willy Hopkins was all wrong. It didn't fit with everything I knew about the man. Willy cutting a deal with the loan sharks was just like him, but the idea that he would use Shooter to throw a tournament was ludicrous.

DiCarlo was relying almost completely on the word of Kenneth Conway, and I had noticed something in Kenneth's biography that the police seem to have missed. Kenneth was the key, all right. But I had a feeling now—a very bad feeling—that he was the key to an altogether different set of answers.

A few minutes after five, with the afternoon sun giving way to a cool October evening, Kenneth emerged from the front door of the jailhouse. I sat up straight and twisted the key in the ignition of my 1972 Dodge Swinger—"the heap," Eileen called it. I often had to remind Eileen that I had known this car a lot longer than I had known her.

Kenneth turned to his right and began walking. Yarmouth was not a big town, and wherever Kenneth was going he seemed to have no need of a cab.

This presented me with my first problem. Surveillance work was not in my job description at the public defender's office. I had never in my life tried to follow anybody. On the other hand, I had seen Jim Rockford do it a hundred times on TV. How hard could it be? It turned out that following a walking person, in a car, without being noticed, was something of a difficult trick. Doing it in a faded orange Dodge Swinger was even more difficult. Obviously, I could not creep along behind him at four miles per hour. Eventually, I improvised a method. I watched Kenneth until he had gone a block or two, then caught up in my car and pulled into a new parking space not too far behind. This would have been very obvious to anybody who was bothering to watch me. I hoped that nobody was watching.

Fortunately for me and my limited surveillance skills, Kenneth did not have far to go to reach his destination, which turned out to be the local NiteTime Inn, part of a chain of inexpensive roadside motels. I drove several blocks past the inn, made a U-turn as discreetly as possible, and pulled my car into a parking spot across the street and down the block. Within a couple of minutes, I saw Kenneth step out of the office, walk a few paces, and turn the key in the door of a room whose number I couldn't make out. I pondered whether I should move closer to get the number of the room, but decided not to risk being spotted for such a minor matter. I should have noticed that just down the block another car had pulled into a parking space.

41

I SETTLED IN FOR some serious waiting. Afternoon passed into evening, and there was no sign of movement from Kenneth's room. The tedium was excruciating. This was something that *The Rockford Files* had not prepared me for. I was completely used up to begin with, and the task of sitting still for hours and not falling asleep was far more than I could manage on my own. The solution, obviously, was to find some coffee. Fortunately, there was a diner at the far end of the block from the NiteTime, directly across from my car.

Trying hard to stay out of sight of Kenneth's room, I crossed to the diner and ordered two large cups to go. At the rate I'd been downing the brew for the last five days, I guessed that my metabolism was now closer to that of a ferret than it was to a human being's. No matter. There would be a nice long sleep waiting for me when I finally got home to Brooklyn. Never mind that I was scheduled to go back to work tomorrow. You can't represent clients if you're unconscious, and I planned to get good and unconscious for a long time as soon as this was over.

Local news on the car radio announced that Madelin Santos had beaten Jack Shea in the final hand of the Northeast Open. I didn't feel glad for her. I kept mentally replaying the hand in which she knocked me out. Obviously, Maddie had wanted to show the jack to make me think she had nothing but a straight draw. How could I have fallen for a stunt like that? And where had Maddie Santos gone to acting school? The whole thing was unbelievable.

When I wasn't brooding over my demise at the table, I also had plenty of time to sort out everything I knew about Shooter Deukart's death. Unfortunately, what I had seen in Kenneth's file didn't leave me a whole lot left to think about.

The drowsiness and the coffee and the murder and the poker chased each other around in my mind until I felt I was going to go nuts. I had to do something. Under cover of darkness, I thought it would be safe to get out of the car and move my body around a little. On the far side of the Swinger, protected from view of the NiteTime, I did some jumping jacks to revive my circulation and my sanity. I felt a little silly doing jumping jacks on a sidewalk in the middle of the night. This was a maneuver that Rockford would never be caught dead performing.

Jumping up and down reminded me that I was still wearing my lucky dice underwear. I toyed with the idea of using the pay phone outside the diner to call Eileen, but decided not to. She was surely wondering why I hadn't called her. Just as surely, she was anxious to ream me out for my role in Jack's little indiscretion. And for not telling her about Binh being killed. Later for that.

I also didn't want to have to explain to her what I was doing at that particular moment. She would've thought I was insane, and quite possibly would have alerted the local police the minute she got off the phone with me. I could hear her now: "Who do you think you are, Humphrey Bogart?"

Eileen would have been right, of course. I *was* trying to act like Bogey, and I was way out of my league. *Damn, I'm a dead money player in this game,* I thought. *All I know is what I've seen on TV.*

Of course I should have gone straight to DiCarlo with my suspicions. But I wasn't going to do that to my friend until I made sure for myself.

It was a little after four in the morning when the door to Kenneth's room finally opened, and the unmistakable silhouette of the powerful man was illuminated in the doorway. Kenneth moved through the parking area in front of the motel, to the sidewalk, where he walked down the block and entered the diner. A few minutes later, a pair of headlights appeared a mile or so up the street. I watched intently as the car slowed in front of the diner and came to rest at the first available parking spot.

One person—wearing a bulky jacket and a baseball cap—emerged from the car and entered the diner. I couldn't see for sure who it was, but I was not in doubt. I felt a little sick.

The diner's windows were the only thing on the block that was lit. Kenneth was plainly visible, sitting in a booth with his face turned toward the front window of the diner. Clearly, there was a lively disagreement going on. Kenneth's face was as expressive as I had ever seen it, and he was waving his hands in obvious agitation. I could see his companion reach out, take Kenneth's hands, and hold them on the tabletop for several minutes as the conversation continued.

Ten minutes later, the pair emerged from the diner, got into the car, and drove out of town to the south. I followed at a distance. When the car cleared town, I had no doubt where it was heading.

I wanted to get there first. I hit the accelerator and passed on the left, turning my head slightly sideways to avoid being recognized. A minute later, I found myself being passed by a different car that was traveling at a reckless speed. "Kids," I muttered.

42

I WAITED IN A soft, upholstered chair in a corner of the lobby of the Humpback Hotel and Casino. The place was deserted. At 4:50 a.m., with the casino closed, the Humpback didn't want their night clerks standing around with nothing to do. Any guest who needed help at this hour could use the phone at the reception desk to call a clerk out of a back room. Other than a parking attendant dozing in a chair outside the main entrance, there was nobody around.

Across the lobby, the entrance to the casino was also unnaturally quiet. The tables had closed at four and the slot machines were silent. The last of the gamblers had drifted out the door, and only the distant whirring of a vacuum gave evidence of another human presence in the place. It was amazing how the sudden absence of gambling action could clear a place out so quickly.

I was surprised, and a little concerned, that the area was so deserted. I caught myself thinking in B-movie dialogue: *Quiet ... too quiet.* This reminded me that I was *not* watching a corny old movie on AMC, and if things got ugly I would not be able to get out of it by switching channels. I knew I ought to be calling DiCarlo's cell phone; it was clearly the prudent move at this point. I wasn't prepared to do that yet, but I wasn't sure why. I also knew that behind the cashier's cage on the far end of the casino there would be people busily counting money—the one activity in a casino that would always be going on, twenty-four hours a day. And where there was cash, of course, there would be armed security guards.

The chair was too soft. Mel Torme was crooning "Too Close for Comfort" over the sound system, and the power of the coffee had finally reached its limit. I found myself drifting into Torme's famous velvet fog, on the verge of slipping into genuine slumber, when I was jolted awake as the front door of the hotel opened and the capped figure in the oversized jacket walked very quickly through the lobby to the elevator bank. It was a measure of the strange silence of the place that the sound of the door had seemed so loud.

I was certain now that I knew the truth. Less than five minutes later, the red light above one of the elevators lit up with a gentle bing. Shortly after that, Maddie Santos reappeared, this time clasping a small gym bag, and hurried back through the lobby toward the front door.

"So, Maddie. I have to give you credit for a magnificent performance," I said. She froze in place and stared around as I pulled myself up from the chair and stepped into the light.

"Oh, Mark. It's you. My God, you scared me half to death." She forced a smile as though she was glad to see me, but even I could see through that one. I walked across the lobby, past the whaling boat, and stopped a few feet in front of her.

"You had me completely fooled," I said. "It was brilliantly done."

She smiled again. "Listen, I'm sorry about that. I guess it was a cheap stunt, but maybe I wanted to win too much. And when the thought popped into my head to show the card, I knew Jack would jump all over it. He's incredibly loyal to you, you know. I hope you don't hate me for it."

"No, I don't hate you. But I'm not talking about the tournament."

She looked confused. "No? Well, listen, Mark, I have a ride waiting for me and I have to get going. I'll probably see you down in Atlantic City next weekend, right?" Maddie began to walk around me, but I moved sideways and blocked her path. She bumped into me. I backed away a couple of feet. She looked me in the eye and made a move to go around me the other way. I stepped sideways, and she bumped into me again. I stepped back.

"I got a look at Kenneth's sheet, Maddie, and something jumped out at me... something that Willy mentioned once and DiCarlo must have missed. Kenneth worked a few years as a mechanic at Saintly Motors in Phoenix. 'Saintly' is an English translation of 'Santos.' Saintly Motors had to be the dealership your father owned before Shooter broke him down."

"Mark, what the hell are you talking about?"

"That's when I finally saw it. You're a great card player, but I didn't realize that you could pull a bluff in real life as well as you do at the table. The same way you showed me the jack and made yourself look vulnerable, you showed DiCarlo your gun. A gambit worthy of a world champion. You knew they'd be looking at you pretty hard anyway, so why not give them something to focus on? You made sure the gun would be found. Nobody could be dumb enough to let her own gun be used in a murder if she had something to do with planning it. And it worked. They never took you seriously as a suspect. Like Jack said, the best place to hide is right out in the open. And you dragged me into it so you could get good intelligence on what the cops were thinking."

Maddie gave me an exasperated look. "Listen, Mark, I know you're upset about losing the tournament, and probably mad as hell at me for it. But why don't we talk about this later." She made another move to step past me, and I blocked her path again. She looked me straight in the eye, and this time her look wasn't smiling or confused or exasperated. It was pleading.

"So you and Kenneth have known each other for years. Tell me something. Has he been in love with you this whole time?"

She nodded, slowly.

"And you've never loved him back. But that didn't stop you from asking him to kill Shooter Deukart for you. When Kenneth told you what Willy was trying to do for Shooter, I guess you saw your chance. Kenneth does the deed, and everything falls down on Willy."

"He hates Willy," she said. "You've seen the way Willy treats him. Enjoys humiliating him."

"Sounds like maybe you *do* care about Kenneth a little."

"Sure I do. Just not the way he wants me to. He was like an older brother to me when my dad disappeared."

"So Kenneth turns on Willy, gives a story to the police, and goes to the can for a few years. When he's out, you pay him off with a share of the money you earned while he was in, right? And everybody's happy. Except Willy, of course. And Shooter. And then you didn't mind dragging your lover Anita into this, either."

Maddie laughed. "Lover! What is this fixation you have with this woman? I don't even *know* her. Kenneth found out about her family from Willy." She looked at me closely and cocked her head with a little smile. "My God, what an imagination you have." Maddie chose that moment to remove the baseball cap, where her hair had been tucked up in a ponytail. Casually, she raised both arms behind her head to undo the ponytail and shake it out. With her elbows back and her hands behind her head, the front of her jacket parted and I had to resist the urge to stare at her breasts.

"Anyway," I said, mentally slapping myself, "neither one of you counted on your picking up a million in cash this week. All of a sudden, doing the time doesn't look so appealing to Kenneth. He wants his money right now, wants to skip bail and never be seen again. Am I right?"

"Well, can you blame him? I thought it would take me at least a couple of years to save two hundred thousand for him, but all of a sudden here it is." She hoisted the gym bag.

"So, Maddie. If you weren't with Anita in your room, who *were* you with that night?"

She looked mysterious. "Oh, Mark, you really don't want to know." She lowered her voice to a sultry growl. "All I can tell you is that there were several people involved. And money changed hands."

"What?!"

Maddie laughed. "Oh my God, do you have any idea how easy it is to play with a man's mind? I was in the *casino*, you jerk, sitting at a Caribbean Stud table, making sure my picture was being recorded by the security cameras. You men are just unbelievable. A pretty girl won't account for herself for a couple of hours and your imagination runs wild. So predictable."

"I don't get it, Maddie. Why did you have to do this? Why take this kind of risk?"

Her voice rose. "I don't think there's any way for you to understand. What he did to my dad—it's like he ripped my heart out. Do you know what it's like to hate somebody *so much* that you don't *want* him dead, you *need* him dead? I'm sure you don't. Let me tell you, it's like a disease. You have to get rid of it before you can start living your life again. I had to find a way to get rid of my hate."

"Did it work?"

"Actually, yeah. It did. It feels good." She stared at me defiantly, as if daring me to tell her she was wrong.

"You got Binh killed."

Maddie looked genuinely troubled. "I never knew anything about him. He was just there, just got in the way. I feel bad about it, but I don't feel like it was my fault."

"So here we are." I stood facing her. Directly behind me was the old whaling boat, and beyond that was the hotel entrance.

She looked me in the eyes. "Yes. Here we are."

There was a moment's silence. Neither of us seemed sure of what we wanted.

"I can't let Willy Hopkins take the rap for this, Maddie."

She took a step closer to me and spoke. "I have to tell you something, Mark. There was another reason why I wanted to keep you involved." I shifted my feet uncomfortably.

"To be perfectly honest, Mark ... I feel something for you. Something pretty strong. I have for a long time. I was hoping if we were caught up in this together, it would bring us closer."

Her eyes locked onto mine, and I couldn't find the power to speak. My head felt suddenly numb, and I was vaguely aware of my face going flush.

"I'm so used to men trying to paw all over me. You were always so ... reserved. Cool. That's sexy. But I know that you've wanted me the whole time. C'mon, admit it. That night up in your room, you were almost ready to go for it, weren't you? If it weren't for that damn kid staying with you, we'd be lovers right now."

She slid her jacket off and let it fall to the floor. I couldn't speak, and my ears were full of buzzing, but a corner of my mind continued to function. Hadn't I seen this happen in a movie?

"It isn't too late, Mark." She stepped toward me again and murmured, "No fooling this time." Now she was breathtakingly, heart-poundingly close, inside the space where thoughts go dim and nothing exists except what the body wants right now. I managed to retreat a step. Just one. My head bumped softly into the side of the whaling boat, which was now right behind me. Maddie moved into me, lifting her arms and spreading her hands across the front of my shoulders. Her breasts grazed lightly against my chest.

Through the fog that was enveloping my brain, I remembered the movie scene. Where the sultry villainess pretends to be in love with Bogey, but he keeps his head and doesn't fall for it. He lets the cops come for her and he walks off alone into the rainy night. Except this was different. Maddie really did want me. Didn't she?

Maddie whispered. "What do you say we climb up into the boat and see if we can get it to rock a little bit." She pulled back slightly, and I made the mistake of glancing down. Her nipples were swollen, erect. This was no phony acting job, it was as real as it gets. If she had glanced down at me, she would have seen that I was as real as it gets too.

I had never betrayed my wife before, hadn't even come close. Now my hands were aching to reach up and take Maddie—with only a small, insistent mote of conscience straining to hold them back.

I never got the chance to tell Maddie no.

Kenneth must have been watching through the front window, and when she drew close to me it was more than he could stand to see. The large front door burst open, and the hulking man stomped into the lobby, glaring at me with what appeared to be murderous intent.

At the same time, something clattered to the floor next to the whaling boat. A ballpoint pen. Zip Addison stuck his head up over the gunwale of the boat, looking sheepish. Then he gave Maddie a twisted smile. "You are so busted," he said.

Maddie stood up straight and looked at me with fury. "You bastard!" she spat, and hit me across the face with her right hand.

I didn't know who to turn to in my amazement. My mind and my senses were still in a muddle from the close encounter with infidelity, which, if the force of Maddie's right cross was anything to go by, was no longer an option in any event. Then Kenneth seized everybody's attention by letting loose a low, guttural bawl and advancing across the lobby. Zip Addison was between him and me, so I liked my odds. Kenneth didn't even look at Addison as he went, not around him or over him, but straight through him. He didn't stop to glance at Addison's mangled body crumpled on the floor as he came directly at me.

"Kenneth! No!" Maddie pleaded, to no apparent effect.

I wasn't going to wait around to see if the beauty could calm the beast. I dashed for the nearest cover, which happened to be behind the reception desk that ran along one side of the lobby.

If surveillance work had been a stretch for me, physical combat was even further out of my league. I grabbed the nearest phone and searched for a button that looked as though it might summon a security guard—or three or four—but Kenneth didn't give me any time. He vaulted over the top of the desk and landed about twenty-five feet from where I was standing. Just above the brute, hanging on the wall behind the desk, was an old maritime belaying pin that was about the length and thickness of a junior-sized baseball bat. Not a papier-mâché decorative object, but the real thing. Kenneth seized it from the wall and advanced on me.

Somewhere inside my brain there was frantic punching at the remote control, trying to shut off the movie and get back to regular life. But as Kenneth came at me, wielding the lethal belaying pin, the best I could manage was to switch from the Bogart film to Indiana Jones. There was an eight-foot harpoon hanging on the wall just to my left. Also not papier mâché. With a burst of desperate courage, I grabbed the harpoon, prepared to do battle. Unlike the belaying pin, though, it was mounted firmly to the wall. It didn't budge.

Like most poker players, I prided myself on my ability to make tough decisions in a very short period of time. Analyze a complex situation, reduce it to a handful of likely scenarios, calculate the probabilities of each scenario, and select an optimal course of action, in just a few seconds. None of these skills were useful here. The situation allowed for no reasoning at all. A far more primitive, instinctive, binary calculation now presented itself. Fight or flee.

This was a decision that was made in no time. With Kenneth less than ten feet away, the portion of my brain in charge of survival seized the remote control, zapped off the ill-conceived Indiana Jones episode, and switched the channel to *Pee Wee's Big Adventure*. I turned and ran, screaming for help.

As a child, I frequently had nightmares of being chased by bad guys. In my nightmare, my legs spun wildly but I went nowhere. My lungs burst with the effort to scream, but no sound came out of my terrified mouth. Fortunately, I now discovered that it is possible to run as fast as your legs will go and scream bloody murder at the same time.

I burst through the swinging door at the end of the reception desk and sprinted through the entrance to the empty casino. Kenneth was momentarily snagged on the swinging door, costing him a step or two, but he was closing on me as we sped down the central aisle of the gambling hall.

Across the casino, two janitors looked up from their carpet cleaning in amazement. They turned to each other, then turned back to gape at the extraordinary scene. It would take them several seconds to gather the initiative to run for a phone and summon security—a reasonable amount of time for a person to process information, when his own life is not in danger, but far too long to do me much good in the present emergency.

Along with surveillance and combat, I could now add running for my life to the list of detective skills at which I did not excel. Fortunately, Kenneth wasn't built for speed either. I was able to keep a few steps ahead, but my ability to maintain speed would be measured in seconds, not minutes. Already my lungs were heaving for air.

We raced past the blackjack tables and the Pai Gow tables. I tried a desperation maneuver, darting to the right down a row of slot machines. Momentarily confused, Kenneth ran down a parallel row. I ducked down, out of Kenneth's sight, and allowed him to overrun my position while I reversed course and ran out the same end of the row that I had just entered, hoping that I had thrown him off, if only to buy a few precious seconds.

It didn't work. Kenneth had also doubled back, and the swinging club just barely missed as I frantically raced around the end of a crap table, with Kenneth nearly on me.

Call it the karma of a game that I dearly loved, or call it luck, but the crap table came to my rescue, if only for a moment. On either side of the center of a crap table is a dealer's station. Because the dealers have to bend and reach far across the table, many find it useful to stand on a small box. Kenneth didn't see the dealer's box in his path; he tripped and stumbled, almost falling headlong, giving me just enough time to put the entire length of the fifteen-foot table between myself and trouble. For a few seconds, we played cat and mouse across the crap table—Kenneth feinting one way while I dodged another, but I was able to leave the length of the table between us. Time was on my side, as the janitors had finally gone to get help, and even if they hadn't it was only a matter of seconds before my yelping would draw attention from behind the cashier's cage.

Kenneth, coming to the same realization, took decisive action. He jumped on top of the table and came straight at me with the club in his right hand. I grabbed the massive table from the bottom and heaved, but it didn't move. Once again I turned and ran, and Kenneth leaped off the edge of the table. I caught the welcome sight of two uniformed guards running toward me from the far end of the enormous room. One of the guards—I thought I recognized my old friend Jimmy from the parking lot—had drawn a gun.

"Stop! Right there!" he shouted. I was alert enough to realize that the guards didn't know good guys from bad guys and, if there was any question of the casino's money being at risk, were likely to shoot at anything that moved. I flung myself face first onto the carpeted floor. Behind me, Kenneth's footsteps kept advancing. "Put it down! Now!" ordered the guard frantically. Kenneth ignored the command.

When Kenneth reached me, he found that my prone figure, stretched out on the carpet, was impossible to hit from a standing position. He crashed down onto his knees next to me, the belaying pin raised to strike a lethal blow. I rolled away just as the sound of two shots came almost simultaneously—one a flat crack and one a cavernous boom.

I had conducted dozens of trials involving shootings, but had never actually seen or heard a gun fired at a human being. I stared as Kenneth's massive torso spun sideways and a bright red stain appeared on his left shoulder. Almost immediately, he lurched back around from some other unseen impact and fell face first onto the floor, the belaying pin sprawling out of his hand.

"Put it down! I mean it!" shouted Jimmy. I looked at Kenneth lying face-down in a spreading pool of blood. The club was on the carpet several feet away from him. *Jeez, how much more down can he put it?* I thought. Then I realized Jimmy wasn't yelling at Kenneth. I looked back in the direction of the casino entrance and saw Maddie Santos holding a small pistol. The little gun in her hands cracked again, and bright red gushed from the back of Kenneth's thigh. A heartbeat later a much louder explosion sounded and Maddie Santos was blasted backward and I closed my eyes and turned my head away.

The next thing I saw was Jimmy and the other guard sprinting past me toward Maddie, whose body was flopped against the side of a slot machine, slowly slumping to the floor. I tried to get to my feet, but the best I could manage was a sitting position. Nobody had laid a finger on me; it was just that my legs felt paralyzed. *So this is what shock feels like.*

"She's hurt pretty bad, Jimmy. We gotta get some help here fast."

"She shot first! You saw that, right?"

"Oh yeah, you have a couple of righteous shoots. Don't worry brother, I got your back."

As it happened, I could have used somebody watching *my* back, because at that moment, unseen by anybody, Kenneth was raising himself onto his hands and knees and groping for the belaying pin. I heard a grunting sound and turned to discover him kneeling over me, soaked in blood, glowering hatefully with the cudgel raised to strike another blow. I tried to yell again, but this time my nightmare was real and no sounds at all were coming out of my mouth. In the bizarre slow-motion world of shock that I had entered, I had plenty of time to think, *Holy crap, he has three bullets in him. Now I'm in a freaking Jason movie!* But the precise form these thoughts actually took in my mind was something more like *Sheeeeeeiiiiiiiiiittttt!!!!* Kenneth brought the club down hard as I raised my arm to fend off the blow, and the sound of Jimmy's shout was swallowed up in the blast of pain that exploded inside my head.

43

Sunday, October 3

"I OUGHT TO PUT you in jail," said Frank DiCarlo. "Obstructing a police investigation, accessory to flight."

I sat up in my hospital bed and looked at him. I couldn't be sure whether the captain was joking. "Bust me for proving you arrested the wrong guy? That wouldn't look so good."

I was still a little addled from the blow that I took from Kenneth, but DiCarlo had been in a hurry to get my statement. My injuries weren't serious—a mild concussion and a sprained forearm. If I hadn't managed to deflect the blow with my arm, according to the doctor, it might well have killed me. Still, I was a lot better off than Kenneth. He had used his last strength in that final attack on me, and he bled to death before the ambulances arrived. Maddie Santos, they told me, had a collapsed lung and came within minutes of dying, but she was out of danger now.

"Well, if idiocy were a crime, you'd deserve a life sentence," said DiCarlo. "I don't get it. Why didn't you talk to me? Why go off and try to be a supercop?"

"Obviously, I made a mistake. But she was a friend, you know? I wanted to be sure."

"Some friend. Now we've got another person dead and three in the hospital, thanks to your silly antics."

Thanks to your shitty police work, more like. I adjusted my position in the bed, trying to get comfortable without crossing up the various tubes that were sticking into my arm. The doctors wouldn't let me fall asleep for twenty-four hours because of the concussion, so they were pumping caffeine directly into my veins through an IV.

"You know," I said, "if I *had* gone straight to you, there wouldn't have been much useful evidence against Maddie. Now you have the admissions she made to me, with Zip Addison and a bag full of cash to corroborate it."

"Okay. So in a blundering sort of way you were helpful," he conceded. "But you're damn lucky you didn't get yourself killed in the process."

"No argument there. I'll have to put Jimmy on my Christmas list . . . and Maddie too, I suppose. She came back to save my life and now I'll probably be the witness who puts her into prison."

"Save *you*? I don't think so. She had to make sure Conway was dead so he could never testify against her."

I thought about that for a minute. "Maybe you're right," I said. Of course he was right. Kenneth signed a confession that implicated Willy Hopkins, not Maddie. With Kenneth dead, there would be no way to challenge him on his statement. Any good defense lawyer could use Kenneth's statement to drive a truck full of reasonable doubt through a first-degree murder case. Maddie would most likely plead down to a lesser homicide charge.

"Well," DiCarlo said, "I'll say this for you—you managed to run like hell when danger called." From the tone of his voice, I could tell that he was only teasing.

"I've always thought courage and stupidity are pretty easily confused. Screaming for help is far more effective than trying to be a hero. But I do feel a little embarrassed about the way my legs froze up there at the end."

"Don't be. It's very common. Your adrenaline kicked in to keep you alive, and when the immediate danger was past, your body locked up. It happens all the time."

"And I thought I was just being a wimp at the sight of blood."

"Well, that happens all the time too."

"Actually, hey…" I suddenly remembered. "Talk about courage. If you dust the harpoon behind the reception desk, you'll find my prints, where I tried to grab it off the wall. Just so you'll know, for one foolish moment I was prepared to go down fighting."

DiCarlo chuckled. "We'll do that. It'll corroborate your story." He rose from his chair. "Get some rest. I'll certainly be talking to you again soon."

DiCarlo walked out. I lay alone in the hospital room, enjoying the fact that I was alive. Some of the details of what had happened in the early morning were still a little hazy, as the doctor had warned me they would be after a concussion. But there were two things that I remembered very clearly. One was almost being killed, and the other was almost being seduced. Either of these would have had a very bad effect on my marriage.

Eileen was on her way up from New York. She'd been relieved to learn I was safe, but relief gave way almost immediately to righteous anger. I hadn't called her, I had put myself in danger for no reason, and I had lied to Brigid about Jack. Guilty on all counts, and she didn't know the half of it yet. I was massively to blame for the near-catastrophe. An idiot for trying to play TV detective. Doubly an idiot for letting Maddie lead me around by the zipper, and a creep for enjoying every minute of it. Still, when the moment of truth came, I did the right thing. That should count for something.

Very soon, I would need to decide how many of the details to share with Eileen. My usual way of describing a gambling trip, giving her the overview and sparing the particulars, was clearly not going to cut it. I would have to come 100 percent clean. Well. Maybe 95 percent clean.

My musings were interrupted by a familiar voice. "Knock, knock." Jack Shea stuck his head inside the doorway. "You decent?" He ambled in and dropped a duffel bag onto a chair. "The spare clothes you asked me to bring."

I was glad for the clothes. My first thought on waking up in the emergency room had been, *Oh no, every one of these people has seen me in my Diceman underwear.* I smiled at Jack. "Thanks."

"No problem. Actually, I came over to check out the nurses. There's nothing to do at the Humpback, thanks to you, Sherlock. The whole damn casino is sealed off with crime scene tape. Must be a thousand people milling around, they're desperate to get at the slot machines. The cops'll be lucky if there isn't a riot."

"Hey, it's Sunday. Those people should all be in church. Kneeling in a pew, praying for world peace."

"I'd rather be standing at a crap table praying for a hard eight, personally."

Jack seemed completely unfazed by the fact that his friend Maddie turned out to be a conspirator to murder. "So, you figured out what you're gonna tell Eileen?" he asked.

"I'm still working on it. If I start with the truth and edit out everything that I'm too embarrassed or ashamed to tell her, I'll be left with, 'Gosh, it was an interesting week.'"

"I advise full disclosure. Complete honesty is the bedrock of a healthy relationship."

This needed no response. Jack was looking distracted, and I didn't have to guess what his problem was. "Where's Brigid?"

"Over at the hotel. Testing the world's record for money spent on spa treatments in a single day." He glanced at his wristwatch. "Right now she's either having her crème de menthe body wrap or her Aztec clay aromatherapy facial treatment. She deserves it all, of course." He looked out the window.

"And?" I prompted him.

"I guess things could be worse. I wouldn't say she's forgiven me, but it'll work itself out. I mean, yesterday she said she was going to tear me a new asshole, right? Today she told me I could keep the one I have. She said it matches my personality perfectly."

"Well, that's like a love sonnet under the circumstances. So what's the bad news?"

"You know the half a million I won yesterday? The money that was going to keep me shooting craps with hundred-dollar chips for the rest of my life? Well, Brigid has her own ideas about that." He pulled a piece of paper out of his pocket and handed it to me.

"You're going to have to open that up for me, I only have one hand."

"Oh, sorry."

He unfolded the paper and placed it carefully into my good hand. It was a printout of an e-mail. The subject read, "Your generous donation." I looked at the text.

Dear Mr. Shea:

On behalf of the thousands of young men and women who gain so much from our programs, I offer you our most heartfelt gratitude for your extremely generous pledge of two hundred fifty thousand dollars. I greatly look forward to meeting you in our offices to discuss the details of the donation and to arrange an appropriate commemoration of your outstanding generosity.

R. H. Gibson
President
Police Athletic League of New York City

Nobody who knew Brigid would be surprised that she had ordered Jack to give away half of his winnings. That Jack would actually *do* it was far more remarkable. I looked up at him. "Wow. So I guess you really *are* in love with her, huh?"

Jack Shea, for the first time in my long acquaintance with him, looked embarrassed.

The awkward pause was broken by a nicely shaped nurse's aide walking briskly into the room, holding a clipboard and a cup of medicine. She stopped short when she saw Jack. "You're not supposed to be here."

He flashed her his most charming smile. "Gosh, I'm sorry. I just stumbled in here by mistake. I don't even know this man. Maybe you could help me…"

I closed my eyes and tuned out Jack's patter. I couldn't wait for Eileen to come. Angry or not, she was what I needed more than anything else. After that, I was looking forward to a few weeks of ordinary life, surrounded by normal people, and no gambling.

Just a few weeks.

ACKNOWLEDGMENTS

Thanks go to my agents, Renee Zuckerbrot and Martha Kaplan, who did a great deal more than simply selling the book. Also thanks to my copyeditor, Wade Ostrowski, for his insightful comments, and to the whole team at Midnight Ink. The book was improved by many people who read drafts, contributed helpful ideas, or provided me with background information: Basil Anastasio, Dan Bell, Mikko Bojarsky, Joe Connors, Brian Coyne, Liz Gordon, Sandra Hutchison, David Liebschutz, Eileen Lynch, Mary Lynch, Greg Mandel, Margie Morris, Mark Multerer, Mike Noble, John O'Hara, Jeff Robinson, Nina Roepe, Brigid Stegemoeller, and Patrick Stegemoeller. Thanks to Eric Blasenheim, Ed Brennan, and Chuck Koon for saving the document when my computer tried to eat it. And special thanks to Mrs. Geisenhoff, who never tolerated anything except my best.

ABOUT THE AUTHOR

Rudy Stegemoeller began playing poker at age six and has never reformed. A former *Jeopardy!* champion, Rudy is a graduate of Haverford College and Duke University School of Law. When he is not playing cards, shooting craps, or watching World Series of Poker reruns, Rudy practices law in the field of public utility regulation. He lives in Poestenkill, New York, where he is happily married and has two children.

WWW.MIDNIGHTINKBOOKS.COM

From the gritty streets of New York City to sacred tombs in the Middle East, it's always midnight somewhere. Join us online at any hour for fresh new voices in mystery fiction, book club questions, author information, mystery resources, and more.

Midnight Ink promises a wild ride filled with cunning villains, conflicted heroes, hilarious hazards, mind-bending puzzles, and enough twists and turns to keep readers on the edge of their seats.

MIDNIGHT INK ORDERING INFORMATION

Order by Phone:
- Call toll-free within the U.S. and Canada at 1-888-NITEINK (1-888-648-3465)
- We accept VISA, MasterCard, and American Express

Order by Mail:
Send the full price of your order (MN residents add 6.5% sales tax) in U.S. funds, plus postage & handling to:

> Midnight Ink
> 2143 Wooddale Drive
> Woodbury, MN 55125-2989

Postage & Handling:
Standard (U.S., Mexico, & Canada). If your order is:
> $24.99 and under, add $3.00
> $25.00 and over, FREE STANDARD SHIPPING

AK, HI, PR: $15.00 for one book plus $1.00 for each additional book.

International Orders (airmail only):
> $16.00 for one book plus $3.00 for each additional book